To Will

C000283864

# En Canot
# and the
# Accidental Artist

*Read and Enjoy!*

*by*

*William Nicoll*

Grosvenor House
Publishing Limited

The right of William Nicoll to be identified as the author of this
work has been asserted in accordance with Section 78
of the Copyright, Designs and Patents Act 1988

The book cover picture is copyright to William Nicoll

This book is published by
Grosvenor House Publishing Ltd
Link House
140 The Broadway, Tolworth, Surrey, KT6 7HT.
www.grosvenorhousepublishing.co.uk

This book is a work of fiction. Any resemblance to
people or events, past or present, is purely coincidental.

A CIP record for this book
is available from the British Library

ISBN 978-1-78623-269-4

# Acknowledgements and Author's Notes

En Canot also referred to as Femme a L'ombrelle, Im Boot, Le Canot and En Bateau is a real painting created by Jean Metzinger (1883–1956), a French artist and a founder of cubism. It was looted by the Nazis and has not been seen since it appeared in the Degenerate Art Exhibition in 1937.

The author has endeavoured to contact the last known owners of the picture, the Alten Nationalgalerie in Berlin and the estate of the late Jean Metzinger to seek permission to use the black and white photograph of En Canot, but with no success. Within the context of fair dealing it is difficult to see how the author's use of the picture has caused any loss and consequently the black and white image of En Canot has been included in the book.

There are also extracts from Wikipedia, the occasional quote from Robert Burns (1759–96) and while some places on the West Coast of Scotland exist, the tale and characters are otherwise wholly fictitious.

# Chapter 1 – En Canot

It was 30° Celsius when the gargantuan Lieu Chang left the cabin of his private Learjet and began to plod down the stairway, his enormous size fifteen feet crashing onto the metal steps, shaking the whole structure as gravity pushed him downwards onto the tarmac of Sheremetyevo Airport, Moscow, where a large Mercedes Benz was waiting to collect him. By the time he had wedged himself into the rear seat beside Siz Long, his elegant female bodyguard, Lieu Chang was a sopping morass of perspiration.

Onwards the car sped along the dual carriageway, around the ring road, over the River Moska before pulling onto the Rublyovskoye Shosse Highway leading into the exclusive enclave of Rublyovka. Once the home of Russian nobility, now a tawdry sprawl of over developed mansions with gaudy architectural features; inhabited by politicians, industrialists, film stars and the likes. In the back of the car Lieu Chang was excited by his imminent meeting while continuing to perspire, with globules of sweat dripping from his nose as his shirt became visibly damp.

Up a side street, through an ornate gateway and the Mercedes ground to a halt on the generous forecourt beside a number of other rather expensive looking cars.

Babek Popovich was waiting to greet them at the grand entrance of the luxurious Palladian styled house owned by his client, Belusha Popvorsky.

'Siz Long, how nice to see you again,' said Babek rather chirpily as the odd-looking couple walked towards them, Lieu Chang still glowing in the heat.

Siz Long nodded but said nothing to Babek as he led them into the hallway, which was festooned with gold Greek statutes, urns, gilt-edged mirrors, porcelain figurines, ceramics and beautiful paintings hanging on the walls. Down the poorly illuminated corridor walked Babek, before resting his hand on the dining room door knob and slowly turning it clockwise. It clicked open. Babek stepped forward, ushering his guests into the murky depths of the room with its shutters still closed and then, after walking a couple of yards to his right, switched on the spotlight which shone across the picture mounted on an easel, standing in the centre of the room; revealing, a wonderful cubist painting with triangular shapes fanning downwards.

The sloth-like Lieu Chang remained motionless for a couple of seconds admiring the painting from afar and then, ever so slowly started to advance forwards, all the time picking up momentum, pulled in like the flux of a magnet, until he came to a halt and stared at the picture taking in its aura, its smell, its being; devouring the beauty which sat before him in silence until suddenly, without warning – Lieu Chang staggered a little to the left. Siz Long moved to assist as Lieu Chang then staggered a little to the right, but before anyone could reach him, his stubby legs buckled and – *kerbuddle*! The titanic of a man plunged forward, crashing into the easel scattering its precious contents across the floor as his jelly-like body mass hit the ground with a shuddering thud.

Babek leapt forward, but he was too late to catch the painting which was now sliding towards the radiator. No one looked to Lieu Chang who lay prostrate on the ground breathing heavily; instead they congregated around the wonderful picture and were relieved to see that no damage had been caused. Babek carefully collected the painting and leaned it against the wall. Lieu Chang sat up. He had fainted.

*

Six weeks later Lieu Chang's entourage of experts examined the picture in Moscow, checking its provenance and scrutinising the tiniest of details. Satisfied with the results, Babek received a payment, US$5 million into the joint bank account he held with Belusha.

# Chapter 2 – Ranald and Elspeth

Ranald Milngavie (pronounced 'Mulguy') gently swept ochre number three and crimson red paint across the canvas with a number fourteen hogs hair brush, while peering out of the open French doors eastwards, towards the Glasgow skyline. It was a view he had painted numerous times before and on each occasion it revealed something new, never the same twice and on this particular September evening it looked, well; stunning, intoxicating, seductive.

Oh, how he pushed and teased the paint. Dabbing, smearing, twirling and pulling as the rich colourful wet pigments revealed themselves, sparkling in the twilight, while his fingers tingled with excitement. Ranald was in a world of his own, oblivious to all around, detached from reality and cocooned within a dreamy bubble of artistic passion. Complete and utter bliss!

He lived on the top two floors of 19 Huntly Gardens, just off Byers Road in the heart of the West End. It was a fine stone townhouse with pleasant views over the pretty communal gardens to the front, and had been gifted to Ranald by his parents when they retired to Bearsden.

He didn't deserve it though. Most certainly not! Ranald was at best lacklustre, had failed his History of Art Degree and since then had wafted between menial jobs with little direction; baker, decorator, furniture remover and so the list went on, hardly what was expected from the son of a successful accountant. His father had been the senior partner at Grigor McDonald, no less.

But, fortunately for Ranald his mother was blind to his many failings, so after some terse discussions with her husband and a cash settlement made in lieu to his younger brother, Ranald was handed the title deeds to the magnificent four storey terraced house which he promptly split in two. Letting the lower half generated an income to support his bohemian life style as an artist and supplemented his meagre picture sales. Understandably his parents had been saddened to see the changes to their splendid old home, but deep down, they knew it was for the best. Poor old Ranald seemed unlikely to ever earn a living under his own steam.

He had drifted into painting later in life, in an attempt to establish a semblance of a career and some modicum of respectability. Self-taught by a process of trial and error, Ranald had learnt how to move the paint on the canvas to good effect and he finished off the sky in heavy oils, with bold horizontal strokes and then gentle flicks of the paint brush to add some lighter clouds. The roof tops in the foreground had already been sketched in and with the darker colours of black, brown and grey hues, mixed impasto, Ranald dabbed on heavy lumps of paint to provide texture, and then softly lightened the scene with brighter shades, mimicking the evenings sunlight. Standing back to view his work in the dwindling autumn light – *braplatta!* Superb he thought. With a bit of touching up here and there he was finished within twenty minutes, whereupon he sat back in his comfy leather armchair, to admire the fruits of his endeavours and drink the rest of his Tennent's lager. As far as Ranald was concerned it had been a successful evening's work.

\*

In due course, he would frame the painting and take it to Hutchinson's Gallery in the Merchant City where his friend, Elspeth McLoughlin, would hang his work for a month or so, although his pictures rarely sold and if they did, for no more than a few hundred pounds.

Elspeth was a slim, sassy brunette in her early thirties with plenty of – *pizzazz* – and in truth had a soft spot for Ranald, who was nearly six feet tall, athletic with deep blue eyes, brown wavy hair and despite being in his early forties still single after a series of turbulent relationships.

They had met at the Western Tennis Club, where their shared interest in the arts had sparked a good rapport, but, despite going on a couple of dates and enjoying a kiss at the Christmas Party; what appeared to be an ideal match, for some inexplicable reason, never quite blossomed into full blown romance.

Ranald, of course, was to blame. Afraid of commitment, he continually got himself into impossible relationships which were inherently doomed to fail. His most recent girlfriend had been half his age, in Glasgow on a gap year and perhaps not surprisingly, only too happy to return to Latvia once her twelve-month work experience was over. The previous had been married and in no hurry to get divorced and so it went on, short term fling after fling, with little sign of him ever settling down. It really was a mystery, what Elspeth saw in Ranald. But then, Elspeth had been going out with Jeremy Brown for four years.

Ah, Jeremy. Drop dead gorgeous, cute beyond comprehension with the dreamiest of dark brown eyes and meticulous short black hair. When they first met Elspeth had been head over heels with dear Jeremy, the computer programmer. But, as time passed her candle for him flickered, until eventually – it went out. There was nothing there. Jeremy was, well, just too serious, too predictable, too nice; whereas Ranald for his faults, and there were many, had something, which she could of course never quite put her finger on, but just something which drew her in. Elspeth fancied Ranald and deep down she knew that he also liked her!

# Chapter 3 – An Invitation

Awaking at his usual time, just after seven, Ranald felt rather bleary eyed, following the previous evenings over indulgence with his friend, Mr Tennent's, although somehow, as he usually did, he managed to roll out of bed to start his day with some exercise! A run would be fitting thought Ranald, wandering around his flat in his underpants, looking for some shorts, running vest and finally the smelly old trainers with holes around the arches.

Round and round the Botanic Gardens went Ranald, past the large Victorian glasshouse, along the perimeter fence running parallel with Great Western Road and then dropping down beside the banks of the river Kelvin. Panting, puffing onwards he ran for a full twenty minutes, lathering himself into a sweat and then grinding to a halt at the busy crossroads on the route home.

Invigorated by his exertions Ranald walked briskly to Huntly Gardens, collected his post from the communal hallway and climbed the stairs to his maisonette, where after a quick shower he enjoyed a bowl of porridge for breakfast. It was the same most mornings, day in, day out and deep down Ranald quite liked the routine.

Sipping his tea while fingering through the junk mail; takeaway flyers, estate agents proposals and faceless brown envelopes addressed to the occupier, eventually, he came to a heavily embossed letter complete with a wax seal of a griffin's head on the back. Raising his eyebrows Ranald smiled to himself. He knew exactly who the letter was from, his uncle, the rumbustious Sir Hector Munro-Fordyce Bt to use the full title.

Sir Hector was a likeable, bustling character, the brother of Ranald's mother who after a moderately successful career in the oil prospecting business, where he sat on the Russian board of Sibernos, inherited not only the family title and baronetcy, but also, the splendid 22,000-acre Fykle Lodge Estate in Argyllshire, just two hours north of Glasgow. It was home to some of the finest scenery on the west coast, including Arragher, a sizeable mountain, which rose from sea level beside Loch Fykle to over three thousand feet, and was widely considered to be one of the most spectacular Munro's in Scotland. The red deer stalking was excellent, as was the salmon fishing on the river Fykle, which ran through the heart of the estate, all of which made it a magical place to stay. Ranald opened the letter to find, as he had expected, an invitation.

On the top left-hand corner 'Dearest Ranald' was scribbled, followed by:

**Sir Hector Munro-Fordyce Bt**

**Cordially invites you for a week of sport and frivolity**

**At Fykle Lodge Estate, Argyllshire.**

**22nd to 29th September**

**RSVP by 1st August**

With, 'yours aye Sir Hector,' hand written on the bottom and a 'p.s. look forward to seeing you next week!'

Ranald's smile widened. This was typical of Sir Hector. Clearly someone had cancelled at the last minute and he was expected to step in and make up the numbers, although he wasn't offended. Regardless that the house was a damp, draughty Victorian pile, where no doubt he would be put in one of the old servant's rooms in the west wing on a dilapidated bed with a shot mattress, the sport more than made up for the domestic arrangements and Ranald was actually pleased to be asked.

*

Chuffed with his invite, Ranald made a pot of coffee and set about framing a picture he had painted the week before and just before lunchtime arrived at Hutchinson's Gallery in the Merchant City. As usual it was deserted apart from Elspeth sitting behind the large mahogany desk, sipping a peppermint tea while she read a trashy gossip magazine and twiddled with her hair.

The doorbell rang as Ranald bounded in with a big smile on his face, ready to chance his luck and see if he could sway Elspeth to take another of his awful paintings.

'My darling, your favourite artist has arrived, the one and only!'

'Oh. It's you, Ranald. I suppose you have bought me one of your dreadful pictures to hang in my fine gallery?'

'Well of course. I mean, who else would take them?'

Carefully unwrapping his work, Ranald neatly folded the brown paper and then handed his painting to Elspeth, who held it up to the light and cocked her head to one side, taking in the scene.

'Ummmm. I think you are actually improving.'

Holding the picture, she walked across the floor, before mounting it on an easel and then withdrew to view it from a distance.

'To be honest, I think it's one of your better works. You certainly seem to have caught the foreground well and I like the bold colours you have used in the sky. How much do you want for it?'

'Well unless you think otherwise,' said Ranald rather optimistically. But, on seeing Elspeth's dead pan face muttered, 'the usual', resigned to the fact, that there was not a queue of gallery owners willing to take his work.

'£250? And it's the standard 50% commission? replied Elspeth, holding her steely piercing stare. Ah, there was something quite brutal and uncompromising about her when it came to business and sensing Ranald frailties, Elspeth went on to deliver the – *coup de grace*. 'And lunch?'

'And lunch!' spluttered Ranald. 'Good heavens. You drive a hard bargain Miss McLoughlin, you're merciless. But, I suppose in the circumstances, you appear to have struck a deal.'

A mischievous grin returned to her Elspeth's face, 'Yes, I thought as much.'

They enjoyed a pleasant lunch at Molly May's, a trendy Glasgow pub not far from the gallery, nestled in a quiet corner with plenty of engaging conversation and banter. There was clearly good chemistry between the two of them, judging by the eye contact and tactile gestures and they really should have been a couple, but, it was Ranald who was to blame. As always, his phobia of relationships, aversion to responsibility, fear of the unknown took hold and he kept Elspeth at arm's length. Argh, it was just so frustrating for her!

Back to the gallery they ambled, gossiping about other artists and discussing the merits or otherwise of painting in gouache. Ranald had a tennis match at four, so once he had given Elspeth a peck on the cheek and said goodbye, he jumped onto his old Raleigh bike and made his way to the Western Tennis Club.

He played with real vigour, deploying his full repertoire of shots: top spin, slice, smash and lob, but despite his best endeavours, rather frustratingly, lost.

A Tennent's in the bar helped quell his ire and by the time a second arrived he had just about returned to his usual frame of mind as he began to subtly flirt with the buxom barmaid. But it was mid-week, a Wednesday evening, not a time to become distracted and lashed to the proverbial mast of drunkenness. Sensibly Ranald finished his pint and made his way home, where he settled down in the living room with Radio Clyde on in the background and picked up the invitation Sir Hector had sent, which bought a smile to his face. Scrolling through his smart phone he quickly typed his reply,

*C U next week* and then after pressing send gazed around at his pictures which adorned the walls. Beautiful works, paintings of urban scenes, Scottish landscapes, sometimes with figures in the foreground and sometimes not, all painted in a laissez faire impressionist style and finished off in his own hand-made frames. Biased as he was, Ranald could nevertheless not help but admire his work. They were all exquisite in his eyes. If only somehow he could sell some, build a name for himself and with that eternal problem on his mind, Ranald retired to bed to contemplate how best to carve out a career as an artist, something he had pondered many times before.

# Chapter 4 – The Licence

The District Office of the Russian Federal Regulatory Service for Mass Media, Communications and Protection of Cultural Heritage was situated within a rather attractive 18th century neoclassical building on Rjepina Street in the Hakarinskyi District of Sevastopol. As Babek approached the main entrance there was a faint chill in the air, not unusual for early September, but he didn't feel the cold this morning. No, he was far too pre-occupied to be concerned with such trifles as he slowly walked up the half dozen steps to the doorway set between two towering columns. Onward he strode into the reception area where there was a long desk and at one end hung a sign – *Export Licences* – but otherwise no one to be seen anywhere, the whole building appearing deserted. Glancing at his watch – 9.15 am, Babek continued to the desk and then struck the bell with purpose. Brrrrrrrrrrrrrring echoed around, but then nothing. Silence returned, until a door clattered in the background and the distant sound of a voice could be heard from somewhere within the depths of the building.

'Olga, Olga, can you take that?'

Rattle, bang, wallop a door burst open and in walked a squat shaped figure with long hair and muscular tattooed forearms poking out from their short-sleeved shirt.

'Morning Comrade,' said Babek as they arrived at the desk, only to be met by a withering scowl and a threatening look.

Glancing at the well filled blouse Babek realised his mistake.

'Sorry. I mean Madam.'

Olga said not a word while continuing to stare at Babek, who removed the paper work from his folder and placed it on the desk.

'Application for an export licence of a non-listed painting,' he said, before pushing the bundle forward.

Olga reached out and started working through the form, ticking boxes as she went, reading the notes and then picking up the cluster of photographs which were lodged in the centre, casually flicked through them, occasionally pausing on some and then looking up, scrutinised Babek through her beady little eyes. He met her stare, not sure what the implication may be, but eventually Olga released his gaze and continued turning the pages until she came to the final section.

Again there was quiet as Olga looked at Babek suspiciously, until at last, she reached to her right and picked up the heavy metal stamp, pressed it on the ink pad and brought it down on the form with a heavy thud:

**Received – Federal Regulatory Service for Mass Media,**

**Communications and Protection of Cultural Heritage**

And then, tearing off the receipt from the bottom of the last page and handing it to Babek, finally Olga spoke.

'Head Office will issue the licence retrospectively within a week, possibly a little longer, but in the meantime you are free to take the picture abroad.'

Babek left the building with a big smile on his face and started making his way to the train station for the eighteen-hour journey to Kiev and then his flight to London.

# Chapter 5 – Fykle Lodge

Sunday the 22nd September arrived and Ranald was surprisingly excited to be embarking on his week's holiday at Fykle Lodge. He had stayed many times before and knew the form well. Sir Hector would be the congenial host dressed in his plus-fours, playing the role of the Scottish laird with aplomb and ably assisted by his wife, the fragrant and vivacious Lady Sally. But, only until around six o'clock in the evening, after which the gin usually took hold. Dinner would be a giggle with Lady Sally's eloquent conversation, ebbing and flowing like the river in full spate, but, as she continued to dispatch the wine with ever increasing intensity, the words would become a little slurred and usually by ten o'clock she would be found in one of the comfortable armchairs in the grand drawing room, slouched in front of the fire, blissfully snoring with her Yorkshire Terriers, Pinot and Grigio, sitting on her lap.

Ranald began by sorting out his clothes, packing his dinner suit, kilt regalia, sports jacket and blazer, with an array of brightly coloured ties and cravats. Next came the sporting wear including a pair of tatty old plus-fours, inherited from a distant relation, tweed shooting jacket, salmon rod and finally his beloved Mannlicher .308 rifle. A beautiful gun with a short floating barrel, encased in an attractive deep grained walnut stock; light and ideal for taking to the hill.

Running a hand along the row of hanging trousers and tops in his wardrobe Ranald pondered what to wear for the journey, until eventually settling on a pair of shabby blue chinos, a faded lilac shirt and a red silk handkerchief which he tied in a knot around his neck. *Chipazaz* – thought Ranald, standing in front of the mirror, running a hand through his wavy brown hair and muttering, 'pure women bait,' to himself, before putting on his peak cap, long overcoat and making his way downstairs.

Out of the front door he marched, onto the private road which ran along the front of Huntly Gardens, where his old MGB GT was parked. A wonderful car, Ranald's pride and joy, 'a classic' as he affectionately referred to the 'old girl.'

He turned the key. Nothing happened. But then, after a couple of attempts, a few coughs, splutters and whines, the engine burst into life with a cloud of smoke belching from the exhaust. He was off, driving down Great Western Road leading out of the City.

\*

It was a bright, sunny day and motoring into Argyllshire was splendid, along the banks of Loch Lomond with the wind rippling over the water and the first signs of autumn appearing, as leaves were gently wrestled from the trees. Ranald felt a sense of liberation, leaving lowland Scotland behind and making his way into the Highlands, with the claustrophobia of city life evaporating and being replaced with fresh air and wonderful views as far as the eye could see. It was Scotland at its finest. Picture postcard beautiful and Ranald pondered why he didn't sell up, buy a wee cottage in the hills and paint to his heart's content.

On reaching Bridge of Orchy, he pulled over to stretch his legs, pick up some flowers for Lady Sally and then wandered over the road to the fish and chip shop to join the queue of Japanese tourists waiting to be served.

'Large fish supper,' Ranald demanded of the sullen, plump, teenage shop assistant when at last he arrived at the counter.

'And will you be having a drink with that?'

'Irn bru, of course,' scolded Ranald, rather too forcefully for a Sunday afternoon. He could be a little irritable if his meals were late. But, on devouring all, his demeanour began to improve and he was soon back in the MG with the stereo at full volume, driving northwards, until eventually turning off the A82 and taking the left hand turn down the single track road to Fykle Lodge. Shortly there would be no phone reception and he instinctively glanced at his smart phone to find a solitary text from Elspeth.

*'Enjoy your hols. E Xxxxxxxxxxxxxxxxx.'*

Ranald smiled. He liked the attention, although wondered how long it would be before she became fed up with him and move on. Probably not long he thought, slightly saddened that her affection would ultimately go elsewhere.

Continuing down the narrow single track road, taking in the wonderful scenery of towering mountains, bathed in sunlight with shadows drifting lazily over the mosaic of colours, Ranald pushed the MG into and around the tight corners, opening the old girl up and within twenty minutes, he passed through the tall stone columns either side of the entrance to Fykle Lodge. Up the worn, potholed driveway he sped and then at the top on the wide gravel parking area beside the east entrance, he swung the car around, scattering stones and came to a shuddering halt. Ranald had arrived and judging by the other cars there he was not the first.

\*

Lady Sally marched out of the wide ornate doorway and greeted him in her usual over the top and well clipped accent,

'Ranald dearest, how lovely to see you,' with Pinot and Grigio following in her wake and yap, yap, yapping at her heels.

'What a delight to be here,' Ranald replied in his nonchalant manner, as he met his Aunt and gave her the flowers and a warm embrace.

'Glad you could make it. Now do come in, your cousins and their families are already here, enjoying afternoon tea,' continued Lady Sally, leading the way into the hall and onwards to the fine panelled drawing room with views southwards across the terraced lawn to the monstrous mountain of Arragher and westwards down Loch Fykle. Ranald was met by Sir Hector who gave his hand a firm shake.

'Splendid you could join us, particularly at short notice.'

'My pleasure,' replied Ranald, moving into the main body of the room, where in the centre was a small table with a large pot of tea and a half-eaten Victoria sponge. A little melee was going on, caused by Sir Hector's cute, but feral twin granddaughters, Flora and Lilly. Now aged six, they ran around the table, chasing each other, giggling and generally causing mayhem. Not that anyone cared. Certainly not their mother, Sir Hector and Lady Sally's eldest daughter, Heather, who appeared oblivious to the destruction and havoc they were creating, as she ignored their wanton behaviour.

Married to Mike, an architect, who Heather had met at Edinburgh University, they now lived on the West Coast close to Oban, from where Mike ran his practice. A little younger than Ranald they were nevertheless, always affable, pleasant and friendly towards him.

'My, the twins have grown since I last saw them,' said Ranald giving Heather a peck on the cheek and shaking Mike's hand firmly. Exchanging small talk for a short while before Ranald moved on to meet the golden boy, Max, Heather's younger brother and heir apparent to both the Baronetcy and Fykle Lodge Estate.

In his mid-thirties, dark haired and annoyingly good looking, Max worked as an insurance broker at Lloyds of London. An admirable profession and one fortunately his father's best friend at prep school – Fatty Forsyth – had pulled a few strings and helped him into. His future inheritance caused a little friction with his sister, but the Munro-Fordyce's had owned the lands for around four hundred years, largely as a result of a well-timed marriage to an American heiress and the practice of primogeniture and there were no plans to change this by settling the estate equally between the siblings. In any event, Lady Sally was of independent means and provided she didn't drink it all away, she would make sure Heather was well provided for.

'Max, nice to see you,'

'Likewise Ranald, and how was the journey?'

'Not bad, not bad at all. The old MG made decent time.'

Max's stunningly attractive blonde girlfriend, Pippa Johnson, had now risen from the sofa and was standing beside them with a kind smile. Still in her twenties, Pippa worked as a florist at a smart boutique in Kensington and had now been with Max for almost three, largely blissful and happy years.

'Hi there,' said Ranald leaning forward and giving her a kiss on the cheek. He had met Pippa many times before and much to Max's annoyance they had struck up a good rapport and Ranald was not averse to a bit of innocent flirting with her, when he had the chance. To be frank, in the early days Pippa had found the Munro-Fordyce clan a little intimidating and in Ranald, the slightly wayward, eccentric first cousin, she unearthed a kindred spirit, a social bolt hole at family events and Pippa was always grateful to Ranald for making her feel welcome within the extended family.

'It's good to see you Ranald,' she replied breaking away, 'now tell me how is your painting going?'

Max seized upon this.

'Yes Ranald, do tell us about your art work. Have you managed to sell any pictures yet?'

It was a rhetorical question, meant to put Ranald down, because Max knew only too well that his work rarely sold. But regardless, Ranald replied with his usual riposte,

'Slow. But then Van Gogh only sold one painting in his lifetime,' before moving around the table, to cut off Max and then admire the fine view from the window. Eventually he made his way back towards Mike.

However, despite minor frictions from time to time, the odd muted row and occasional falling out, by and large they all rubbed along pretty well together and even though Ranald found the landed gentry way of life a bit pretentious, on the whole he liked his mother's side of the family and he actually quite enjoyed these gatherings.

After finishing his cup of Earl Grey, Ranald excused himself and went outside to collect his luggage with Pinot and Grigio following.

'Top of the back stairs, last room on the left at the end of the corridor,' shouted Sir Hector when he arrived back in the hallway with his bags.

Ranald knew the room well. It was his usual haunt. A little cramped and damp but at least had decent views westwards down Loch Fykle and beyond.

# Chapter 6 – Sir Hector's Present

At around six o'clock Ranald was sat on the stone bench outside the Lodge's east entrance with Lady Sally enjoying a generous gin and tonic, a little conversation and the vista across the mountains, when there was the familiar sound of tyres on gravel as a vehicle could be heard approaching. Suddenly, a gleaming brand new black Range Rover swept into view, scattering gravel when it turned in an arch to join the row of other parked cars. It looked exceedingly expensive.

Sir Hector was soon bustling out of the entrance and walking over to meet his new guests, when the passenger door opened and a pair of black stiletto heels appeared, followed by a set of long elegant legs, wrapped in a delightful short skirt. Ranald was gob smacked. Lady Sally muttered, 'Now don't stare,' while getting up and walking towards the new arrivals.

The owner of the long legs was now out of the car and an impressive sight, standing over six feet tall, with delightful curvaceous shapes, dark wavy hair and looked to be in her early thirties. Hesitating, she had clearly not met Sir Hector and Lady Sally before, but at this point, a short round balding man appeared from behind the back of the Range Rover, followed by an equally rotund lady dressed in a hideous pink suit.

'Babek and Jacinta how lovely to see you,' boomed Sir Hector, approaching the spherical couple and grasping Babek's hand, gave it a hearty shake before turning around to give Jacinta a kiss on the cheek. Ranald watched Sir Hector and Lady Sally be introduced to their attractive companion and when they started walking towards the house, he stood, ready to greet them.

'Ranald' boomed Sir Hector, 'meet Babek and Jacinta Popovich, my Russian friends who I have known for many years, dating back to my time on the Sibernos board. And Babek's daughter Ursula.'

Ranald shook their hands in turn, 'Nice to meet you'.

Captivated by Ursula's deep piercing blue eyes, he lingered with her hand in his palm for a split second longer than it was polite to do so. Ranald was simply awestruck by her striking good looks, all of which left him in a bit of a fluster. He hadn't expected to meet anyone as glamorous as Ursula at Fykle Lodge!

They ambled into the entrance hall with Pinot and Grigio circling around their feet, merrily yapping and then moved to the drawing room, where Max and Pippa were seated in the armchairs beside the fire, reading their books and enjoying a drink. Standing up to meet the new arrivals, they were soon joined by Mike, Heather and the twins. There was now quite a hubbub in the room, so Ranald decided it was time to slip out and change for dinner.

*

Lying down on the uncomfortable single bed, staring up at the cracked ceiling with its lopsided shabby central pendant, Ranald pondered the guest list so far. He had never met Babek and Jacinta before, but had heard much about them over the years and he knew they were regular visitors to Fykle Lodge. However, Ursula had been a real surprise; tall, elegant, sophisticated, and potentially available? Often Sir Hector and Lady Sally would invite single females when he came to stay, but usually they were not at all to his liking. Local girls, well fed, shapely, as his mother would kindly describe them.

However, Ursula was already causing Ranald a dilemma, as his thoughts turned back to Elspeth. He had no ties with either of them, but, Ranald suddenly felt guilt ridden and that in some way his instant attraction to Ursula was a betrayal of Elspeth. The gin and tonic had clearly over stimulated his emotions, so he went for a bath in the hope that the warm water would clear his head. Unfortunately not. Ursula and Elspeth continued to play on his mind.

\*

Dressing for dinner Ranald slipped into a pair of check trousers, shiny cream shirt and blazer with an over the top bright paisley cravat, before admiring his look in the small mirror sat on the chest of drawers. He felt the whole occasion was a pretentious farce and he saw no reason why he shouldn't enjoy himself, play his part as the artisan and dress appropriately. By half past seven Ranald was back in the drawing room enjoying another gin and tonic while everyone congregated, before the gong would be struck at eight, signalling dinner was ready to be served.

\*

A couple of new guests had arrived, Hamish and Rhona McCall who Ranald had met before. They were around his age and Hamish was the newly appointed Estate Factor, after the long suffering previous incumbent, the dour Mr Grieve, had eventually retired. Like Ranald, they were frequently summoned to make up the numbers although rarely stayed at the Lodge. Instead, Hamish and Rhona would drop in and out during the course of the week to fit in with their other work commitments and as requested by Sir Hector.

Hugh and Janet Robertson were also there. Contemporaries of Sir Hector and Lady Sally, and long-established friends of many years. Hugh was a pedantic retired lawyer from the well-respected Edinburgh firm of Robertson and Watson, which his grandfather had founded in the 1920's. He had worked slavishly for Sir Hector's late father, dealing with estate matters and the family's affairs and had been delighted, shortly after Sir Hector succeeded to the Baronetcy to be appointed a trustee. Oh, how he liked the perceived elevation of status the role brought. Hugh wasn't averse to letting his position be known at Morningside drinks parties, if he felt the occasion required, 'Of course, I'm a trustee for the family,' were his usual words of choice, typically delivered through a smug conceited smile.

Nevertheless, the close working relationship with Sir Hector had strengthened their bonds and they had over the years become very good friends.

The doorbell rang and Sir Hector dashed to the entrance hall to welcome his final guests the stately and rather self-important Count and Countess Von Kelheim. With Pinot and Grigio barking in the hallway, there was a general kerfuffle while coats were taken and hung up in the cloakroom. Ranald, was standing close to the doorway, watching Sir Hector swoon over the Count in a rather over the top and self-demeaning way.

'Absolutely delighted to see you.'

The Von Kelheim's rented the neighbouring estate, Tumult Lodge and usually spent August and September in the Highlands stalking and fishing to their hearts content, before returning to their medieval castle, deep in the Bavarian Black Forest, to hunt boar and while away the winter months.

There was also a mistress on the scene, Camille Jankers, a much younger and rather attractive Belgian lady who always joined them on their trip to Scotland. According to Sir Hector she had been kicking around for a few years and would reside in a suite of rooms in the north of Tumult Lodge while the Count and Countess occupied the rest of the tatty old Victorian house. The Countess and 'Das Fraulein' – as she was affectionately known – tolerated each other, although it clearly put a strain on the marriage.

'Meet Count and Countess Von Kelheim,' said Sir Hector rather grandly, introducing them to Ranald.

'Please do call me Egbert,' replied the Count, as he stooped to shake Ranald's hand while rather annoyingly twiddling with his grubby little moustache, before sweeping past and heading straight for Babek and Jacinta. Judging by the warm embrace, they clearly knew each other as they began to speak in Russian. Sir Hector struck the gong to announce that dinner was ready to be served.

\*

There was a set seating plan and a lot of toing and froing while everyone circled the dining table looking for their place, apart from Ranald. He knew exactly where he would be seated and made his way to the far end of the table, well away from the older generation and sat down waiting for his neighbours to arrive. Within a couple of minutes, who should turn up to sit on his left? None other than the exceedingly attractive and rather glamorous – Ursula! Ranald had popped in earlier and changed the place names around. This confused Sir Hector, who thought he had put Ursula beside her father, as Babek had requested and it was causing a bit of angst at the other end of the table, until he looked around and caught Ranald's eye; who simply raised his glass and winked. Sir Hector muttered under his breath, 'Damn Ranald.'

It was plain to see what had happened, but now that everyone was seated, Sir Hector, who was feeling the effects of the gin simply let it go.

'Hello, I'm Ranald. We met briefly earlier.'

Ursula turned, flashing her piercing blue eyes which she ran up and down him, before teasingly settling on his gaze, 'Nice to meet you, so tell me, what do you do?'

'I'm an artist. A painter. Not the most demanding of careers admittedly, but it keeps me out of mischief and occasionally helps pay the bills.'

'Oh really, how interesting, so what is your thing. I mean what do you paint?'

'Landscapes. Unsurprisingly, mainly Scottish Landscapes. I suppose living here why would I want to paint anything else? The scenery is spectacular, the light subtle and the colours more varied than you might imagine for the northern edge of a damp, dreich, little island, stuck in the Atlantic.'

'That's a coincidence. Arts my thing, particularly paintings. As it happens, I studied on your damp, dreich little island. Three years at the Chelsea Art School, followed by two more at the Royal Academy. Then a short spell at the Hermitage in St Petersburg and home to Moscow, where I now run a small gallery with my father. We sell mainly contemporary Russian paintings, artist such as; Chernigin, Hades, Pavlensky, all of whom we have exhibited. Do you know them?

Ranald shook his head, not really sure what to say.

Ursula continued, 'Their work is popular in Moscow and developing a global following. Nowadays, we frequently sell their pictures into the America's and the Far East, especially China.'

Wow, Ranald was impressed. Not only was Ursula a walking demi-god, but she also had artistic leanings and plainly knew a lot about paintings. Reaching for his smart phone he quickly flicked some of his pictures onto the screen and passed it to her.

'Here, have a look at these. Not quite Lavery, but let me know what you think?'

'Umm interesting. I like your skies. And your textures.'

'It's the view from the top floor of my Glasgow flat. They really ought to be half decent, I have painted it enough times,' replied Ranald with a wry smile.

'So where do you sell them, and how much?'

A small gallery in town hang my works and they ask a few hundred pounds.'

Ursula paused momentarily, while she did the calculations.

'Really, that's cheap. Well, we will buy some at those prices and take them back to Russia to see what the Muscovites make of them.'

A little taken back by the prospect of a sale, Ranald was lost for words, until on recovering his composure, he raised his glass and clinked Ursula's.

'Deal.'

*

Babek was restless at the other end of the table constantly turning around, staring at Ursula and not concentrating on the conversation he was flittingly engaged in. As the chatter ebbed and flowed, during a momentary lull, Jacinta, suddenly piped up and said, 'Now Babek, tell Sir Hector about the gift you have bought him from the gallery. You know the...'

'Good heavens,' riposted Sir Hector, slurping messily from his wine glass before continuing.

'Last year it was a sculpture, the year before a bear skin, so what on earth have you bought this time?'

'Well, it's just a small token of our appreciation for your exceedingly kind hospitality,' replied Babek, with a smirk appearing on his face, 'and anyway, it will smarten up your dreary old house.' Everyone laughed politely.

Count Von Kelheim suddenly started taking a keen interest in the conversation, while he continued to gently massage Lady Sally's leg. Oh, how he preferred her well fleshed thighs to his wife's stick like pins, as his thoughts turned to the more generous proportions of his mistress, Camille, whom he would not see until the middle of the week. Lady Sally was oblivious to the Count's attentions, continuing to dispatch the wine at an ever increasing tempo. She had around an hour of conversation left within her, after which it would be a fireside seat and Sir Hector, only too aware of this, pressed everyone to keep eating while the cook, Fiona Cockburn the Ghillie's wife, rushed courses in and dirty plates out.

\*

Ranald turned back towards Ursula, 'So then, how does Scotland compare to Russia? What do you think?'

'It's my first time here. It seems nice, albeit I know it rains a lot. I like the men in the skirts, that's novel. Is it true they wear nothing underneath?'

Ranald raised his eyebrows, 'Well, I will be wearing mine before the weeks out. So if you play your cards right!'

Ursula threw her head back, laughing heartedly and then as she leant forward with her hair flopping over her forehead, looked up and stared into Ranald's eyes with a burning intensity, before a big wide grin enveloped her face. That was it, blue sparkling eyes and generous smile. Ranald was smitten!

Pudding and then a cheese board followed and once the plates were cleared, coffee was served as the port was passed around the table. Suddenly, Babek appeared behind Ursula and began massaging her shoulders.

'So sweetie, please tell me, who is this charming scotsman?'

Leaning her head backwards and closing her eyes, Ursula muttered,

'He's called Ranald and he wears no pants under his kilt!'

Babek smiled, while bending down and kissing his daughter on the neck, before leaving to visit the cloakroom.

Ranald was momentarily lost for words, not really believing that he had seen a father and daughter being so openly intimate! He was perplexed, confused by the relationship and not really knowing what it all meant, decided to make his excuses and retire with his port to the drawing room. Lady Sally was already there, mouth wide open and fast asleep, gently snoring in a fireside chair with Pinot and Grigio sat on her lap.

*

With the rest of the party gradually moving through, Sir Hector filled tumblers with whisky. There was a little disturbance in the hallway and suddenly Babek and the Count appeared with a large wrapped, rectangular object, which they carefully placed on the floor, resting it against the sideboard. Babek shouted out, 'Sir Hector, now come and get your present.'

Looking up from the drinks trolley, Sir Hector grinned like a little schoolboy on Christmas day, sipping his whisky before replying, 'Oh my word, let's have a look then,' while starting to walk towards them.

Babek and the Count were in high spirits and particularly jovial, continuing to chuckle and laugh between themselves.

Sir Hector began to tug at the wrapping paper, eventually ripping off a small corner.

'Gently now,' urged the Count, 'We don't want you damaging our precious gift, now do we?'

'Piffle, precious indeed,' muttered Sir Hector, who after becoming stuck with a piece of sellotape, decided to put a bit of vigour into the whole exercise and with both hands now applied to the task, began tearing off huge swathes of paper which piled up on the floor. He looked up to see what had been revealed and unexpectedly there before him sat ... a large cubist painting!

There was silence. Everyone looked on bemused, until eventually Sir Hector spoke,

'Well goodness gracious me. That pictures' even worse than the sculpture you brought last year!'

The room erupted in laughter. Babek fuelled on by a generous helping of whisky was almost in tears while trying to contain his mirth.

'It's very special,' he eventually said when the laughter started to die down, 'and I want you to promise me that you will treasure and look after our present.'

Babek took the picture out of the room and put it on the dresser in the hallway for safe keeping, before returning with a big smile on his face.

'Babek, you never cease to amuse us with your quirky gifts,' said Sir Hector, filling up the whisky glasses, yet again. 'Every year something different. I have no idea where we are going to put all this niff naff and trivia you keep bringing us.'

Babek and the Count continued to chuckle.

*

Ranald, like the rest of the party had been amused by proceedings, but, there was something about the painting which intrigued him, so, with everyone now settled down and entwined in conversations, he slipped out of the room to take a closer look.

The picture was not framed, which he thought odd and on peering at it closely, took in the shapes and colours, while naughtily running a finger across the canvas. It was plainly a good quality painting, that was clear to see, even through his eyes, but surely it must be a copy of the original? Pulling his smart phone out, he took a photo and then another of the signature, before retiring to bed up the backstairs to his pokey little room in the west wing to reflect on the day and contemplate the events of the evening.

# Chapter 7 – Lieu Chang

Lieu Chang nodded to the security guard as he entered the well protected gallery situated within the grounds of his enormous house in the Chaoyang Park District of Beijing, home to China's elite, fitting for Lieu Chang the country's sixth wealthiest person. He was grotesquely fat, weighing over twenty stone and had made his fortune processing iron ore in the Shangdong Province, which had boomed during the nineties on the back of China's growing economy. Next came property development and Lieu Chang was responsible for building huge swathes of poky little flats in and around Beijing. They were usually poorly appointed and often badly constructed, however none of this concerned him one iota, because he lived a life of luxury with his seven wives, one for each day of the week.

The manservant behind the gallery bar popped a bottle of Pol Roger champagne as his master approached and by the time he arrived there were plates of sushi laid out in front of him. Lieu Chang's cumbersome hands came out of his pockets, elevated upwards in a mechanical manner and then picking up the chop sticks, he started shovelling the sushi towards his salivating mouth. Back and forth the sticks went in a whirr, as the big man proved surprisingly dexterous, not dropping so much as a grain of rice, while slaying the indomitable dragon of his insatiable appetite. Within a couple of minutes the plates were cleared and then smiling at the manservant, Lieu Chang raised the champagne flute to his lips and quickly drained the contents before putting the glass back on the bar and then letting out an almighty – 'buuuuuuuuuuuurrrrppp!'

The flute was refilled and then Lieu Chang walked off with his champagne in his hand.

Around the corner he waddled into the early China Dynasties, firstly the Tang pausing to look at the Dong Yang early landscape

– Shanshui (mountain and water), before continuing to amble through the Song and Yang phases and into the Ming Dynasty. Taking a sip of his champagne while the man servant waited tentatively behind him, ready to replenish his glass, Lieu Chang enjoyed Wen Zhengming's triptych of magnolia trees and song birds. Early Quing paintings, late Quing art, New China, Communist and finally Avant-Garde contemporary pictures and suddenly Lieu Chang was into the European section where he paused allowing the manservant to top up his champagne flute. Lieu Chang appetite for art was no less than his appetite for food – insatiable. Through Europe he trudged: Baroque, Renaissance, Romanticism – Turner, Delacroix, Constable, Friedrich – into the Impressionist barely glancing at the Monet, Renoir, Degas, Manet or Van Gogh which lined the walls. Onwards he waddled, before grinding to a halt at the post impressionists – Cubism. Here he stared at the Picasso, Braque and Delaunay under the gentle lights. His favourite section. Lieu Chang became absorbed, lost in a world of his own while contemplating the irregular shapes, confused structures and subliminal messages the paintings conveyed.

Without being prompted the manservant topped up his glass yet again, whereupon Lieu Chang raised it to his lips and then in one motion poured the champagne down his throat, belched heartedly and let the glass drop to the ground, shattering on the concrete floor.

Walking out of the gallery Lieu Chang climbed into the waiting limousine, to take him to Beijing Airport where his Learjet was being prepared for the flight to London.

# Chapter 8 – A Revelation
## on the River Bank

Ranald awoke at around seven in the morning after a poor night's sleep. The whisky had over stimulated his mind which along with Ursula and that wretched painting had set his thoughts racing and he had remained awake, tossing and turning in his uncomfortable little bed, until well after one in the morning. He gingerly arose, crossed the room to the sink in the corner and sloshed some cold water around his face before shaving. It had rained during the night and there was a good prospect that the river would be up and the fishing decent. Within twenty minutes Ranald was dressed in his plus fours, putting his salmon rod together in the game room when Max walked in.

'Morning. You seemed to be enjoying yourself last night, sat beside the glamorous Russian.'

'Yes, she was rather interesting. Do you know anything about her?' enquired Ranald, rather hoping to get some information out of Max.

'Well, apparently she is Babek's daughter through a previous dalliance with his PA in Moscow. It was hushed up at the time, but according to Dad, it all came out around five years ago and since then they have been gradually getting to know each other. Why do you ask? Are you keen?'

'Well possibly. I mean she was easy on the eye and runs a gallery in Moscow, so we have a common interest. She could do worse!'

'Not by much though,' replied Max with a smile, 'and has she agreed to take any of your paintings?'

'Well yes, as it happens, she did say she would buy some.'

Rather surprised, Max quickly spun around and looked at Ranald, 'Well there you are then. A match made in heaven.'

The door burst open and Sir Hector bounded into the game room, like a small whirlwind, whistling all around.

'Ranald, what on earth were you playing at last night, swapping the place names around?'

'Just making sure your new guests were made welcome,' replied Ranald with a wide grin.

'Well in future leave the guests entertainment to me. Ursula is Babek's only daughter and he is terribly protective of her.'

'Yes, Max was just giving me the lowdown.'

'Well then, you can see its sensitive.'

Sir Hector opened the door and stepped outside to check the weather. The rain had stopped. It was warm with some low hanging clouds shrouding the mountains, a little breeze to keep the midges away and looking up to the hills, he cocked his head backwards and breathed in through his nostrils, sampling the scents of the highlands; moss, heather, bracken with the lingering fragrance of rhododendrons in the background. Walking back into the game room, Sir Hector continued, 'Plenty of rain, the river's up, so it ought to be perfect for fishing,' before making his way towards the tackle chest to ensure there were plenty of rods, nets and salmon flies for all.

\*

Breakfast was being served in the dining room and the smell of bacon and eggs wafting throughout the downstairs began to draw in the guests. Ranald took a seat beside Hugh Robertson, who had been a contemporary of his father's and their professional paths had crossed on a number of occasions. The pedantic lawyer and the precise accountant, both of whom had jostled over matters, with ever spiralling fees at their clients' expense.

'And how is the old man enjoying retirement? Has his golf improved?'

'I'm not sure. I never play the game, although Dad and Mum seem quite happy, now they have settled into Bearsden.'

Mike and Heather arrived with the twins, who promptly started to excitedly run around and around the table, giggling and chasing one another, until Lady Sally intervened and managed to get them sat down with a bowl of cereal in front of each of them. Fiona was scurrying back and forth, serving out the cooked breakfast and once Sir Hector was seated at the head of the table he was joined by Ewan, the Head Ghillie and Stuart his underlining.

'Tea?' asked Sir Hector.

'Aye we don't mind if we do,' replied Ewan as he and Stuart helped themselves from the pot on the sideboard.

'There's been a good drop of rain over night and the rivers up, so I presume you will want to be fishing today?' enquired Ewan.

'I think so, although let me double check with the Count,' who had just entered the room and was sitting down next to Janet Robertson.

'Egbert, what would you like to do today? The cloud is down so it is not a good day for the hill. Are you happy to fish the river?'

The Count paused, not rushing to reply. He would have much preferred to take his chances with a rifle in the mountains, rather than with a rod on the river, but he could see that Sir Hector was not keen. He went with the flow. The stalking could wait for another day.

'Of course, I'm happy to fish.'

Ewan and Stuart now knew that they would be required on the river to make sure everything ran smoothly and Sir Hector's guests enjoy their day.

\*

Ursula arrived for breakfast wearing brand new tweed plus fours, waistcoat and looked the part, still as strikingly glamorous as she had been the night before. Effortlessly, she circled the table, gliding around, looking for a seat, before eventually sitting down beside Heather. They chatted briefly before she glanced over, caught Ranald's eye and longingly held his gaze with an inviting smile. Oh, she was a tease. Ranald was flattered, in fact embarrassed, blushing momentarily, before quickly turning back towards Hugh and continuing their conversation.

Sir Hector had now stood up and with his tea cup in hand was walking around the table to do some introductions.

'Ursula, meet Ewan and Stuart who will look after you today.'

'Have you ever fished before?' asked Ewan.

'No, never.'

'Well not to worry. We will sort you out with a rod and give you some tips. You'll be reeling in salmon before you know it.'

'Thanks, I think I will need it,' replied Ursula with a nervous look on her face, not quite so confident as Ewan, on the prospects of catching fish.

\*

At ten thirty everyone was eagerly waiting outside the Lodge in their fishing wear, with rods in hand, when Ewan and Stuart returned in the estate Land Rover. Hugh and Janet knew the form and not wishing to waste any more time climbed in, followed by Max, then Pippa and finally Ranald, who squeezed himself into the back seat before slamming the door shut. Tossing the keys to Stuart, Ewan sent him to the top beats, while Sir Hector was busy corralling the rest of the guests and working out how to get them all to the river. Eventually, he decided that Ewan would take Babek, Ursula and the Count to the lower beats, while he gathered the final waifs and strays together; Mike, Heather and the twins, whom along with Lady Sally, jumped into the battered old Subaru and set off for the middle section, where they would have a leisurely fish and some family time together.

\*

Spreading his guests out at the various pools, Stuart's plan was to swap them all around after forty minutes, to add a little variety, stop everyone becoming stale and make sure the best pools were not being monopolised. The cloud was beginning to clear from the mountains and in between squalls of wind, the sun was occasionally poking through, lighting up the sparkling rocks and gushing streams on the hillsides, exposing their beauty for all to see. Ranald was on the top pool Sylvia's and after tying an alley shrimp fly to the end of his line was ready for action.

Starting at the head, where the river was narrowest and the water most turbulent, he found it easy to flick out a cast with his fifteen-foot salmon rod. But my, how the current, whirlpools and eddies dragged the line one way, then another, before it was swiftly pulled under by a strong down force, as the river toyed with his pitiful efforts. Such power thought Ranald, watching the water pounding down in full spate, in awe of its strength and only too aware of the hidden dangers it held. A careless slip on the wet rocks and the wicked current would surely drag him under the dark peaty water and to his wretched end. Ranald reckoned his chances of clambering out would be slim at best!

As it happens, he never found the head of the pool much good in these conditions. There was just too much water, sweeping the fly away before it had chance to gently sink and after a few minutes, he allowed himself to be drawn down the bank, where the river was a little calmer.

Moving on to Spey casts, with some nimble hand work performing a neat figure of eight, he thrust his rod forward and threw out the line in a lovely sweeping arch. What pleasure to watch it elegantly riding across the water. After a couple more casts, Ranald had managed to work his fly over the river and was now fishing to much better effect. He was enjoying himself, content with his efforts, allowing yet more line to be drawn out, while watching the bright, orange alley shrimp dancing in the current, whipping through the eddies and all the time moving down the riverbank until he was at the tail. According to Ranald, this was by far the best place to fish, because often a tired, weary salmon would rest, once it had entered the pool. Again he cast his line expectantly and watched in anticipation while the fly was quickly pulled across by the current, darting through the water, surely a tantalising meal for a tired, hungry fish. But, despite his best efforts it was all to no avail. Ranald wound in his line and sat down on the small bench overlooking the river.

'Any luck Ranald?' asked Max, who had just arrived with Stuart to swap pools.

'No, nothing. Not even a nibble.'

'That's a shame. What have you been fishing with?'

'An alley shrimp, I always do. It usually delivers the goods on this river.'

'A shrimp is okay, but, I use a silver stoat tail when the river is in spate,' advised Max as Ranald collected his rod and began walking downstream to the next pool.

'Silver stoat tail indeed,' he muttered. It was typical of his cousin Max, he always had to have something a little better and flashier than everyone else, or so he liked to think.

'Well, we will see at the end of the day if that silver stoat's tail is up to much,' Ranald mumbled to himself, as he strode on down the riverbank.

\*

Ewan was delighted by how well Ursula had taken to casting. Diligent, consistent and eager to learn she was managing to master the unwieldy rod with her firm but gentle hands; working the drag of the line and whipping out casts with ease. Ursula was a natural, looked the part on the riverbank and was fishing the water rather well for a novice. She had a genuine prospect of catching a fish.

Ewan left to see how the Count was getting on, only for Babek to appear and provide some tuition of his own. Fumbling around behind Ursula he gently put a hand on her hip and an embracing arm around her waist!

\*

Alders was Ranald's favourite pool on the whole river. The mature trees over hanging the far bank were pretty and with plenty of open ground behind, the casting would be much easier. Standing at the head of the pool the water looked perfect and he started his routine, with short flick casts, wielding his rod with elegance, like a conductor commanding the orchestra, while all the time extending the line and gently ambling downstream. Soon, he arrived at the tail and with keen anticipation and hope in his heart, Ranald cast his line expectantly, letting the current whip his fly across the water, when suddenly... there was a couple of tugs on the line and the tip of his rod began to twitch. Quickly taking up the strain, Ranald realised he was into a fish!

Initially, he was quite matter of fact about it all, while reeling in as the salmon swam upstream, but with the rod now bent and flexing, Ranald could feel butterflies starting to circle in the depths of his stomach and the nervous tension begin to build. It felt like a jolly good fish indeed; solid and swimming strongly, even though every now and then it appeared to be violently tugging on the line, trying to dislodge the fly and then without warning there was a whoosh of turbulence, just beneath the surface and – *traplonk*. Everything went slack. Ranald knew only too well what this meant. His fish had gone!

'Blast.'

Reaching for his flask, he poured a cup of coffee and had a few quiet moments of reflection. Understandably saddened, not to have landed, what most certainly felt like a very good salmon indeed; to have been thwarted by the Piscine Gods, as so cruelly they can do. However, with the sun now shining over Arragher and the peaty smell of the river in his nostrils, it was hard to be downtrodden for too long. Ranald packed up and began walking towards the fishing hut where they were due to meet for lunch.

*

Pippa was already there with Sir Hector and Lady Sally, who had brought a basket of sandwiches, now laid out on a trestle table beside the hut.

'Successful morning?' enquired Sir Hector.

'Almost. I had a decent fish on in Alders. Solid as a rock and swimming strongly, a real beauty. But, somehow, it managed to wriggle free.'

Sir Hector smiled. He knew the feeling all too well.

'That's fishing for you I'm afraid.'

Ranald settled down to chat with Pippa, who was looking rather lost on her own, but Max soon appeared with a decent cock salmon of around 8lbs and a smile as big as his ego, which Ranald found rather sickening.

'There you are Ranald, what do you think of that?'

'Nice fish,' he said reluctantly.

'Yes it is, isn't it. Are you sure you don't want to borrow a sliver stoat's tail for the afternoon? I could lend you one if you like?'

Ranald paused, feeling a little annoyance grow inside while he pursed his lips, 'Thanks, but no thanks.'

'As you like,' replied Max with an ever widening smile. He just couldn't resist winding Ranald up, particularly when he found him chatting up his girlfriend.

*

The Count, Babek and Ursula were enjoying the picnic lunch which Fiona had delivered to the hut on the lower beats. Ham sandwiches, pork pies, plenty of crisps and the whiff of some healthy food in the token gesture of a couple of tomatoes and some rather limp lettuce leaves packed into a tupperware container. Large tumblers of white wine were poured and it was proving to be a merry little gathering; the sustenance of food and drink raising their spirits as they jovially chatted in Russian, while Ewan looked on.

Getting up to stretch his legs, the Count had his back to the party as he ambled towards the path running along the riverbank while Ewan was chatting to Stuart on the estate radio. Babek leant over, stroked Ursula's leg and planted a wet kiss on her lips. Brushing his hand to one side Ursula quickly withdrew as she looked around. But then smiled invitingly and returned the gesture, running her fingers across Babek's lips and caressing his cheek.

*

Ranald finished his lunch with a Tennent's. Pippa was now cuddling up to Max on the bench, so he decided to leave them to it and work his way down the river, fishing the pools on the way back to the Lodge.

First it was Junction, a long meandering stretch of water where he found Hugh Robertson and Janet thrashing away. They had pretty much exhausted their efforts, were ready for a break and only too happy to let Ranald swiftly cover the water as he majestically threw out his Spey casts.

'Lovely casting,' shouted Hugh.

'Thanks,' replied Ranald while continuing to move down the river. He always cast better after a Tennent's at lunchtime.

Ranald fished with real intensity for a couple of hours, going from pool to pool, skipping some where they were busy and lingering longer on others when he had more time, however, despite his best efforts, little luck. He could of course, have changed his fly, but, after his earlier exchanges with Max, Ranald was not inclined to do so and instead, stuck resolutely to the alley shrimp. He never found swapping flies made much difference anyway.

At the Graveyard pool the river was bathed in sunlight, sparkling on the water. A pied dipper flew back and forth in short intermittent busts over some rapids, looking for flies and it was a pleasure to be outside, enjoying the fresh air in such idyllic surrounds. Ranald was in no hurry, continuing to roll out his line and as it was swept across the tail of the pool, he again felt a tug and the rod begin to flex – bang! Ranald had hooked another salmon.

The surge of excitement began to build and the nervous tension within him swelled, while all the time he wound in the line as the fish swam strongly upstream. Suddenly, Ranald saw a flash of silver when it wriggled, showing it's under side and then not content with jostling in the water, leapt clean out of the river and writhed in mid-air, trying to break free. Ranald made his way down to the river bank, but when he approached, the fish went on a run across the pool, diving deep seeking to escape his clutches in the murky depths. Sensibly, he let out more line, rather than risk wrenching the fly free, and try as the fish did, it could not shake off his shackles.

Eventually, beginning to tire, the salmon slowed and again Ranald reeled in the line.

By now, the fish was swimming limply, just a couple of feet from the bank and with the rod held high in his right hand and the net lowered into the water with his left, Ranald began to pull the weary salmon towards its end. But, when only six inches from the net, the fish became gripped by its impending doom, had one last burst of energy and went on another run, diving deep and swimming across the pool, in what would surely be its last act of defiance.

Unfortunately Ranald slipped on the wet rocks, momentarily dropping his rod, allowing the line to slacken; the fisherman's cardinal sin, and by the time he had recovered his balance and raised his rod to take the tension back on the line... it remained flaccid, coming clean out of the water and wafting in the breeze. Ranald's fish had escaped again!

Disappointment soon turned to annoyance. He scrabbled back up the rocks and away from the river's edge.

'*Rollocking rollocks*' – cursed Ranald, looking back at the Graveyard forlornly. To have lost one salmon was annoying, but two. Well that was just downright vexing. He was done with fishing for the day. Ridiculous sport, he remonstrated to himself before sitting down to pour a cup of coffee from his flask

\*

Trotting along the river bank Ranald was rather hoping to find Ursula as he made his way back to the Lodge, but on reaching Big Pool he had still not found her. He was beginning to think that perhaps she had already packed up and left, although while walking along the path beside the river, contemplating if he should have one last thrash of the water, he noticed a couple of rods leaning against the fishing hut and what was that? Banging noises coming from inside?

Not sure what was going on, he approached with caution and heard the distinct tones of a foreign tongue, interspersed with some giggling and laughter as it sounded like there was a right – *royal frolic* – going on inside. However, nothing could have prepared him for what he saw, when he poked his curious little head around the entrance and into the hut. There was Ursula in a state of partial undress, sitting on the rough wooden bench with her clothes hanging off her shoulders and her eyes closed shut; while Babek, who had his back to Ranald and trousers around his ankles, was pawing her all over, nibbling her neck and flexing his saggy buttocks!

Ranald froze with his mouth wide open, unable to move or speak while taking in the passionate scene in front of him, before sensibly taking a step backwards so he was out of sight. Clearly he had not been seen as they continued with their tryst, so Ranald retraced his steps along the river bank to the footpath leading over the bridge and on towards Arragher. Now a couple of hundred yards from the hut he paused, reflecting on what he had just witnessed.

It was a bit more than fatherly affection, that was for sure and then, the light bulb came on. Ursula wasn't Babek's daughter at all. She looked nothing like him in the slightest. Tall glamorous, athletic while Babek was short fat and balding. No doubt he was rich though and he wouldn't be the first wealthy patron to have a much younger mistress. Ursula was plainly his lover, not his daughter.

However, Ranald had been quite taken by Ursula and suddenly he felt a sinking feeling, realising his romantic overtures had been dashed and she was not quite so single, footloose and fancy free as he had originally thought. He was no longer interested in going back to the Lodge, so instead left his fishing tackle on the bridge and decided to climb up Arragher to the lip of the burn and escape what he had seen. There would be mobile phone reception at the higher altitude and Ranald suddenly felt a pang to reconnect with Elspeth and his life in Glasgow.

\*

Ursula was busy straightening her clothes in the fishing hut as Babek fastened his trousers and did up his belt. There were small beads of sweat on his brow which he wiped away with the sleeve of his shirt while looking at Ursula and grinning. She returned his look, smiling sweetly and then gazed out of the doorway across the neatly cut riverbank towards the tail of big pool where the water was still swirling around and contemplated, the joys of fishing. Ursula was hooked!

\*

Sitting on a rock beside the burn Ranald could clearly see the Lodge in all its splendour, stood within the mature grounds, a magnificent house which looked every bit the classic Victorian shooting lodge it was. His smart phone buzzed as messages arrived, indicating a few missed calls and also a text from Elspeth.

'How's your holiday going? E xxxxxxxxxxxxxxxxx'

Ranald smiled. He felt in need of some love and was delighted that Elspeth had shared her affection with him.

'Missing you! R xxxxxx p.s. what do you think of this?' attaching a photo of the painting which Babek had given to Sir Hector.

The day was still warm and while lying down with the sun's rays warming his face Ranald watched the clouds drift lazily overhead, casting shadows over the hillside. He let his eyes close and there in the fresh air with beauty all around, he found peace with himself. Calmness returned.

# Chapter 9 – Elspeth's Discovery

It was half past four and tea was being served in the drawing room with freshly made drop scones and the remains of yesterday's Victoria sponge. Not a sign of Babek or Ursula anywhere, just Max and Pippa sitting in armchairs beside the fireplace and the twins who were aimlessly running around making a din. Mike, who was reading the paper tried to keep them in check.

'Quiet girls, please do be quiet.'

It of course, had no effect whatsoever. The twins continued to create havoc.

'Any luck Ranald?' asked Max.

'Hooked another in the Graveyard, a nice fish. Played it well and almost had it in the net, but...' no more needed to be said.

'Not been your day has it old boy?' replied Max with a smirk.

'Well no. I suppose not. Did that silvery stoat thing entice any more fish onto your line?'

'Well you won't be pleased to hear this, but, yes as it happens. A nice cock salmon of about 12lbs. Its lying in the utility sink if you want to take a look.'

'Well done,' replied Ranald through gritted teeth as he sat down on the sofa beside Mike to escape Max's torment.

'The twins seem to be enjoying themselves.'

'Yes,' replied Mike, hardly moving his paper.

Ranald finished his tea and retired to his room for a bath and a quick nap before dinner.

*

Elspeth received Ranald's text just as she was shutting the gallery and leaving for home. It bought a smile to her face, but she didn't have the patience to wait for the photo to download. Instead,

Elspeth caught the 54 bus to Hyndland in the midst of the West End and her comfortable two bedroom flat in one of the lovely old stone tenement buildings. It was home to many fond memories; late nights and wild house parties of fun, decadence and excess. But, when her most recent lodger had left to buy their own place, Elspeth decided not to find a replacement. Time had moved on and she now preferred peace and quiet in her home, rather than flatmates creating a disturbance all night.

Throwing her bags onto the kitchen floor, Elspeth put the kettle on and an Earl Grey tea bag into a mug, while fiddling with her smart phone to open Ranald's text and start the download. Scrolling back and forth across the screen to see what he had sent, Elspeth was surprised to find, what she thought was a cubist painting? It was difficult to view on the small screen, so she emailed it to: elspeth@hutchinsons.com which would enable her to have a better look on the laptop, which sat on the old antique desk in the sitting room.

Continuing to unpack her bags, Elspeth carefully stacked some groceries in the tall cupboard beside the kitchen sink and after helping herself to a chocolate cookie from the biscuit tin, sat down with her mug of tea and hit the return key on her laptop. There was the email sitting at the top of the inbox and once open she took a closer look. Interesting, bizarre even, most definitely an unframed cubist picture sitting on a rather nice old dresser. Elspeth was unsure what to make of it. Mystified as to its relevance, she zoomed in for a closer look and then with little idea what to do next, copied the image, dropped it into google and hit the return key, waiting while the icon circled and circled. Dozens of images flashed before her, different colours, shapes and sizes, but there in the middle of the screen was a match. They appeared identical, even down to the smallest of detail. Elspeth copied the title – *En Canot* – pasted it into the search bar and again hit return. Voila:

*Jean Metzinger, 1913, En Canot (Im Boot), oil on canvas, 146m x 114 cm (57.5in × 44.9in), exhibited at Moderni Umeni, S.V.U. Mánes, Prague, 1914, acquired in 1916 by Georg Muche at the Galerie Der Sturm, sold to the Nationalgalerie,*

*Berlin in 1936, confiscated by the Nazis and displayed at the Degenerate Art Show, Munich during 1937 and missing ever since.*

CONFISCATED BY THE NAZIS! Elspeth read it again and took a long sip of her tea. What on earth was Ranald up to sending her an image of a stolen painting?

Picking up her smart phone, she sent him a text:

*Jean Metzinger 1913 looted by the Nazis! Glad you are enjoying your hols. E xxxxxxxxxxxx.'*

Peering again at the picture Elspeth pursed her lips and shook her head, confused as to why Ranald should have sent the photo. Yes, he had always been eccentric, quirky on occasions and not averse to the odd practical joke when the opportunity presented itself, but, she just couldn't fathom what he was up to this time.

\*

Ranald had managed a brief snooze and was now fully bathed after his day on the river. The discovery of Babek and Ursula enjoying their romantic liaison in the fishing hut, played on his raw emotions and still pained him. But, he was now more balanced and measured in his outlook and on reflection was determined to have a bit of fun on the back of it. Slipping into his kilt for dinner, he was fully aware that it would provide a talking point with Ursula.

\*

In the drawing room Ranald looked around to see that almost everyone was present, enjoying gin and tonics and recounting the tales of the day. Max was holding court at one end of the room, blathering on about the merits of his wretched silvery stoat fly and the size of the fish he had caught, which seemed to be growing by the minute.

'Rod bent double,' were the words Ranald overheard as Max held his little posse captivated with his riverbank tales. He was growing more and more like his father all the time.

Babek, Jacinta and Ursula were nowhere to be seen, so Ranald sidled up to the Count and Countess who were deep in conversation with Hamish and Rhona McCall, who had come along for dinner at Sir Hector's request. Ranald knew them well, so had an easy entry into the group and just as he had planned, Babek, Jacinta and Ursula soon arrived to join them.

'Рад Вас видеть,' greetings were in Russian and Ranald found himself standing beside Ursula. Intentionally, he avoided her gaze, appearing aloof and distant, until inevitably he was drawn back to his exotic Russian belle. Their eyes met. Still as gorgeous as ever, Ursula smiled innocently, holding his attention, until she let her eyes run up and down dear old Ranald. Her face crumpled up into a big wide smile.

'Wow, you have your skirt on!'

Ranald grinned, the fish had taken the fly.

'Well kilt actually. But hey, I will let you off that small indiscretion.'

Babek and Jacinta looked surprised and Ranald, now fortified with gin, spun around with his kilt rising, stamping his feet on the ground as if he was at a ceilidh performing a Highland set. Ursula laughed.

'You are a funny man. Now tell me, are you wearing anything under your dress?'

'Well there is only one way to find out. Now you tell me. Are your hands warm?'

Ursula smiled and laughed again. Ranald was brazenly flirting and despite his discovery earlier this afternoon, Ursula seemed to be lapping it up. Babek looked disgruntled, but before Ranald could continue his assault they were saved by the dinner gong. Sir Hector led the party into the dining room where Ursula was restored to her intended place, beside Babek, while Ranald was left at the far end of the table to continue his conversation with Hamish and Rhona. He had had his fun for the evening and once dinner was over, Ranald enjoyed a quick dram of whisky, before retiring early to bed.

Walking through the hallway towards the backstairs he looked at the painting and shook his head. What on earth was that cubist picture doing here at Fykle Lodge?

# Chapter 10 – Mischief

Billy Murray, the Harbour Master at Port Glasgow was casually browsing the sports section of the *Daily Record* while sipping his Whisky/Baileys mix from the hip flask he kept in the second draw of his laminated desk. Rangers lost again 2–1, Dundee equalising two minutes before the final whistle and then scoring the winner in extra time. Dismal he thought, taking another swig from his flask before continuing to read the article. But, while soaking up the torrid details of his team's demise, he became aware of a shadow falling over the room and the papers pages losing their lustre. Billy looked up, tilting his head backwards to take another gulp, although before the liquor reached his lips, he caught sight of some movement out of the corner of his eye. Turning around he stared out of the window.

\*

Calumn Mackenzie was also staring out of the window of the Harbour Bar, 'Jimmy, Hamish, come and look at this.'

\*

The captain sat proudly on the bridge watching the pilot ship direct them inwards to the harbour side. He glanced around the well-equipped station; radars, sonar's, depth gauges, distance gauges, every conceivable device and mod con with lights flashing all over the place. His diligent crew busied themselves, while the first mate took control of the ships wheel and eased her in.

The captain settled his gaze on the six framed pictures hung beside the entrance, the monochrome images showing the Remi

Tessier designed boat's sumptuous shapes, clean cut hull and the lovely concentric oblongs of the upper decks matched by the curve of the stern. Beautiful.

*

Billy was now flicking through the ledger book sat on his desk and there scribbled under arrivals was 'Super yacht – registered Port of Tainjin, Beijing, China.'

*

Calumn had led his friends out of the Harbour Bar onto the quayside where they were stood between the bollards staring up at the sleek four hundred and fifty-foot yacht. The crew, dressed in blue and white tunics were scurrying around on deck, before eventually lining up on the side and saluting to the small crowd below, as the boat gently touched the quayside and the ropes were thrown to the harbour staff.

*

Billy looked at the stern with the red flag of China flapping in the breeze and the yacht's name emblazoned across the rear fenders. *Mischief* – named after a coral reef in the South China Sea – had just completed the month long voyage from Beijing.

# Chapter 11 – A Royal Fiasco

Ranald awoke with light streaming in through the window. He was in no rush to get up and instead pondered the events of the previous day. The revelation of Babek and Ursula still tortured him a little. It seemed odd that they had gone to such great lengths, concocting what was quite an elaborate lie, just to conceal a mistress. Ranald assumed Jacinta knew all about it and thought it strange that they hadn't simply introduced Ursula as a personal assistant, or something of that ilk. In any event, he had not warmed to Babek and found it highly irritating that he usually spoke with the Count in Russian and insisted on having both his wife and lover sat either side of him at dinner. Jacinta never said much of any note and Ranald could not understand why Sir Hector was so fond of them. Contemplating life for a little longer from his uncomfortable bed, eventually, Ranald arose and opened the curtains to see what the day held. Bright and sunny with some light wispy clouds drifting slowly overhead. Without any mist shrouding the mountains, it looked to be a perfect day for stalking. Surely there would be a party going to the hill. No doubt, the Count would be first gun, although there may be time for a second stag so Ranald changed into his tweeds, collected his rifle from the game room and walked to the range within the woods for a practice shot.

*

Fortunately, there was a target on the mid-rift of the cut-out plywood stag which he casually examined through the scope of his rifle. Three bullets closely grouped in the bottom left corner and what appeared to be two stray shots at the top. Ranald readied himself, lying down on the damp mossy ground with his rifle resting on a hillock of grass and pushing the bolt forward cocked the gun. Without even the faintest whiff of a breeze, rather irritatingly – *culicoides impunctatus* – the common highland midge decided to join him and they began buzzing all around. Somehow, Ranald managed to ignore the wee tormentors and keeping his breathing steady, placed the cross hairs on the bull's-eye and pushing the safety catch off, pulled the trigger – click! He always started with a blank shot to calm himself down.

Ranald loaded his gun, took in a deep breath and was now ready for action. Aiming, at the bull's-eye he again squeezed the trigger and – *'kerrbang.'* The gun barked and a loud booming shot rang around the glen, as it recoiled into his shoulder and left his ears ringing.

Now, driven to distraction by the ruddy midges, he leapt up and started walking briskly down the range to inspect at first hand where his bullet had hit. About an inch above the bull, but plum in the centre. He was content with his first shot, but the wretched midges were showing no sign of letting up and with a cloud of them following in his wake, Ranald marched back along the range and in the circumstances settled himself down as best he could to repeat the whole exercise. After a couple more shots, a grouping within a few inches of each other, he was sufficiently pleased with his performance and only too happy to pack up, return to the Lodge and escape the curse of the West Coast – the nauseous highland midge!

*

'How was your shooting?' asked Sir Hector, who was lingering in the game room when Ranald entered.

'Fine. The old Mannichler is firing true, but good heavens the midges are ravenous, just awful today.'

'Yes, they usually are bad at the range. But, there will be a little wind in the mountains which will keep them away, so can you go as second gun to the Count? I think Babek and Ursula will join the stalking party and I suspect Ewan will go to the Drum in these conditions. It's a southerly wind. Oh, and do please try and keep your hands off Ursula. Babek is terribly protective of her you know.'

'Very protective indeed,' muttered Ranald, remembering the previous days frolicking scene in the fishing hut, while following the smell of cooked breakfast into the dining room.

*

All were seated at the table so Ranald took the only place available, beside Max.

'Was that you letting off some lead down the range this morning?' he asked.

'Yes, it was, as it happens. Thought I ought to clear the cobwebs out of my rifle, and make sure I can still shoot straight.'

The Count looked up, concerned that perhaps Ranald would monopolise the Ghillie today, but on seeing this, Sir Hector intervened,

'Don't worry, Egbert. You will be first gun with Ranald as back up.'

'Babek, you mentioned that Ursula and you wanted to join the party for the walk? You would be very welcome to do so. It's a nice day and the views will be splendid in the hills. '

Babek hesitated, appearing unsure of what to do, until Ursula nudged him.

'Yes of course. Why not. We would be delighted to.'

'Good, that's all settled then. I think the rest of us will try some loch fishing and have a picnic lunch?' suggested Sir Hector while raising his eyebrows questioningly. There was a muffled agreement from the other guests.

Ursula looked up at Ranald and smiled kindly. He returned the compliment only to see Babek fix his gaze with a scolding stare and momentarily Ranald wondered if Babek realised that he knew their secret. On reflection, unlikely he thought as a plate of bacon and eggs arrived in front of him.

*

Stuart was already on his way to the hill, trudging through the plantation on the long arduous slog towards the top of the Drum. On reaching the open ground beyond the forest he paused, while enjoying the fine views down Loch Fykle and had breakfast; a packet of cheese and onion crisps, washed down with a can of coke. After a hearty belch, Stuart continued making his way up the south west side towards the ridge from where he would spy the ground in search of stags.

*

By ten o'clock the group had gathered outside the Lodge when Ewan pulled up in the estate Land Rover with the eight-wheeled amphibious Argocat towed in a trailer. It was an unusual square looking vehicle with skid steering, the most rudimentary of cabs and not at all a glamorous way in which to travel. But practical, ideal for ferrying guests up the gentle slopes of the Drum and would mean the highland ponies would have a day off to save their legs for later in the week, when they would be stalking on steeper ground.

The party clambered in and Sir Hector shouted,

'Enjoy your day!' as they set off up the glen.

There was a little polite chatter as they travelled and after a couple of miles Ewan parked on the road verge. He retrieved the estate radio from the dashboard, jumped out of the Land Rover and called Stuart.

'Hi there, its Ewan, can you see anything?'

There was a pause and no reply.

'Stuart, come in. Can you hear me?' Again silence.

'Stuart, come on answer, please,' said Ewan, becoming increasingly exasperated.

'Ewan, is that you?' came the reply.

'Aye it is. Now where are you?'

'About half way up on the southwest side.'

'And can you see any shootable stags?'

'No, not yet.'

'Can you see any stags?'

'No.'

'Okay, I will be in touch once we are through the plantation and on the hill.'

Ewan finished the call and turned towards the Count,

'Aye, we should find you a good stag today!'

Ranald smiled to himself. The banter was standard fare. There was a new under ghillie every year and he pitied Ewan who spent so much time training them, for so little visible reward.

*

Sitting in the back of the Argocat, Babek and Ursula spoke in Russian while Ranald looked on inquisitively, wondering what they were discussing, until Ewan started the engine which quickly curtailed their idle chat. Over the rocks they bounced, along the rough track, through the stream and into the plantation, where they did their best to avoid being scraped by low hanging branches.

The noisy engine grunted and groaned, billowing out fumes from the exhaust as on it toiled and within ten minutes of steep ascent they burst out of the woods and arrived on the hill. There was at last some peace and quiet when Ewan turned the engine off.

'What do you think Ursula?' asked Ranald, waiving his hand towards the scenery of rich russet autumn colours, against a back drop of blue sky and hazy views down the loch as far as the eye could see.

'Do you have anything like this in Russia? I mean, it's simply awesome on a day like today, would you not agree?'

'Beautiful, that I would not dispute,' replied Ursula with a gentle smile.

Babek chatted with the Count in Russian, while Ewan called Stuart again.

'Are you there?' he hissed into the radio.

'Aye, I'm here all right'.

'And have you seen any shootable stags yet?'

'Aye. There is a group of seven on the scree about five hundred yards in front of me. If you get yourself up to the ridge you should be able to stalk them from here.'

'Okay, thanks,' replied Ewan and withdrawing his Gray's telescope from its case, placed it to his right eye and scanned below the ridge, methodically, working back and forth across the rocky terrain, until he picked up the mature stags basking lazily in the sun. He soon came to the conclusion that there would be no harm in taking an old one off the hill.

'Count, there's some good stags for you. It will be an hour's walk to the ridge and we should be able to stalk into them from there.'

He nodded, indicating his approval and with all their belongings collected together they began the trek.

\*

Ewan lead the way, followed by the Count, Babek, Ursula and finally Ranald bringing up the rear with his rifle and game bag slung over his shoulder. As a seasoned veteran of the hill, he walked leisurely, at his own pace and knew not to rush, for this was no sprint. They would reach the ridge in their own time and judging by the way the Count was slipping around on the damp grassy surface in a pair of ridiculous looking wellies, completely inappropriate for walking in the mountains, it was not going to be any time soon. Babek huffed and puffed, plainly not conditioned for the hill, as his fat little face began to glow and his shirt became visibly damp with perspiration. Ursula, of course had no such problems, elegantly gliding over the uneven surface in a feline manner. Oh, what buttocks thought Ranald, looking up to see the tweed plus fours deliciously wrapped around her shapely bottom. It put a little spring in his step and a big smile on his face.

\*

An hour and a half later they summited the ridge and met Stuart.

'What kept you Ewan. Did you get lost?'

'I do the jokes, you cheeky wee loon,'

Ranald smiled to himself while listening to the exchanges between Stuart and Ewan and then sat down and looked over towards Babek, who was flushed red and still sweating profusely. What on earth did Ursula, see in him? Money of course. What was the expression his father had always used; *money can't buy you happiness, but, at least you can be miserable in comfort.* Out of frustration, Ranald kicked a stone which was lying in front of him. What a waste he thought, while un-wrapping a sandwich and taking a bite.

Ewan had crawled to the edge of the ridge and spied the stags through his binoculars to see that they were still lying down, enjoying the warm autumnal sun. In a couple of weeks the rut would begin in earnest and it would be a different scene altogether. Matted testosterone driven stags, would stomp, bellow, charge and fight to keep hinds. Primeval really, and when Ranald looked around at Ursula and then at Babek he couldn't help but draw parallels. If they were stags, then surely he would see that old sod off and claim his prize.

Ewan scrambled back to rejoin the group.

'Stuart, I want you to stay on the ridge, until I call you on the radio. If we get a stag you can help gralloch it and with the drag back to the Argocat.'

'Count, can you come directly behind me and the rest of you follow on. We are going to approach down a gulley to the left and then crawl out over the top to take the shot.'

'How much crawling?' asked Babek.

'That depends on a number of things. There could be quite a bit. The truth is at this stage we don't really know how it will all pan out. If you are unsure whether to come or not, I suggest you wait here with Stuart and walk down with him later.'

'Okay, Ursula and I will stay.'

Ursula quickly turned towards Babek and frowned, clearly disappointed with his decision and on seeing this Ewan intervened,

'Ursula will be fine to join us. She is fit and won't hold us up, so there is no need for her to remain on the ridge.'

Babek was surprised at having his decision questioned. Caught off-guard by Ewan's directness and not wishing to cause a scene on the hill, he paused and then relented.

'Okay, okay, Ursula can go and I will wait here.'

Delighted with the turn of events, Ranald smiled as Ewan led the stalking party along the ridge and then dropped into the gulley which ran down the front of the face.

*

Slowly, they descended, using their hands to steady themselves on rocks as they went. It was proving to be hard work and with the tension of the stalk beginning to build after around three hundred yards, the Count slipped and sent some scree tumbling down the mountain. Rattle, bang, clash went a rock, gathering momentum and bouncing for almost a couple of hundred yards, clattering as it went, before eventually coming to rest in a boggy patch of rushes with a squelching splat! Ewan halted, signalling to the party to stay put, while he climbed out of the gulley and onto the face to see if the stags were still there. Unsurprisingly, a couple of the larger males had their heads up and were looking around, clearly spooked, but fortunately they had not kicked up their heels and taken flight. Ewan crawled back and in hushed tones began to speak.

'They are a bit unsettled. If we could just continue for another hundred yards then we should be in a position to make the final stalk. You need to be careful though, we don't want to disturb them again.'

Everyone nodded and Ewan set off at a slower pace. Amazingly, the feckless German aristocrat managed to stay on his feet and within fifteen minutes they had reached a point from where Ewan thought they should be able to make the final push out of the gulley to see if they could bag a stag. He whispered,

'Ranald, Ursula. I want you both to remain here while the Count and I go over the top and see what we can find.'

Removing the Count's gun from its sleeve, Ewan was impressed to see a beautifully engraved Carlos Gustafsson 30-06 bolt action rifle with a wonderful dark, rich grain running through the walnut stock, complete with a Swarovski scope on top. He quickly filled the magazine, gently placing it in the gun, before tapping the Count on the shoulder and quietly saying, 'Follow me.'

They both crawled towards the face in search of a suitable place to take a shot and Ranald knew from experience that this was unlikely to be a quick event, so he settled down with Ursula to while away the time.

\*

The weather had remained sunny and surprisingly warm for the time of year. Grass tufts gently fluttered in the breeze as the light cirrus clouds, drifted calmly overhead. The views westwards towards Loch Fykle were enchanting, the flat calm of the water and haze in the distance, kept Ranald spellbound for a time, as a raven croaked noisily when passing overhead. But, after admiring the scenery for a couple of minutes, he became restless and on reaching inside his pocket found an old packet of polo mints which he unwrapped. Tapping Ursula on the arm, Ranald offered her one. She looked around a little bemused at first and then broke into a smile. Gracefully accepting, Ursula delicately teased a mint out of the packet and seductively popped it into her mouth.

Ah, poor Ranald, suddenly became engulfed in the romance and beauty of the Highlands. He turned around to look at Ursula who was sitting closely beside him. They caught each other's glance and Ranald found himself being drawn into her deep blue hypnotic eyes, while she returned his gaze. Here they were at the start of the rut, together on the side of a mountain and Ranald, like a virile stag in his prime, suddenly felt an overwhelming urge to take this young hind off her ageing master.

His right hand fell onto Ursula's leg. He began to gently massage her firm thigh, caressing, pressing, flexing her lovely flesh, while he worked his hand up and down. Suddenly! He felt a tingling sensation on the back of his neck as Ursula gently ran her hand through his hair, responding to his touch. She held his gaze, offering no resistance and with a brooding atmosphere in the air, Ranald realised it was now or never. Seizing the moment, he lent forward to kiss Ursula. Their lips met, tingled, electrified by the connection and just when Ranald thought he had bagged his hind, Ursula suddenly pulled away and pushed Ranald's hand from her thigh as she sat bolt upright! Looking directly at him, she shook her head and mouthed in hushed tones,

'Sorry, my life is just too complicated for this.'

*

Ewan and the Count had crawled around twenty yards from the gulley onto the face of the slope and reached a point behind a boulder, from where they had a clear view of the stags about two hundred yards below. Carefully placing his tweed deer stalker on a rock and the beautiful Carlos Gustafsson on top, Ewan looked around at the Count and with his left hand beckoned him to move forward, up to his rifle. He did so and once the gun was firmly mounted into his shoulder, Ewan whispered,

'Can you see the stag to the furthermost left?'

There was a pause.

'He has his back to us and head down grazing.'

There was further silence. Eventually the Count whispered,

'Yes, I see him.'

'Well, come two stags up and you will spy a large one with an awful switch head. No points on his right-hand side and only one on the left. Now, that's the stag I want you to shoot. He's not quite broadside, although in your own time, just take him.'

The Count did indeed see the stag he was supposed to shoot, but out of curiosity, moved his gun further up the hill to spy the other stags in the group. Scanning quickly he covered the ground and there to the right stood a magnificent beast, big solid body with a fine head and a broad set of antlers, standing sideways on with his head down, nonchalantly chewing some grass.

'Don't take too long now,' said Ewan.

'Give a whistle,' replied the Count.

Ewan gave a fox screech. All the stags looked up and a split second later the Count squeezed the trigger – *'kerrboom'* – echoed throughout the mountains.

'Missed,' said Ewan, watching the startled stags gallop off down the hill.

The Count smiled to himself,

'I think not.'

'No, definitely not hit.'

The Count still had his gun mounted and the scope to his eye when he said,

'Look around twenty yards further up the hill.'

Slightly confused, Ewan did as he was told and there lying in full view was the magnificent beast with his broad set of antlers. The Count had just shot the best stag on the estate!

Ewan's heart sank. It was a trick as old as the hills which surrounded them, to mistakenly shoot a good stag and brush it off as an innocent mistake with a barrage of apologies. In any event, the Count hadn't even muttered a sorry and was now getting up and beginning to walk towards his prize. The radio crackled,

'Hi Ewan. Have you got one?'

'Yes,' he said with a deep sigh and heavy heart, 'walk on down with your guest.'

\*

Ranald and Ursula waited a little longer in the gulley in case there was a second shot and after a couple of minutes they appeared on the face and started walking towards Ewan. The Count had reached the stag and was delighted with his trophy, lifting the head to inspect the antlers.

'Twelve points, a fine Royal, Ewan. I am very pleased that you found this one for me.'

Remaining stony faced Ewan never said a word. He was seething deep down, livid at the injustice of loosing such a fine young stag. If anyone was to shoot a Royal then it surely should have been the Laird, not some jumped up German aristocrat from the neighbouring estate.

Ranald and Ursula soon arrived on the scene.

'That's a fine beast Ewan, twelve points. It's a Royal! I am surprised you decided to take that one off the hill just before the rut.'

Turning around to look at Ranald, Ewan simply shook his head, while pulling his knife from its sheath and starting to cut open the belly. Sensing the hostile mood, Ranald soon realised what had happened. This clearly wasn't the stag which Ewan had wanted the Count to shoot.

Stuart and Babek arrived and Ewan handed his knife to Stuart to finish off.

'What a magnificent trophy,' exclaimed Babek, also examining the stag's head.

'Yes, it will sit well in the Lodge alongside the other Royals I have shot over the years,' replied the Count cheerfully.

Stuart looked at Ewan and shrugged his shoulders, his way of asking, so why this one? Without saying a word, Ewan simply shook his head and Stuart realised all was not well.

Babek and the Count chatted sprightly in Russian, appearing unaware of the crime committed while the rest of the group were solemn and silent, mourning the loss of the beautiful stag, taken out in his prime. It really was a tragedy.

*

They were soon dragging the beast off the hill and once on the shallower grassy slopes the haul became easier. The pace quickened and the Count struggled to stay on his feet while Babek was finding the descent no easier than the earlier climb, as his little round face became increasingly flushed. Ursula had now taken up her dutiful role at his side and helped where she could and within the hour they reached the Argocat. By three o'clock they'd loaded the stag.

'It's not too late to go and find another if you are keen Ranald?' said Ewan.

Ranald looked at his watch, screwed up his face in contemplation about what to do, but in truth, after the events of the morning, he now had no stomach for the kill.

'It's still early in the week. There will be other opportunities, so let's just get this one back and into the game larder for today.'

Ewan set off in the Argocat with the Count, Babek and Ursula, leaving Stuart and Ranald to walk through the plantation. They arrived on the single track road at the bottom of the glen, just as Ewan was manoeuvring the Argocat, onto the trailer.

Despite being cramped on the back seats of the Land Rover, somehow, Ranald managed to retrieve his smart phone from his jacket to catch up on messages which had come in on the hill, to find Elspeth's text. He suddenly felt a pang of guilt and regret, that his earlier actions were in some way a slight on her, but regardless, he read it.

*Jean Metzinger, 1913 looted by the Nazis 'Glad you are enjoying your hols! E Xxxxxxxxx*

LOOTED BY THE NAZIS! – *holy jack fish* – Ranald stared at the small screen in amazement and re-read the message again. Yes, definitely looted by the Nazis! He was barely able to comprehend the news and while he knew that many great works of art went missing during that era, never to be seen again, surely it couldn't be the original.

Ranald was in a complete spin, not sure what to make of the information he had just received and what the implications were. The week was becoming more bizarre as it went on. Firstly the discovery of Babek and Ursula and now the picture. Fake or otherwise, it was a splendid piece of work and Ranald quickly decided it was worth a closer examination, once they got back to the Lodge.

# Chapter 12 – Ranald's Discovery

Ewan informed Sir Hector about the loss of his Royal on their return to Fykle Lodge.

'He did what?'

'Aye, he just shot the stag without any warning. It's not what I would expect of a gentlemen.'

'Ruddy Kraut,' bellowed Sir Hector slamming his fist firmly on the desk in his study, scattering a scruffy pile of papers onto the floor. '*Popscotch*' – he shouted in heated breath, kicking the papers, while fuming and cursing some more.

Ewan sympathised and after another tirade, Sir Hector started to calm down.

'It's outrageous behaviour, however, let's make sure it doesn't spoil the week. I have never really trusted that pipsqueak German Count, but he has become good friends with Babek and Jacinta over the years and I don't want to spoil their holiday.'

'Okay,' replied Ewan as Sir Hector stomped off, still smarting over the loss of his fine stag, to join the rest of the party for tea and cake in the drawing room.

\*

There was a general melee with the twins continuing to create havoc despite Lady Sally's best interventions. Fiona had baked a dark rich chocolate cake, which sat on the coffee table in the middle of the room which everyone seemed to be enjoying and Ranald made sure he grabbed a slice before the twins moved in for yet more. Janet Robertson kindly poured him a cup of tea.

'So how was your day Janet?'

'Wonderful Ranald, absolutely wonderful. We fished at Loch Skeen, had a picnic, and I managed to sketch a few pictures on my pad, while Mike and Heather played hide and seek with their little girls.'

'Yes, I remember you draw and paint. Can I see your sketches sometime?'

'Well they're not very good, but certainly, I will let you have a browse before the weeks out.'

Lady Sally, who had become fed up shepherding the twins, wandered over and joined them.

'Almost time for something a little stronger?'

Ranald glanced at the clock on the mantelpiece. It was half past four!

'Now Ranald,' continued Lady Sally, 'I've heard a rumour from a little birdie that you have… well, developed a soft spot for Babek's daughter?'

Hardly a daughter thought Ranald, smiling to himself. However, despite his earlier rejection on the hill, he decided to play along with his Aunt's little game.

'She's a fine lassie and likes paintings, in fact she has agreed to buy some of mine.'

'Has she now. Well that will be a first.'

Ranald wasn't offended. Lady Sally had a playful side and in any case he was used to some gentle ribbing about his work.

'Well she clearly has an eye for beauty,' he replied matter of factly.

'And do you think the same eyes will be drawn to you, Ranald?'

'Well. She's human isn't she?'

Lady Sally threw her head back and laughed,

'Ranald, what are we going to do with you? Will you ever settle down? I'll wager you a tenner that she manages to resist your wicked charms over the course of the week.'

Ranald held out his hand and shook Lady Sally's, 'Deal,' he said before making his excuses and retiring to his room to contemplate what had been an interesting day.

\*

Unbelievably the Count had shot a Royal stag and despite this, Sir Hector did not seem too concerned. However, Ranald suspected that deep down he would be fuming, livid at losing such a fine beast just before the rut.

Ursula had resisted his advances on the hill, but, he felt that still had a little way to play out and his ten-pound bet wasn't lost just yet. However, the picture perplexed Ranald most of all. He scrolled back through his smart phone and re-read Elspeth's message;

*Jean Metzinger, 1913 looted by the Nazis. Glad you are enjoying your hols! E xxxxxxxxxxxx*

A joke perhaps? Elspeth could, of course, be winding him up, but for some reason Ranald didn't think so. She had a good sense of humour, but this was just, too precise, too premeditated and not off the cuff as was her style.

The whole week was becoming more bizarre by the day and while he lay on the bed letting his mind wander, Ranald eventually decided to run a bath and let the hot water ease his aching limbs. Twenty minutes of being partly submerged in dark peaty water did little to crystallise his thoughts though and after pulling the plug, Ranald returned to his room and dressed for dinner, sporting a fine navy blazer and an awful pink paisley tie. Chintz, even by his standards!

*

In the drawing room Heather was sitting in one of the large armchairs beside the fireplace with Pinot and Grigio at her feet while she read the paper. Mike was on bath duties with the twins and Heather was enjoying a welcome respite, flicking through *The Times* and sipping a gin and tonic. Ranald helped himself to a drink and after exchanging pleasantries, picked up a copy of *Salmon and Trout* and skimmed through the pages, looking at the pictures and browsing the headlines.

The drawing room began to fill and soon there was a merry throng with everyone gathering before dinner to share the day's stories. There was a muffled under current of disapproval about the Count shooting a Royal, although no one was brash enough to say anything derogatory in his company for fear of offending him. In any event, he was engrossed with Babek, as they rather secretively huddled in a corner and chatted in Russian, clearly not wanting to be disturbed.

Eventually, the gong was struck and there was a shuffling of feet and general kerfuffle while everyone took their seats and Ranald found himself sitting beside Max, yet again.

'How was your day?'

'Excellent. We had a good stalk on the hill and the Count, as you know, bagged one of your father's Royals. In fact, probably the only one you had on the place.'

'Yes, I heard. Dad seems to have taken it rather well, all things considered.'

'And are you making any progress with your Russian belle?' continued Max, quickly changing the subject.

'Well, Lady Sally and I have a small wager on that. I have until the end of the week to work my irresistible charm and win the princely sum of ten-pounds!'

'Good luck. But be warned, Mum has an excellent track record on the horses. Do you want to double the stakes on that one?'

'And how is Pippa enjoying the week?' replied Ranald, ignoring Max's proposal.

'She's had a quiet day. In fact, spend much of it in the Lodge, reading her book.'

'Well, I may have a day off tomorrow and pop into Oban, paint a harbour scene and view the galleries. Pippa would be very welcome to join me if she's at a loose end.'

'And can I trust you with my girlfriend?'

'You seemed quite happy to bet against me and Ursula. Are you afraid I will whisk Pippa off her feet?'

'The stakes are higher. I would lose more than a tenner if I lost that one.'

Ranald smiled while turning to look at Max.

'Don't worry, your girl will be safe with me.'

'Well in that case I will ask Pippa. She may want a trip out of the glen.'

The soup starter was quickly cleared and Fiona brought in game stew which she left on the sideboard for everyone to help themselves. Lady Sally did the honours, filling plates which Heather handed to the guests. However, there was a slight lackadaisical feel to the party, something Sir Hector put down to a busy day, outside in the fresh air. He wasn't quite his usual bon viveur self or the congenial host at the dinner table that everyone had come to expect. In truth, he was rather deflated by the loss of his Royal, which still riled him.

They galloped through the courses and were soon onto cheese and biscuits as the port was passed around the table and by ten o'clock everyone was back in the drawing room for a night cap of whisky. As Sir Hector brushed past, Ranald tapped him on the arm.

'Sir Hector, where has the painting gone? It's no longer on the dresser in the hallway?'

'Upstairs on the main landing. We'll hang it there somewhere.'

'And what do you think of it?'

'Well I don't know Ranald, you tell me. You're the expert on these things.'

'I don't know a great deal about cubism, although, I must say it does fascinate me. Do you mind if I pop up and take another look?'

'By all means, help yourself.'

*

Rather surprisingly, Ranald had never been on the first floor within the main body of the house before and he quite admired the generous proportions and sweeping hand rail of the cantilevered staircase while he climbed the steps. The landing was wide with a tatty old sofa situated beside the grandfather clock and there was the picture, standing on the floor at the far end.

6 5

Walking towards it Ranald took in the artefacts which adorned the walls; a couple of sizeable stag heads, coats of arms and typical mid 19th century Scottish landscapes of cattle drinking from lochs and drovers with their sheep. 'Pastiche,' he muttered, thinking how well one of his more contemporary pictures would pimp up the decor and smarten the place up.

Kneeling down he let his eyes roam over the picture, examining the precision of the brush strokes, the blend of colours, irregularity and mismatch of shapes which defined the work. My, how the picture had grown on Ranald since he first saw it and now as he looked closer, naughtily letting a finger run over the canvas, he really began to appreciate its charm and quirkiness, while he let himself be absorbed within its aurora. Turning the painting around and looking closer at the old frame, he found some faded stickers – *Degenerate Art Exhibition Munich 1937.* What did that mean he wondered, retrieving his smart phone and taking a snap. Lingering a little longer and continuing to admire the work, Ranald then stepped back for one last look. Who was Jean Metzinger, he pondered and then mumbling to himself, still unable to understand why the painting should have turned up here, at Fykle Lodge, began to retrace his steps back along the landing.

But, not having been in this part of the house before, curiosity got the better of Ranald. He stopped, pushed open one of the bedrooms doors and looked inside. It was poorly lit from the corridor, but nevertheless, Ranald could see it was a good size, far more generous than his own, with a double bed and two windows looking out over the front lawn. Allowing time for his eyes to became accustomed to the dark, as they flittingly roamed around, he suddenly saw, what appeared to be another picture propped up against the wall. This seemed odd and without thinking he flicked on the lights and blinked while his eyes readjusted to the bright central pendant. Ranald stood motionless, stunned by what sat before him – *Jeremiah* – there was another painting identical to the picture sitting on the landing!

Staring in disbelief, completely befuddled why there should be a second cubist painting in the house, he glanced over his shoulder to double check he was not going, completely and utterly mad and the original was still where he had left it. Acting on impulse, Ranald entered the room, squatted down to examine the picture more closely and then for some unfathomable reason picked it up and retreated back down the corridor, placing it beside the original to compare then. They were most certainly an exact match, even down to the faded, worn stickers on the backs.

*

Suddenly, there was some noise downstairs in the hallway as the party broke up and good nights were being said and all too aware that he was soon likely to be disturbed, Ranald realised that he must act quickly. Perhaps, it was the generous helping of whisky which Sir Hector had dished out earlier which clouded his judgement, or possibly his inherent mischievous nature took hold, but for whatever reason, he swapped the pictures before quickly scampering back to the bedroom.

By now, footsteps and some chatter could be heard on the stairs, so Ranald slipped into the room, quietly shutting the door behind him and switched off the lights. Pausing to allow his eyes to readjust, he was breathing hard and with the nervous excitement building within, Ranald felt his heart pound yet faster. The footsteps and voices became louder. Quickly, returning the picture to the original position, against the wall, he could now hear voices just outside the door and with nowhere else to hide, Ranald entered the en suite bathroom, quietly closing the door behind as the occupant walked into the room and put on the lights – *jillopy jerrepers*! Ranald realised he was in a fix, while considering the ridiculousness of his situation. He could hear footsteps in the room and to his alarm, they appeared to be heading in his direction. Within seconds he would surely be found out and with little alternative, Ranald rehearsed his excuses. A water leak, yes, a water leak. He would say he heard running water and when he came to investigate, simply found a tap left on. It wasn't very convincing and with light now streaming in under the bathroom door he looked around for inspiration, to discover he was in a Jack and Jill bathroom with a second doorway leading to another bedroom. Ranald opened the door and slipped into the adjoining room as he heard someone enter the en suite and the light switch click on behind him. Momentarily, he breathed a sigh of relief!

However, when his eyes readjusted to the subdued light, Ranald looked around the attractive, well-furnished bedroom and suddenly saw the Countess, lying in the double bed, illuminated by a dim side light as he recalled she had left shortly after dinner.

'Egbert, Egbert is that you?' she said, gradually raising herself upright and moving her hands towards the sleeping mask over her eyes. Ranald was living by the skin of his teeth and moving swiftly across the floor, replied in his best guttural German accent,

'Ya, my Darling, ya,' gently taking hold of her hands and kissing her squarely on the lips. Rather alarmingly, she didn't resist. Ranald ever so slowly pushed her hands away from the mask while she lingered in his embrace, appearing to enjoy the intimacy, as he tried desperately to extract himself from her squid like mouth and the acrid taste of cigarettes on her lips. But, it was a price worth paying and bought Ranald sufficient time to suddenly pull away and escape through the main door, back onto the landing before she realised whom it was.

Phew! Close thought Ranald, pausing to collect himself together and then realising he was not yet out of the woods, quickly made his way to the staircase and the hall below, where he met Sir Hector on his way to bed.

'What on earth have you been up to Ranald?'

'I'll tell you in the morning,' he replied continuing towards the back stairs and his bedroom.

*

The Countess removed her eye mask to discover the room was empty. She could hear the Count in the bathroom fiddling with his toothbrush and although slightly mystified by his sudden departure, pulled her mask back down and rolled over to try and sleep.

*

Ranald was now even more confused than ever. One cubist painting in the house was in itself a bit of a mystery, but for there to be two, exactly the same, was a major conundrum. After retiring to bed he just couldn't settle down, tossing and turning and recounting what he had just found, until eventually, he got up and went to the drawing room and helped himself to another whisky.

Putting a log on the fire Ranald enjoyed watching it smoulder and smoke before finally sparking into life. Oh, how he tried to make sense of events, but, however Ranald cut and shuffled the facts in his head, his instinct always took him back to the same conclusion, and that one of the paintings may just be the original!

# Chapter 13 – The Plot Revealed

At half past three in the morning, Mischief, moored up in deep water, just outside Oban harbour. Lieu Chang was on board, with two of his six wives – Suki and Mor – having arrived at Glasgow airport the previous evening, before being flown to the Super Yacht in the Augusta 109 helicopter which usually sat on the stern of the boat. Their reunion had been polite, courteous even, although muted, which was perhaps hardly surprising given that it was a functional relationship rather than one of love. But, regardless, they enjoyed a seven course dinner together while Mischief had cruised up the coast, before retiring to bed, where Lieu Chang now peacefully slept, snoring to his heart's content.

*

Ranald awoke from a restless night's sleep slightly regretting the extra whisky he had drank after his adventure with the paintings. He was fast coming to the conclusion that he was either privy to an elaborate hoax or an international art smuggling scam and was delighted that he had managed to swap the pictures without being caught. Whatever was going on, it amused him to think that it could yet backfire as a result of his intervention. His thoughts turned back to the kiss he had given the Countess and the vile taste of cigarettes which had lingered on his lips. Yuck! Ranald still couldn't quite believe that he had not been caught, slipping out of one door, just before the Count entered via another and all in all felt pleased with himself. He got out of bed feeling rather chipper.

*

Breakfast was in full swing downstairs. Mike and Heather were endeavouring to coax the twins to eat, while Janet and Hugh were eyeing up the cooked kippers which had just arrived on the hot plate. Sir Hector entered the dining room with his usual bustle, followed by the Count and Babek and they all sat together at the top of the table in a little huddle. Surprisingly, the loss of the Royal appeared to have been forgotten.

'Any ideas what you would like to do today gentlemen?' enquired Sir Hector.

The Count finished pouring his coffee before speaking,

'I have a friend who has a boat in Oban and he's offered to collect me from the pontoon on Loch Fykle and take me for a cruise. I think Babek and Ursula are keen to join us.

'What about the Countess and Jacinta?'

'The Countess has decided to go back to Tumult Lodge for a day or so,' replied the Count, looking towards Babek, who placed his coffee cup on the saucer as he started to speak,

'Jacinta would prefer to keep her feet on dry land, so she is going to stay in the Lodge and read a book.'

'Well that sounds as if you are all sorted then. The weather is fine and the barometer is moving up, so you should be in for a sunny day on the water. If you get a chance to drop into Oban there is an excellent fish restaurant on the quay I can recommend. Would you like me to book a table?'

'That's very kind of you to offer, but I am not sure what my friend has arranged. Probably best to leave it,' replied the Count

In any event, Sir Hector wasn't too bothered about helping out. Despite appearing unconcerned, deep down, he was still mourning the loss of his Royal.

'Hugh, what about you? Do you fancy a day on the hill with Ewan?'

'Where is he likely to go? I would love to, but, I wouldn't be able to climb Arragher, if that is where he wants to stalk.'

'It's still a southerly wind, so you can go to the Drum and we can give you a good start in the Argocat.'

Ewan entered the dining room to see what plans the Laird had for him, just in time to hear Hugh reply,

'Why not? Let's see if I can bag a stag.'

Janet looked towards him and gave an approving smile.

'Grab yourself a cup of tea Ewan. It's back to the Drum for you with Hugh,' said Sir Hector.

'That'll be fine, there should still be plenty of stags there.'

Sir Hector and Ewan caught each other's eye and nodded, acknowledging there would be no Royals bought back today. Hugh would behave himself.

*

Ranald arrived late for breakfast after everyone had left and managed to scrape together a bowl of porridge and some leftover kippers which he ate, while browsing over an old copy of the *Sporting Times* and sipping his tea. Pippa walked in.

'Ah, there you are Ranald. Max mentioned you may be going to Oban today and if I wanted, I could tag along?'

'Certainly, I would be delighted to have some company. I wasn't planning on doing much other than perhaps painting a seascape from the harbour side and visit Finnian's Gallery to see what rubbish they are displaying.'

'Great, give me ten to get ready and I'll join you.'

'No rush, I haven't even finished breakfast yet. Let's meet in the hallway in say twenty minutes?'

Ranald enjoyed some peace and quiet in the dining room, much preferring to gaze absent mindedly out of the window, across the lawn, than make polite conversion at this time in the morning. Once finished he collected his wallet from his room and met Pippa downstairs.

'You set then?'

'Yes, I'm looking forward to visiting Oban. It will make a change from hanging around the Lodge with my head stuck in a book.'

'What are you reading?'

'Romantic novel, Olga Dopski, set in Russia during the Crimean War.'

'Sounds interesting,' replied Ranald, rather unconvincingly.

*

The MG turned over a couple of times and then sparked into life and on pulling away Ranald accelerated hard kicking up gravel at the rear. Max who had been watching from the game room looked on and suddenly felt pangs of jealously grow within, as he wondered to himself, why he had ever suggested to Pippa to have a day with Ranald in Oban.

'Don't worry,' said Lady Sally, who had just walked in and caught her son observing the scene. 'It's only Ranald. He's unlikely to take Pippa away from you.'

'I hope not, I quite like her.'

'Good, I'm pleased for you both. I doubt a day with Ranald in Oban will change anything.

'Yes, I suppose you are right,' replied Max, not feeling wholly reassured.

\*

The Countess had a drag on the Silk Cut cigarette casually hanging from her lips, while driving the Range Rover quickly along the single track road out of the glen, back towards Tumult Lodge, although she slowed when she saw a little Peugeot approaching with the familiar face of Camille Jankers sat behind the wheel. With the wee French car, respectfully pulled onto the verge, the Countess flashed her lights and accelerated past.

'Das Fraulein,' she muttered, knowing that Camille was on route to meet her husband and prone to the occasional outburst and tirade from time to time, mumbled through gritted teeth, 'zee bitch'.

Camille continued down the beautiful glen, enjoying the gorgeous scenery, draped in sunshine and within fifteen minutes pulled up close to the pontoon besides Babek's black Range Rover. The doors opened and the Count jumped out rather sprightly, followed by Babek and Ursula.

'Camille how good to see you, it's been too long,' said the Count, 'I have missed you over the last few days,' and wrapping his arms around her, planted a kiss on her lips and playfully squeezed her generous bottom.

Camille smiled back in her dutiful way,

'I know, I've missed you too.'

In reality, Camille was becoming bored of being the Count's mistress. When their relationship first started she had genuinely been drawn to his tall elegant looks and dark brown eyes, but now, after a number of years of being dragged around Europe the initial attraction was on the wane and Camille was looking for a way to extract herself from the arrangement.

'Nice to meet you,' she said, shaking Babek's and Ursula's hands.

Further down the loch they could see a powerful day boat approaching and within five minutes a forty-foot Portofino pulled alongside the pontoon and tied up, while the landing steps were lowered. Babek collected the painting, which was wrapped in a soft woollen blanket, as a well-dressed Chinese gentleman, all in black, stepped off the boat to greet them.

'Hello,' my name is Wran Chin. Lieu Chang has sent me to collect you,' he said with a smile, while bowing in turn to the guests and shaking their hands.

'Nice to meet you,' replied Babek, leading the party onto the small deck beside the bridge, where another well-dressed Chinese man nodded in their direction to welcome them aboard. Within a couple of minutes the boat was cast off and the powerful engines burst into life and began thrusting them back up the loch towards Oban.

*

It was a glorious day, the water glistening in the sunlight and with the faint whiff of the sea in their nostrils it would have been lovely to stay on deck and admire the scenery. However, there wasn't much room, so Wran Chin ushered his guests downstairs to the cabin and carefully stowed the picture, before leading everyone to the central table, where a couple of bottles of Pol Roger Champagne were chilling in a bucket of ice. Placing a bowl of the Caspian's finest beluga caviar on the table, he said, 'Please help yourselves. Lieu Chang would like you to enjoy the trip.'

Babek's piggy little eyes lit up with a gluttonous smile appearing on his chubby little face and ignoring everyone else he sat down, picked up a spoon and devoured a mouthful of the fine sturgeon eggs.

'Wonderful, absolutely wonderful.'

The Count popped a bottle of Pol Roger and within a few minutes they were all gorging themselves as they began to relax and enjoy the journey. The champagne worked its magic and after a refill, Babek turned to the painting, raised his glass and proposed a toast;

'To Jean Metzinger. He's about to make us US$25 million dollars,' with a big smile breaking out across his face.

The Count grinned before taking a generous swig of champagne and raising his glass, 'to Metzinger,' he repeated.

\*

Babek had come by *En Canot,* within the last six months. Its provenance was well documented during the early years; exhibited in Prague in 1914, acquired by George Muche at the Galerie Der Sturm, before being sold in 1936 to the Nationalgalerie, Berlin. Then confiscated by the Nazis where it was exhibited at the *Degenerate Art Show* in Munich during the summer of 1937, Hitler's way of mocking modernism, which ironically proved to be a surprisingly popular exhibition with his countrymen. After that however, its whereabouts becomes less clear, until it surfaced at the Lavidia Palace, the summer home of Tsar Nicholas II, in the Crimean. How it came to be in Russia was a mystery, but some believed it had been taken there by General Erich Von Manstein when he led the Nazi's successful campaign defeating the Russians in 1942. It was thought to have remained at Lavidia for a number of years until the Palace became an asylum, whereupon it was sold, along with many other artefacts, to help raise funds to repair the roof.

Gradually as time passed, *En Canot* became known on the Russian black market and had traded a couple of times in Moscow between wealthy collectors. Babek had become friendly with the current owner, Belusha Popvorsky, a chirpy little man and modern-day oligarch, having made his fortune when the state-owned power network was privatised. Now in his seventies, he wished to cash the picture in, so it wouldn't be a burden to his family after he had shuffled off this earthly world and was no longer with them. In any event, his much younger, but eccentric wife, Jolga, hated the painting and swore she would throw it out as soon as he was gone.

'*Traplush*'! – for the garden fire,' she would remonstrate after a shot or two of vodka!

\*

In Moscow, *En Canot* would make about US\$10 million max and may take some time to sell, although on the global black market it could potentially make nearer its full value of around US\$50 million. Strangely, some investors preferred to acquire art in this way, without the publicity of big auctions and also because it gave their private collections an air of mystique, if they had the odd painting which was not well publicised or known about. Babek knew the workings of the black market well and with his accomplice and occasional lover, Ursula, they had forged many links throughout the world and were instructed by Belusha to sell the picture for the best possible price.

Delighted with their appointment, Babek had scoured his contacts looking for a buyer and eventually, Lieu Chang had come to him through one of China's more salubrious underworld operators, Siz Long a glamorous and elegant female in her mid-forties. She was commonly known as – *latrodectus tredecimguttatus* – the 'Black Widow', because of her propensity to murder the partner of anyone who crossed her, leaving them to suffer bereavement in widowhood, before she would eventually kill them as well.

Life had not been kind to her, though. Orphaned at birth the Black Widow had grown up in the red-light district of Beijing with a dysfunctional and ruthless aunt, Madame Tutong. It had been a difficult and often a sad childhood, learning to fend for herself and survive in an adult world inhabited by some rather unsavoury characters, which in part, probably went some way to explaining her psychopathic tendencies. Well, how else was a young girl to get by in the deprived slums of Beijing?

However, fortunately Babek and the Black Widow had managed to strike up a working rapport and between them arranged for Lieu Chang to view the painting in Moscow and after a little toing and froing, haggling and an arm wrestle over a bottle of vodka, they eventually agreed a price of US$50 million. It had taken a few weeks to complete, but in Babek's own words, 'The best deal he had ever done,' when finally the Black Widow and he shook hands.

As agreed, Babek would take fifty percent of the proceeds, leaving Belusha with US$25 million, which was far more than he would have obtained if he had sold the picture to another Muscovite and gave him a decent return on his original investment of US$2 million. Everyone seemed happy with the arrangement, but, this did leave one not inconsequential problem. How to smuggle the painting out of Russia, a chore which fell to Babek and was the reason why his cut was so generous.

*

*En Canot* was known to the Russian authorities; The Federal Regulatory Service for Mass Media, Communications and Protection of Cultural Heritage who were responsible for national treasures and the issuing of import and export licences. They knew Belusha owned the painting and that he kept it at his house in Rublyovka, however, they never took any action because they weren't bothered about repatriating the picture to its rightful owner and simply wanted it to remain in Russia. As far as the Federal Regulatory Body were concerned, Belusha was free to sell the painting to another

Muscovite, so long as they were kept in the loop and he didn't try to take the picture out of the country.

However, *En Canot* had never been officially authenticated by the Wildenstein Gallery in Paris, the authority on such matters, because they would have simply confiscated it. Babek was aware of this and as a consequence, the *Unauthenticated En Canot* was not on the official list of national treasures, which meant the export licence procedure was less onerous. Provided good photographs accompanied the forms, then so long as they were submitted prior to the date of export, the painting could be taken abroad and the licence issued retrospectively.

Babek knew that once the Head Office of the Federal Regulatory Body in Moscow saw the application they would realise what had happened and seek repatriation, so he decided to submit the paperwork to one of the district offices, Sevastopol, who would be unaware of the significance. It would take the hic rustic country officials a few days to process the forms and forward these to Moscow, by which time the picture would have left the country, meaning the Federal Body would have to go through Interpol to obtain a confiscation order. Babek reckoned they would have at least a week before anyone would catch up with them.

In the meantime, his friend and intermittent business associate, the Count, had arranged for a notorious Dutch forger to make a copy, which they would swap with the original, so when eventually the authorities apprehended them, the picture would be found to be a fake and all the fuss would die down. But, of course, by this time *En Canot*, would actually be on its way to China. It was like money laundering really. Passing ownership through a couple of hands, throwing a fake into the mix and generally muddying the waters. Sir Hector was simply the innocent stooge and completely unaware of the significance of his present. Ingenious, they all agreed, drinking yet more champagne and scoffing the remnants of beluga caviar, while the Count and Babek pawed their giggling mistresses. Wran Chin looked on with repulsion.

*

Ranald and Pippa were having a less successful journey and were pulled over in a lay by at Ballahulish, with the MG belching out steam from under the bonnet.

'Blasted car has overheated,' said Ranald stating the obvious.

'I can see that.'

Jumping out he opened the bonnet and checked the oil, which despite being low, at least didn't have white streaks, indicating water ingress and a blown head gasket. With a cloth, Ranald managed to remove the radiator cap as hot steam hissed out and then from the bottle, he always kept in the boot, topped up the water and managed to get the lid back on before inspecting under the engine. He could see a small leak – tap, tap, tap, it dripped onto the tarmac.

'Blast,' cursed Ranald, pulling himself out from under the car and then adding some more oil for good measure, before climbing back into the driver's seat and firing up the old girl. The engine spluttered back into life. Pippa looked at Ranald a little apprehensively.

'Don't worry yourself, it's only a wee leak. We should get to Oban and once the engine cools I will drop a couple of raw eggs into the radiator, which should seal it for the return journey.'

'Raw eggs?' questioned Pippa.

'Yes, raw eggs. Its ingenious really. They get drawn to the leak and when the water heats up they cook and plug it. Who would have thought a simple egg could be so useful? It's not a long-term solution, but it should get us back from Oban in one piece.'

'Raw eggs,' repeated Pippa, sitting in the car and looking out of the window with a bemused expression on her face.

\*

As Ranald had thought, they reached Oban within the hour with steam beginning to seep out from under the bonnet.

'There you are, I told you we would make it.'

Pippa looked at Ranald and smiled. The day was at least going to be an adventure, regardless of whether the old MG got them back to the Lodge or not.

'Let's go for a coffee. I need a caffeine hit and know a little place on the harbour side which does a decent brew.'

'Okay, I'm in your hands today Ranald. You call it.'

Once inside McGregor's, a dated old cafe with formica table tops and a juke box in the corner, they placed their orders and Ranald became aware of a gathering of people, jostling outside on the quay. When he looked closer, he spotted Mischief moored just beyond the harbour walls.

'Holy Moses, look at that Pippa,' he exclaimed, staring at the sleek four hundred and fifty-foot super yacht with four decks and a helicopter parked on the stern. It was massive, opulent, vulgar really and Ranald doubted the likes of which had ever been seen in Oban before. Pippa was more matter of fact about it.

'It's just a big boat Ranald,' she replied while collecting the coffees.

Ranald looked around at Pippa, with a surprised expression on his face, and shook his head.

'Come on, let's go outside and take a closer look.'

*

The water was flat on Loch Fykle and the Portofino was making swift progress, occasionally touching on twenty knots, serenely gliding over the sparkling surface, leaving a rippling wake as it went. However, Lieu Chang did not want to receive his guests until just before midday, so Wran Chin did a small detour to waste a little time and made sure they arrived alongside Mischief at quarter to twelve. Babek and the Count were oblivious to having reached their destination, while they finished off a second bottle of Pol Roger and yet more Beluga Caviar.

*

There was now quite a crowd on the quay and Ranald, who had become more curious walked away from the main throng towards one of the permanent telescopes, further along the front.

'Where are you going?' enquired Pippa.

'Just follow me, we will get a better view from over here.'

Pippa watched Ranald rummaging through his pockets, until eventually he found a twenty pence piece, which he placed in the slot, before putting the telescope to his eye.

The landing steps had been lowered onto the front deck of the Portofino and Ranald directed the telescope left, then right, up, then down, trying to find the super yacht and then, more by accident than good judgement, picked up Mischief in the view finder and scoured all around. Eventually he let the scope rest on the Portofino and his eyes focus – *galloping grhinos*! He was dumbstruck. There was the Count, Babek and Ursula, with a man dressed in black carrying a large rectangular shape wrapped in a blanket, climbing the steps which had been lowered onto the boat. It was the painting!

The telescope shutter suddenly snapped shut.

'Damn,' shouted Ranald, while searching his pockets for some more loose change.

'Pippa have you got any twenty pence pieces?'

'Yes, I think so. Let me have a look. Here's one.'

Once Ranald had re-focussed, he could see them all making their way up the steps. The man in black with the picture first, followed by Babek, the Count, another woman whom he didn't recognise and finally Ursula. Wow! What legs he thought, watching her taught shapely thighs elegantly carry her upwards as he slavishly stared at her short skirt and curvaceous bottom.

'Can I have a look?'

Yes, yes, just a minute,'

'What's so interesting?'

'Well nothing really. But here, have a go.'

Pippa put the telescope to her eye. It took her a little while to direct it and when she eventually picked up Mischief, she saw an empty deck with the Portofino bobbing up and down alongside the mother ship. Swivelling to the left, then the right and then – snap! The shutter closed again.

'What did you see?' enquired Ranald.

'Nothing really, just the boat.'

Ranald pondered, if he should divulge all to Pippa. The events of the week were beginning to play on him and he had toyed with the idea of letting Sir Hector in on his secret. However, for some reason something had held him back. He was not sure why, but there was just this niggling feeling in the back of his mind, which cautioned him from doing so. Ranald was inherently secretive anyway.

'What now then Ranald?'

Slightly thrown by events, Ranald's head was a whirr of speculation, while he tried to reconcile the recent happenings and work out what on earth was going on. He was now more convinced than ever, that one of the pictures was the original, probably very valuable and it appeared to him that quite by chance, he had stumbled into a plot to smuggle the painting somewhere. But, if so, who was in on it? Sir Hector? Babek and the Count were his friends after all.

'Ranald, come in? Are you listening?'

'Yes. Sorry Pippa my thoughts were elsewhere. Let's go and have a look around Finnian's Gallery and see what the opposition are up to.'

# Chapter 14 – The Race is On

Once inside the gallery Ranald and Pippa browsed the works, mainly contemporary Scottish Landscapes, modern day impressionism with the paint usually applied with a palette knife in deep rich swathes of colour. It harked back to the great Scottish Colourists: Peploe, Cadell, Leslie, Hunter and as Pippa swooned over some paintings, Ranald passed disparaging comments about others. In truth though, he knew that his work fell a long way short of what his contemporaries could do. Ranald was in some ways too traditional, remaining faithful to the hog's hair brush and belittling the palette knife as a blunt and inferior instrument, suitable for tradesmen and manual workers. However, in reality, he lacked the confidence to be bold and too often became bogged down in a minor detail, say a solitary figure in the foreground, which was of no consequence to the overall impression. How he would fiddle and tinker with his paintings, gently softening, when he really should have been daring and brave, splashed some colour onto the canvas and release his creative flair, in a gushing fountain of spontaneity and extravagance. He needed to have – *chutzpa!* And in reality, deep down he knew it.

However, Ranald appeared to be in a world of his own unable to concentrate on any given picture for more than a few seconds, incapable of having a coherent conversation and was proving to be a tedious companion. Eventually, Pippa decided to take matters into her own hands.

'Ranald, I'm going to have a look around Oban. Why don't you go and paint a picture and I will meet you back at the car in say an hour, an hour and a half?'

'Okay that sounds like a plan,' replied Ranald who was not particularly enjoying the gallery and rather pleased to escape and have some time on his own.

*

Wran Chin had carried the painting up four flights to the main reception gallery. It was a beautiful room with circular glass windows on three sides, lined with intricately carved oak panelling and in the centre was an open fire with flames flickering around the burning logs. Beyond was a large round table where Lieu Chang sat on a massive chair which had been specially designed to accommodate his gargantuan size. It looked like a throne. He was flanked either side by Suki and Mor and never said a word, as Wran Chin led everyone in and placed the picture on an easel, before pulling the blanket off to reveal it.

There was complete silence. Not a whisper or a rasping breath could be heard, until Lieu Chang's chair noisily scraped across the wooden floor as he stood up and then slowly waddled towards the easel. He paused, letting his eyes roam over the painting and eventually raising his right hand, ran his fingers over the surface and then stared at the picture for what felt like eternity. Suddenly, Lieu Chang quickly span around with a broad smile on his face and nodded, indicating his approval.

Wran Chin looked relieved and also nodded, acknowledging his master and then turned to Babek and the Count.

'Lieu Chang is very grateful to you for delivering the picture. Now, please do sit down.'

The tension appeared to dissipate from the room as everyone shuffled towards the table and took a seat. Lieu Chang waddled back to join them.

\*

The door opened and in walked the Black Widow. Babek had not been expecting her. He was all too aware of her fearsome reputation and would have much preferred she was not around, just in case something went wrong. Plainly that was not to be.

'Hello, nice to see you,' he said as they both greeted each other with a bow.

But, the Black Widow didn't linger to exchange pleasantries with Babek and after the briefest of encounters walked on past him to greet Lieu Chang. They bowed and spoke quickly in Mandarin, before she continued around the table towards the easel and collected the painting. Babek and the Count promptly stood up and Wran Chin sensing their concern began to speak.

'Please, this is just a formality. Lieu Chang simply wants his experts to check it's the same painting they saw in Moscow.'

It was a fair point and in the circumstances not an unreasonable request, but, Babek had been in the art industry long enough to know the tricks of the trade and he wasn't overly keen to lose sight of the picture, until the deal had completed.

'Okay, but the painting doesn't leave the room. The experts can do their work in here.'

Wran chin spoke with Lieu Chang, then the Black Widow and eventually Lieu Chang smiled and nodded towards Babek, signalling his agreement.

'That's fine,' said Wran Chin. 'The painting will remain in the room. Now, please do sit down and enjoy lunch.'

Waiters arrived to serve Vintage Pol Roger Champagne with small spoons of foie gras.

*

Ranald had returned to the MG, retrieved his easel and paint bag and set up on the quay ready to start with a sketch. But, try as he did, his heart just wasn't in it. Instead, he reached for his smart phone and started searching in his browser for more details on the painting. Round and round the icon circled and then – *failed connection* – appeared on the little screen. Becoming frustrated with the wiles of modern communication, Ranald decided to phone Elspeth instead.

*

Sitting in her gallery, Elspeth was surprised to see the call come through.

'Ranald what a pleasant surprise. How is your holiday going? Caught any fish?'

'Well almost. I mean I've hooked a couple, but, unfortunately not managed to get them onto dry land. Frustrating really.'

'Ah, the one that got away.'

'Well yes, I suppose so.'

'Anyway Ranald, you haven't phoned me for a general chat. What can I do for you?'

'It's a strange request. The photo of the picture I sent through.'

'Yes, I remember. Looted by the Nazis, so the internet said.'

'Well, do you know anything else about it? It's just that, I think the original may have turned up at Fykle Lodge.'

'Oh! Are you sure you haven't been drinking too much whisky, Ranald?'

'Well, I don't think so. Could you give it another google search and see if you can find anything else about it? Does the – *Degenerate Art Exhibition* – ring any bells?'

'Ah, yes. I do recall that, now let me have another look. What was the name of it again?'

'Try Jean Metzinger, he was the artist.'

Elspeth's screen icon circled while it searched.

'Here we are. *Jean Metzinger 1913 En Canot exhibited in Prague 1914, acquired in 1916 by the Galerie Der Sturm, sold to the Nationalgalerie, Berlin, then confiscated by the Nazis around 1936 and displayed at the Degenerate Art Show in Munich.*'

'And what was the *Degenerate Art Show*?'

'Not sure,' said Elspeth, clicking onto the link.

'Okay, here are some details. It ran from July to September in 1937 and was Hitler's exhibition of anti-modernism. The picture has been missing ever since.'

The doorbell of Hutchinson's Gallery rang and a customer walked in.

'Sorry Ranald, must dash, someone's popped into the shop. You never know they may buy one of your paintings. Bye, bye.'

Elspeth hung up and left Ranald to digest what she had told him.

\*

After the taster of foie gras, another small spoon arrived with quails' eggs in a rich truffle sauce and the champagne glasses were topped up yet again. Oysters Rockefeller followed as the wine sommelier uncorked a 2012 Ramonet Montrachet Grand Cru and a little chatter began to flow, before freshly caught Scottish lobster in a rich bouillabaisse sauce arrived with more Grand Cru, as the mood continued to improve. Lieu Chang grinned from time to time, nodding at his guests, while Suki and Mor smiled as they looked on.

Venison Wellington was the main, served with a decanted 2004 Roumier Musigny Grand Cru while all the time, Lieu Chang's experts poured over the painting and discussed matters amongst themselves. Babek began to relax. What was there to worry about? Lieu Chang and his people had been over the picture before and with the Grand Cru slipping down rather nicely, a smile returned to his face. He began to enjoy lunch.

*

Ranald put his canvas away without even applying a dash of paint. He just wasn't in the mood and in any event, whichever way he looked out to sea, that ruddy great yacht dominated the vista and he had no wish to paint the huge monstrosity, which he considered little more than the vanity of a rich person's ego. Ranald racked his brains, thinking about the picture. He was now more certain than ever, that one of the paintings must be the original and since he had swapped them last night, there was a distinct possibility that it would still be at Fykle Lodge. He suddenly felt a sense of urgency to return and get hold of the picture, although exactly what he was going to do with it, was not particularly clear.

It was half past one and he was wondering where on earth Pippa had got to and becoming impatient to leave, Ranald walked down the high street to try and find her. If his hunch was right and the original was still at the Lodge, then those on the yacht, may also realise this and send Babek and the Count back to collect it.

'Ranald, Ranald,' he suddenly heard, turning around to see Pippa's head sticking out of the newsagents.

'Ah, there you are Pippa. Come on let's get going, it's time to go back to the Lodge.'

In truth, Pippa was bored and quite happy to leave, but she was surprised by the sense of urgency in Ranald's voice.

'What's the rush?'

'Don't ask, we just need to get going. Trust me.'

They marched to the car in silence and Ranald was in the driver's seat with the engine running before Pippa had even managed to close the door.

'Haven't you forgotten something?'

Ranald turned around with a perplexed look on his face.

'Eggs?'

Pippa reached inside her bag and passed half a dozen to Ranald.

'For the radiator!'

'Oh, yes. Well remembered,' replied Ranald, switching off the engine, clicking open the bonnet and taking the packet from Pippa. Two will do, he thought, cracking the shells and dropping them in, before hastily jumping back into the driver's seat and again firing up the old girl.

'Why the urgency?' asked Pippa for a second time. 'We were having a relaxed, leisurely day and suddenly there is a desperate rush to get back.'

Ranald considered the question and again pondered if he should let Pippa know the reason for their sudden departure, but instead, decided to stone wall it.

'We've exhausted Oban, seen all there is to see and in any event, my painting wasn't going well. Artistic temperament I'm afraid.'

Revving the engine, Ranald set off. Pippa simply shut up and resigned herself to the journey home.

\*

The second bottle of Grand Cru was drained as the plates were being cleared to make way for the dessert, a delicate cappuccino and raspberry soufflé, as the sommelier decanted a Sauternes dessert wine from the Chateau d' Yquem. The pace of eating had picked up and Babek loosened his belt a notch while looking out of the window, longing to take a short stroll around the deck to aid his digestion. But there was no respite. Lieu Chang appeared to be hitting his stride, effortlessly gobbling up all that was put before him.

Suddenly, there was a little disturbance surrounding the painting at the far end of the room. The Black Widow stood up and purposefully walked over and after what appeared to be a heated conversation with the experts, they called for Wran Chin. Looking on apprehensively, Babek and the Count were not entirely sure what to make of the abrupt change in mood and what it all meant, but, after a couple of minutes Wran Chin walked back to the table and spoke with Lieu Chang. The mandarin flowed between like molten lava, erupting from a volcano and for once Lieu Chang appeared animated, gesticulating with his hands while his brow became furrowed, plainly disturbed by what he was hearing and then all of a sudden they stopped talking and turned to face Babek and the Count. There was complete and utter silence in the room, not so much as a clink of cutlery could he heard.

Babek and the Count returned their stare, still not sure what was going on, until after a further period of deathly quiet, eventually, Wran Chin cleared his throat and with his eyes held firmly on Babek, spoke,

'The painting's a fake.'

Babek stood up.

'It can't be. It's the same picture you saw in Moscow. It's simply not possible.'

'It's a good copy, but the brush strokes in small areas don't match the high resolution images we took when we last saw it.'

Lieu Chang's chair scraped noisily across the wooden floor as he raised his massive bulk onto his short fat legs and without saying a word, waddled out of the room, quickly followed by Suki and Mor. Babek looked back towards Wran Chin to provide further explanation, only to see the Black Widow approach the table with a henchman either side, brandishing AK47 assault rifles.

'There must have been a mix up,' said the Count. 'I'm not sure how it has happened, but somehow we must have brought the copy by mistake and left the original at the Lodge.'

'Yes of course,' continued Babek. 'That must be the reason. It's easily resolved.'

Wran Chin didn't smile.

'Lieu Chang is a very honourable man; however, he doesn't take kindly to being trifled with. He paid you a US$5 million deposit, which you still hold. You have forty-eight hours to deliver the original.'

'Or what?' asked the Count.

Wran Chin simply held out his hand in the direction of the Black Widow. No more needed to be said. Babek gulped. He fully understood the implications and it was not a pleasant thought.

Within five minutes, they were all back on the Portofino with the fake picture travelling at 20 knots towards Loch Fykle.

*

Ranald had his foot to the metal, pushing the MG along as fast as he dare and by the time they reached Ballahulish, the temperature gauge was hovering dangerously close to the red. He knew they should stop, let the engine cool and add a little more water, but Ranald now had the bit between his teeth and he was determined to get back to the Lodge as soon as possible and get his hands on the painting, come what may. With steely resolve he kept his foot hard on the accelerator, while Pippa sat in silence.

Continuing to eat up the miles the MG roared on and within twenty minutes they reached the single track road down the glen. The temperature gauge was now firmly in the red with the oil light intermittently flickering red and when Ranald slowed to turn off the main road, he saw wisps of steam, seeping out from under the bonnet.

'Blast it,' he muttered. The eggs hadn't done much good. It was touch and go if the car would make the eight miles to Fykle Lodge, but, Ranald reasoned to himself, that there were many old, clapped out MG BGT's, but only one *En Canot* by Jean Metzinger and while he knew it would probably be terminal, he pushed his foot yet harder on the accelerator, as the old girl bounced over rises and screeched around corners on their way down the glen.

*

The water on Loch Fykle was calm and the mood in the Portofino equally subdued as the twin engines purred, powerfully driving the boat along. They had made good time and were nearing the bottom of the loch with the pontoon almost in sight.

'I don't understand it,' said the Count. 'The copy never left my room. How on earth it became mixed up with the original is beyond me.'

'Who knows,' replied Babek, 'possibly one of the cleaners moved it. However the most important thing is, that we get back and our hands on it, or…' he hesitated, not sure what to say next.

'We are in big trouble?' asked the Count.

'Yes, to put it mildly. The women with the two henchmen. Do you know that in China she is known as the Black Widow?'

The Count looked at Babek vacantly.

'Firstly, she kills the partner of her victim, so they suffer grief and then as they are getting over their bereavement, she kills the victim. It sometimes takes months, even years, but you can be sure of one thing, the Black Widow always gets the job done.'

The Count gulped. He wasn't too concerned about the Countess, but if they didn't get the original painting to Lieu Chang, the omens weren't looking good.

The Portofino began to slow on the final approach to the landing pontoon and once on dry land they would be within a couple of minutes' drive of the Lodge.

*

Ranald was no more than quarter of a mile from the entrance drive with the green verges and trees lining the road, flashing by in a haze. The MG twisted and roared, hugging the tarmac and flexing around the corners, when all of a sudden – bang! All the lights on the dashboard began to flash and there was an abrupt loss of power with steam flooding out from beneath the bonnet. But miraculously, somehow the car kept going, with a loud clunking noise coming from the engine and the vile smell of burnt oil, drifting throughout the inside. Ranald turned in past the two tall columns, limped up the gravel track and ground to a halt in his usual place, just outside the east entrance. Looking around, Pippa glared at him in a daze.

'You are absolutely bonkers.'

'I know,' replied Ranald, jumping out of the car and running towards the house.

Babek's black Range Rover was entering the drive and hurtling towards the Lodge as Ranald ascended the main staircase and grabbed the painting before bounding back down. But, when he reached the hallway, he heard voices in the porch and with no alternative, ran for cover into the drawing room and hid behind the sofa. He could hear footsteps quickly climbing the staircase, Babek and the Count remonstrating in Russian and then someone else enter the porch. Ranald felt trapped and feared he would soon be discovered, but, when he looked around, he saw the three-quarter length window ajar and an escape route.

Quickly crawling over the tatty old faded carpet, Ranald gently pushed the window open, slid the picture through and then wriggled out. Picking up the painting he sprinted around the side of the Lodge, towards the game larder and on opening the door entered, to find himself standing beside the Royal stag, which the Count had shot the previous day. Oh, what on earth was he to do with the painting now. Around the room he peered, but there were no obvious hiding places in the clean sterile environment and Ranald found himself staring at the hollow insides of the stag for inspiration, while he racked his brains. Alas, devoid of ideas, he let his eyes be drawn upwards, along the sleek carcass, until eventually they came to rest on the hook and chain in the ceiling and there he found the answer he had been looking for. A hatch into the roof space!

With the help of an upturned bucket and heavy metal hook, he managed to open it and with a little huffing and puffing, carefully pushed the picture into the loft, before shutting the door and then briskly walking around to where the cars were parked.

Pippa was still in a state of shock from the journey and only just getting out of the steaming wreck as Ranald looked on admiringly at his old MG. Such resilience in the face of adversity. The old girl had not let him down.

'Pippa let me give you a hand.'

She returned a stare of bewilderment.

'Ranald, you could have killed me at the speed you drove back.'

'Now come, come, it wasn't that bad.'

They looked up to see Ursula disappearing into the house with the fake picture, partially wrapped in the blanket, under her arm.

'Ursula how nice to see you,' said Sir Hector who had heard everyone arrive and surprised that they should all of been back so early, walked through to investigate.

'What's all the hubbub about,' he asked, confused to see Ursula holding his present with a blanket loosely hanging around it.

'Nothing really. But, I just had to admire the picture in the daylight,' she replied, before continuing up the main stairs.

Sir Hector shook his head and wandered back towards his study in silence while thinking, what a load of old – tosh.

# Chapter 15 – An Innocent Mistake

It was mid-afternoon and tea was still to be served in the drawing room. Sir Hector was back in his study not sure what to make of the kerfuffle, while Pippa made her excuses and retired to her bedroom with a romantic novel to recover from a morning with Ranald. The fake picture was placed on the landing floor and there was much toing and froing upstairs, as doors were opened and shut. Babek and the Count could be heard discussing matters in Russian and by the tone of their exchanges, Ranald concluded that all was not well. It was time for a bath and a dram of whisky.

*

Immersed in the hot, dark, peaty water with his feet hanging over the side and whisky tumbler in his right hand, Ranald felt quite chuffed with himself, in fact tickled pink by how events had played out. It had been close, but, he had beaten Babek and the Count to the painting, although what he was going to do with it now was not yet clear. Ranald had no idea how much it was worth and to whom it rightfully belonged, but he quickly made up his mind that he would hand it in to the police at the earliest opportunity and let the authorities sort it out. It was really just a question of how he should go about it. Ranald took another sip of whisky and began to weigh up his options.

He could of course simply leave it in the game larder and tip the police off at the end of the week, which in many ways appealed to his lackadaisical and often lazy disposition. Why make it difficult for himself, he thought, lying in the bath and contemplating some more. However, this concerned him a little. There were still quite a few days to go and always the possibility that someone else may find it, and in any event, he didn't want to drag Sir Hector into disrepute, as would surely happen if the picture was discovered at Fykle Lodge.

The alternative was to smuggle the painting out of the glen and leave it anonymously at a police station, which surprisingly, excited his adventurous side. He felt the hairs on the back of his neck begin to tingle, as the romantic idea gained traction and very quickly enveloped him. How difficult could it be? Imagine the dash and daring of foiling Babek and the Count's, undoubtedly dodgy scam, by smuggling the long-lost picture out of the glen and back to its rightful owners. What excitement, what trepidation, what fun, a far more attractive proposition than simply leaving the painting in situ and keeping his fingers crossed. Draining the tumbler, Ranald pulled the plug out with his toes and watched the water start to whirl at the bottom of the bath, gurgling and then quickly disappear. He had reached a decision. Ranald was going to smuggle the picture out of the glen as soon as possible. It was just a question of how?

*

Jacinta was having a siesta in her room. She always found the stay at Fykle Lodge dragged a little and by mid-week she was only too happy to have some downtime and relax. Babek burst in to find the curtains drawn and her curled up under the duvet, so he left hastily and reconvened in the Count's bedroom to try and work out what to do next.

'So where on earth could the original be? I can't believe we can have lost it,' he remonstrated.

'Well don't blame me,' replied the Count, 'I fulfilled my part of the bargain and got you a copy. It was pretty good by all accounts, even the Chinese thought so.'

Babek looked at the Count in disbelief. He really didn't seem to understand their predicament, so he decided to spell it out clearly and concisely to make sure he was in no doubt how precarious their future was.

'I'm not necessarily blaming you, but in addition to the Black Widow coming after us, if the painting is not found and with Lieu Chang within the next forty-eight hours, we will also have Belusha to answer to. He let us take the picture on trust and is expecting his share of the proceeds or the painting returned. If he gets neither, then he is not going to be particularly happy!'

'Well it's not even officially his, so I am not sure what he has to complain about,' riposted the Count forcefully.

'I doubt Belusha will see it like that. You really don't get it do you? Belusha is not going to stroll into his local police station and report the picture missing. He will simply put a bounty on our heads and wait for someone from the underworld to deliver our scalps. That is of course, if the Black Widow doesn't get us first.' The Count remained silent, quietly considering Babek's words.

Camille and Ursula entered the room and joined them. Looking at Ursula, Babek asked, 'Any ideas?'

She shrugged.

'What about this Ranald character. He's an artist and may have twigged something. I don't particularly like him and I certainly wouldn't trust him."

'I don't know. Possibly. It all seems a bit beyond him though, but I can't be sure either way.'

'Well can you find out as much as you can from him? Work your charm and see if he reveals anything. In the meantime, let's start discreetly searching the house. Most of the guests are out, so we can split up and have a good look before everyone returns.

\*

Ranald was in his room getting dressed and contemplating how best to smuggle the picture out of the glen. The MG had served him well today, but the old girl had played her part and realistically was unlikely to go anywhere, unless it was on the back of a rescue truck. Now that was a thought. What could be simpler than being effortlessly towed away. Shame, he didn't have breakdown cover!

This left Ranald with few options, other than to walk out across the mountains to Bridge of Orchy station and catch a train to Glasgow. It was around an hour's drive by road and Ranald reckoned it would be the best part of a day's walk over Arragher and the more he thought about what he should do, the more he came to the conclusion that this was his only realistic option. As much as he racked his brain for an alternative, he was struggling to come up with anything else of any note.

*

It was around four thirty, teatime, and Ranald was ravenous after missing lunch. Wondering what Fiona had baked, he descended the back stairs and went to the drawing room. It was deserted, apart from a cake and plates in the centre of the table with a fresh pot of tea. The large three-quarter length window was still open, with the curtain blowing in the breeze, so Ranald casually walked over and closed it. Turning around, he came face to face with... Babek, who had quietly entered the room.

'You had a good day?'

'Yes fine,' replied Ranald, a little taken back by Babek's sudden appearance, 'and how about you?'

Babek didn't reply, but instead walked over to the window and looked out.

'And do you like the painting I gave to Sir Hector?'

'It's unusual. Where did you get it from?'

Babek paused before answering.

'I came by it in Moscow. It's a copy of course and not worth much. But, I like the picture and thought it would make an interesting present.'

It was Ranald's turn to hesitate. He slowly walked to the table and started to pour the tea.

'Would you like a cup?'

'Yes, why not. Milk no sugar.'

'Ursula tells me you both run a gallery in Moscow?'

'That's right. I've always been interested in art and when I retired from Sibernos, I ploughed some money in and set up the gallery with her. We've been reasonably successful and managed to keep trading over the last seven years.

'And you, I hear you are an artist?'

'I certainly paint, although perhaps 'artist' may be too grand a word for what I do.'

There were footsteps in the hallway. Lady Sally arrived with Pinot and Grigio following.

'Good afternoon gentlemen, and how has your day been?'

Babek and Ranald were momentarily silenced by the sudden intrusion. Eventually Ranald spoke, 'Excellent thanks.'

'Pippa mentioned you had an interesting time in Oban, particularly the drive home. Why the rush to get back?'

'Nothing really, other than half a day in Oban is enough for anyone.'

Babek's ears pricked up.

'So, you were in Oban today, Ranald?'

'Yes, Pippa and I drove there this morning and had a look around Finnian's Gallery. Some interesting works, mainly contemporary Scottish. You ought to go and have a look, they might go down well in Moscow.'

Mike, Heather and the twins arrived and there was suddenly a little more background chatter in the room as the girls giggled and laughed while Lady Sally cut them some cake.

Hugh, still in his plus fours and with a big grin on his face, walked in with Janet.

'Successful day Hugh?' enquired Ranald.

'By Jove yes. I got a nice stag on the Drum just after two o'clock. It had a poor head and was aged around twelve years, according to Ewan. He's taken it to the game larder to be hung up and weighed, if you want to have a look.'

'Well done. A good stalk?'

'Splendid. We spied him at midday, but the stags were spooked and moved on, around the hill. It took us a couple of hours to catch up and get a shot in.'

Babek realising the conversation had moved away from him managed to slip out and return to his bedroom.

\*

Jacinta was reading her book and after exchanging pleasantries, he left and went to see the Count. Knocking on the door he walked straight in to find him lying on the bed with Camille in a passionate embrace.

'There is no time for that nonsense,' he said firmly as Camille jumped off the bed and straightened her clothes. 'Have you seen Ursula?'

There was an incoherent grumble, so Babek walked down the corridor and knocked on her door.

'Ursula, Ursula are you there?'

The door opened and her head appeared from around the side.

'Come, we need to have a meeting with the Count.'

Camille had sorted herself out and was sitting on the sofa at the end of the double bed beside the Count, when Babek and Ursula entered.

'Did anybody find anything?' asked Babek.

The prolonged silence answered his question.

'Look, I don't think you all fully appreciate the seriousness of our situation. We have to find the painting or we are as good as dead!'

'Well, you are, retorted the Count. We didn't smuggle the picture from Moscow, so I don't see why we should be blamed when it goes missing.'

Babek swivelled around, pulled out a Russian type 54 pistol from his jacket and pointed it straight at the Count, who gulped as an air of panic spread across his face.

'Listen Kraut, I think you need to start understanding how the underworld operates. No one is really interested in the rights or wrongs and apportioning blame. If you get caught up in the cross fire then you will probably get hit and if you think I'm going down on my own, then you have another thing coming. Do I make myself clear?'

The Count simply stared back, too afraid to speak.

Babek returned the gun to his inside pocket and continued,

'Anyone have any suggestions, where the picture could be? Any thoughts? Any leads?'

Again, Babek's questions were met with silence. He looked around forlornly as it slowly started to dawn on him, that he wasn't getting much help from this lot. Babek was fast coming to the conclusion that he may as well have discussed it all with Jacinta instead.

'Does anybody know anything about this artist chap, Ranald? Ursula you sat beside him at dinner one night, did you learn much about him?'

Ursula shrugged her shoulders.

'Other than he paints and sells a few pictures from time to time, nothing really'.

'He was in Oban today and apparently in a rush to get back. There is something about him. I'm not sure what, but I just have my suspicions. Ursula, can you get to know him a bit better? You know what I mean. See if you can find out anything from him which may help us?'

Ursula knew full well what Babek meant. They were first and foremost business associates and she was now being asked to use her feminine charms to the best of their effect. Ursula would get US$2 million if the deal came off, so she resigned herself without any questions. In any event, she quite liked Ranald and the alternative of not finding the picture wasn't particularly appealing.

'Okay, I will see what I can do.'

'Good, I will make sure you sit beside him at dinner tonight.'

*

Downstairs, Ranald was enjoying afternoon tea and cake. Janet had bought her sketches for him to browse and Lady Sally had inquired how he was getting on with Ursula. She was clearly enjoying the little wager. Max and Pippa turned up and appeared particularly affectionate towards one another and Ranald wondered if Pippa had recovered yet, from their journey back from Oban. He decided to avoid her in case of any repercussions and managed to slip out of the drawing room and go for a walk to collect his thoughts together.

*

Ranald wandered down the drive, through the entrance columns, onto the public road, turning right towards the landing pontoon on Loch Fykle. It was a couple of miles and he found the walk bracing, while he thought about how he was going to get to Bridge of Orchy with the painting. Realistically, it was going to be on foot, but the picture was large and would be difficult to carry. He could possibly strap it to his rucksack, although it would be cumbersome and Ranald wasn't entirely sure how he would fasten it securely. Approaching the pontoon, he saw Stuart fishing for slob trout from the landing area.

'Evening, had any luck?'

Quickly turning around Stuart looked a little startled. He hadn't heard Ranald, but, on regaining his composure replied, 'Plenty of nibbles and the odd decent fish,' nodding in the direction of a bucket where there were a couple of trout around a 1lb each.

'I hear you had a good day on the hill?'

'Aye, we managed to get a stag for Hugh. It took a bit of stalking, but the old fella stuck to it and got a shot in.'

'Well done, I am sure Sir Hector will be pleased with that. What about tomorrow? Is anyone going to stalk?'

'Not sure yet. I doubt it though, we've been to the hill for two days on the trot now, so I expect it will be something different. Perhaps a trip down the Loch and a picnic, we don't know yet, it all depends on what the Laird wants to do in the morning.'

'Yes, a cruise on the Loch is usually one of the day's activities, in which case, I may borrow a pony and go for a stalk myself. Sir Hector and Ewan are usually happy for me to go on my own.'

'Okay, I will mention it to Ewan later, if I see him. I don't suppose he will be too bothered, provided you don't shoot a Royal! He's still a bit sore about the one he lost yesterday.'

'Yes, I'm sure he is. Not surprising really, it was a magnificent stag. Look, don't bother Ewan about the pony tonight. I will speak with him in the morning. In fact, if you could keep quiet about it, I would be grateful. I don't want any of the others joining me, because it's a pain looking after them and I can cover the ground much quicker on my own.'

Stuart was silent while casting his fly onto the water and considering Ranald's request. If word got out, then Ewan and he would be expected to lead the stalking party and Stuart quickly decided he would much prefer to have an easier day.

'I won't mention a word to anyone.'

'Thanks,' replied Ranald, leaving Stuart to get on with his fishing.

*

In the drawing room Max was playing the congenial host, serving gin and tonics, while everyone congregated before dinner. The Count was there with his mistress, Camille and there was no sign of the Countess, who had decided to stay the night at Tumult Lodge. The substitution caused no angst. Camille was known and had previously stayed at Fykle Lodge on a number of occasions. In any event, Lady Sally got on with her rather well and much preferred her gentler nature and pleasant disposition to that of the stuffy old Countess.

Sir Hector was deep in conversation with Hugh, not only about his splendid stalk, but also estate matters. Babek and Jacinta arrived and spoke with Mike and Heather and despite Babek's dire situation, he seemed able to cover up his underlying worries.

Ranald was later than normal and once Max had thrust a large tumbler of gin into his hand, he wandered over to speak with Pippa.

'Sorry about the drive back from Oban. I was a bit hasty. I'm not sure what got into me.'

Pippa had spent the afternoon reading her book and with a more attentive Max than usual, had almost forgotten about the events of the morning. She smiled, 'Don't worry. It was an adventure. It's not every day that I get driven around the Highlands by a mad Glaswegian, in a clapped out sports car, with eggs boiling in the radiator.'

Ranald retuned her smile. He was glad there were no hard feelings.

'And is your car likely to recover?'

'Not sure really, it looks pretty terminal. I suspect the head gasket's blown.'

'So how are you going to get back to Glasgow?'

'I haven't a clue, but I will sort something out before the end of the week.

Pippa smiled, 'Never a dull moment!'

Max joined them and put a caressing arm around Pippa, which was rather more doting than he usually was and Ranald began to wonder if there was anything going on behind the scenes. However, he was soon distracted by Ursula entering the room – *frolicking flamingo's.* Wow! She looked; stunning, swaggering across the floor in high heels, dressed in a short black, skin tight frock, which showed off her delicious curves to best effect. It was a miracle she could breathe. Ranald's jaw dropped while watching her elegantly shimmy towards Babek and Jacinta, as momentarily the conversation within the room seemed to dip, until Ursula started to speak and the background chatter picked up again. Lady Sally looked over at Ranald, caught his eye, smiled and raised her eyebrows to the ceiling. He replied with a grin and a wink.

'What do you make of that, Ranald?' piped up Max.

'She's. Well. Hot!' he replied, without even thinking. Ursula's entrance had taken him by surprise.

'Well Ranald, you'll never get a better chance at Fykle Lodge. It makes a change from the local frumps Mum usually invites for you.'

Ranald let his eyes roam up and down Ursula. He just couldn't contain a smile, 'It certainly does, it certainly does.'

Glancing over, Ursula caught Ranald's gaze. He was gobsmacked, in a complete spin until Max managed to catch his attention and bring him back down to earth.

'Pippa tells me you had an interesting morning in Oban, particularly the drive home.'

'Yes, I'm sorry about that. I'm not sure why I was so impatient, but we did make it back in one piece.'

'And I hear there was a super yacht moored just outside the harbour wall. Pippa said it was huge.'

'Yes, amazing really. Very opulent, compete with a helicopter parked on the stern.'

Sir Hector signalled for Max to hit the gong, announcing dinner was ready be served.

*

Filing through the double doors into the dining room Ursula caught Ranald up.

'How was your day?'

'Good thanks,' he replied, moving towards the bottom end of the table where he was usually placed. Ursula followed and found herself sat beside Ranald with Max to her right.

'Dad thought I ought to join the younger set tonight.'

'Well that will be fun,' said Ranald looking up to see Sir Hector staring in his direction with a foreboding look.

'And how about you Max, how was your day?' asked Ursula.

'Nothing out of the ordinary. Janet and I went loch fishing in the morning while Pippa was in Oban with Ranald.'

Ursula looked beyond Max to Pippa and enquired, 'So, what did you do in Oban?'

'I just tagged along with Ranald. We had a look around Finnian's Gallery and I then left him to paint a picture on the harbour side, while I browsed the shops.'

Turning back to Ranald, Ursula asked, 'So how did your painting go? Can I see your work sometime?'

'To be quite frank, I didn't really get started. Artist's temperament I'm afraid. I just wasn't in the mood.'

'Yes, the same artistic temperament which drove me back at hundred miles an hour,' piped up Pippa.

'Why the rush?' asked Ursula staring into Ranald eyes. He met her gaze.

'Red or white?' he asked, reaching for the wine bottles to deflect the question.

Ursula held his eye contact, 'Red please.'

'Interesting. I had you down as a chardonnay girl.'

'Well, there are many things about me you would find interesting,' she replied teasingly.

Salmon terrine arrived on a large silver serving tray and was passed around the table while the hubbub of background conversation increased and the cutlery tinkled on the china plates. Ursula and Ranald were in awe of each other, chatting back and forth, both careful not to divulge too much information, while they gently sparred with one another.

*

At the far end of the table Lady Sally was in full flow, attacking the white wine with her usual gusto, but otherwise, it was a somewhat more sober mood. Jacinta made polite conversation with Sir Hector, but he could sense all was not well with his guests, particularly Babek and the Count who were both very quiet.

'How was your trip to Oban?' he enquired.

'Yes, good thanks. We had a nice cruise up the loch and lunch on the boat just outside the harbour,' replied the Count.

'Pippa mentioned there was a large yacht moored there.'

'Indeed there was. Enormous, with a helicopter parked on the stern.'

'That's unusual for Oban, do you know who it belongs to?'

The Count simply shrugged his shoulders and shook his head, in an apathetical way.

*

Grouse arrived on the sideboard, which Sir Hector had ordered from a friend's estate near Fort William. There were none at Fykle Lodge, so it was a treat and Sir Hector adored them cooked rare, still pink on the inside. Vegetables and potatoes were placed on the table, while plates were passed around and Hugh topped up the wine glasses.

Likewise, Max did the honours at the other end of the table where the mood was considerably more jovial. Ursula was proving a hit with all, chatting back and forth between her neighbours, while Ranald enjoyed the extra attention she was giving him. It was clear that he was being plugged for any information on the painting, but Ranald held his cards close to his chest, careful not to give anything away and simply enjoyed the flirting.

Pippa cut into the grouse and blood began to ooze out,

'Ugh, it's not cooked.'

'That's the way Dad likes them I'm afraid. Just try a bit, it's not as bad as it looks,' replied Max.

Pippa put a small morsel in her mouth, chewed it a few times and then spat it out into her napkin.

'Don't worry,' said Ranald, 'concentrate on the potatoes and veg and we will finish off the grouse for you,' looking towards Max, who smiled at Pippa and nodded.

'You like this?' asked Ursula, glancing at Ranald while holding her grouse slightly elevated off the plate with a knife. The wine was beginning to take hold and Ranald was drawn into her deep blue hypnotic eyes, as she let an inviting smile spread across her face.

'Yes I do, it's delicious,' he replied, cutting into his bird.

Ursula was much less prudish than Pippa and began to make inroads into the grouse, all washed down with plenty of red wine.

'Lovely,' she declared after finishing most of it.

*

By the time the grouse was cleared, Lady Sally had been through her window of sobriety and was now into the witching hour, continuing her vigorous onslaught on the wine. It was all part of the evening's entertainment and Sir Hector looked on helplessly, in the full knowledge that she was now beyond intervention. Her conversation was becoming less coherent and the words occasionally slurred. Everyone knew within the hour, Lady Sally would be slumped in a fireside seat fast asleep with Pinot and Grigio sat on her lap.

*

Sponge pudding came and went and finally the cheese plate arrived as the port was passed around the table. Despite the inquisition from Ursula, Ranald had enjoyed the evening and while sipping his port and smiling inanely to himself, he suddenly felt a hand stroking the inside of his leg! He looked around expectantly at Ursula.

'So, Ranald do you have a girlfriend at home?' she asked looking into his eyes and letting her hand stray further up his thigh.

'Well, no, not really.'

'What do you mean, not really? You must know if you have someone or not?'

'Well then, no, as it happens.'

'Good,' mouthed Ursula strengthening her grip on his leg,

'And would you like a girlfriend?'

Slightly taken aback by the direct approach, Ranald hesitated, not really sure what to say.

'Well yes, I suppose so.'

'What do you mean you suppose so?' replied Ursula, smiling and squeezing his thigh yet firmer. She was almost laughing at Ranald, playing with his insecurities and continuing to tease him, while allowing her hand to creep ever higher. To be quite frank, Ranald was relieved when the chairs started to scrape across the parquet floor as Sir Hector stood up and began to lead his guests towards the drawing room.

Lady Sally made it to her usual fireside seat and within five minutes of sitting down, had her head flung back with her mouth wide open and began to gently snore. Sir Hector poured drams of whisky, while everyone sat down and made themselves comfortable.

Ursula waited for Ranald to take a seat, before plonking herself beside him on the small sofa at the far end of the room. The springs had lost much of their zest and as they both sunk into the cushions, Ursula's already short dress rode up a little higher when she crossed her legs in Ranald's direction and smiled at him. Like her prey, Ursula also took a whisky and continued to toy with poor old Ranald.

'So why no girlfriend then?'

Ranald pondered the question he had been asked many times before and as always he struggled to find an answer.

'I suppose I haven't met the right girl yet,' which was his standard response.

'And what is your right girl then?'

'I don't know exactly. That's probably half the problem, I don't really know what I am looking for.'

Ursula leaned forward in Ranald's direction, letting the top of her black dress plunge to reveal a generous cleavage. Her perfume wafted under his nose and she allowed her hand to drop and rest against Ranald's leg. He returned Ursula's gaze as they stared into each other's eyes.

'And do you think a Russian girl could be the right girl for you?'

'That depends,'

'On anything in particular?'

Unable to answer, Ranald just smiled as Ursula swivelled around so her legs were resting against his, while all the time holding eye contact and letting her tongue delicately circle her lips.

'So Ranald, tell me. Which is your room?'

There was lengthy pause. The silence continued, until eventually. Ranald spoke,

'Top of the stairs, first door on the right.'

Ursula smiled and moving to stand up, looked at Ranald and said,

'Well lover boy, looks like your luck's in tonight. I will see you later,' and squeezing his leg stood up and walked off.

My, it had been a brazen assault, but Ursula appeared to have caught Ranald within her web and all that remained, was for her to devour him!

*

No one had really noticed their flirting, apart from Babek who had kept a close eye on them, and after watching Ursula fawn all over Ranald, he now detested him even more.

'Scottish pig,' he muttered, while waiting for Ursula to join him. She gave a wink, which was sufficient for Babek to know that all was set for later.

Sir Hector kept everyone's glasses topped up, but as the night wore on Mike and Heather were first to retire, which proved to be the catalyst for everyone else to throw in the towel and make their excuses. Slowly the numbers began to dwindle. Ranald and Sir Hector were last to leave and after placing the guard in front of the fire, they left Lady Sally to sleep, snoring contently in her usual chair. She would come to bed soon enough, once she awoke and found herself in darkness.

*

Babek quietly tiptoed down the corridor, turned the door knob and entered Ursula's room. He handed her a cheese wire, a gruesome tool which had recently become a popular appliance to dispatch the unwanted in Moscow. Babek gave Ursula a quick lesson on how to use the deadly instrument and some helpful advice.

'Only try it, if you think it's absolutely necessary and for god's sake don't choke him to death. We will never find the painting if he's dead,' before he returned to Jacinta to hope and pray that Ursula would manage to uncover something and find out where that annoying little artist had hidden the picture. He was sure that Ranald was implicated.

Poor Ursula had mixed thoughts about the plan. Her share of the proceeds was sufficient to set her up for life in Moscow and she fully understood the importance of getting the painting to Lieu Chang before the deadline, or their lives would be in peril. But, she actually quite liked Ranald and although she was more than happy to pay him a visit in the depths of the night, Ursula had no wish to hurt him. She sighed and shrugged her shoulders. Realistically it was not going to be a social visit!

Taking a long hot shower, Ursula stood in the cubicle letting the foam bubbles run down her elegant lithe body, while contemplating her approach and how best to get information out of dear Ranald. Seduction was obviously the answer, but, if that didn't work, then she would have to be prepared for more drastic measure. There would be no alternative, other than of course – the cheese wire!

\*

Ranald was in his pyjamas, tucked up in bed, wondering whose room was at the top of the stairs first on the right. He smiled to himself.

\*

After drying herself and splashing on some Chanel No 5, Ursula slipped into a skimpy, black silk negligee and her slippers. She admiringly spun around in front of the full-length mirror before applying some lipstick, pulling on her dressing gown and then carefully stepped out into the poorly lit corridor. At the far end a side lamp shone over the fake painting, although it did little to cast light further along the landing in her direction of travel. But, as befitting Ursula's athletic frame, she elegantly glided over the worn-out floor rugs and rested her hand on the door knob of the first room on the right. Gently turning it in a clockwise direction, she felt the catch release and quietly slipped inside, carefully shutting the door behind her.

Ursula paused, allowing her eyes to become accustomed to the dark. She could make out a large double bed to her left and on approaching, heard heavy breathing coming from the body, which lay under the covers fast asleep. As her vision improved, Ursula saw there was much more room on the far side, so she quickly tiptoed around, allowed her dressing gown to fall to the floor and then slipped between the sheets.

*

Downstairs, Lady Sally became aware of a hot wet tongue licking her face as Pinot showed his affection. It was almost pitch dark, apart from the gentle glow from the dying embers in the fireplace and she cursed under her breath, why oh why, had Sir Hector not left a side light on. Slowly pulling herself out of the chair, Lady Sally carefully made her way to the hallway and the stairs beyond.

*

Ursula had now snuggled up to the body which was lying with its back to her. She ran her hands across their shoulders and gently caressed the neck. It was all a bit bony, not the broad muscular frame she had been expecting. Undeterred, Ursula continued massaging and then ran her hands down the back, before moving on and gently caressing the buttocks. Oh dear, they were disappointingly flabby and not at all pert as she had hoped. However, her attentions seemed to be having the desired effect, as the body began to stir and slowly rolled over onto their front. Ursula ran a hand through their hair and then looking to capitalise on her position, straddled the dozing lump so she was on top. Not sure what to do next she panicked and decided to wrap the cheese wire around their neck and gently tighten the noose. She suddenly felt empowered!

Sir Hector, had been in a deep sleep, although gradually became aware of a not insubstantial weight on top of him and a sharp penetrating pain around his neck. Realising he was awakening, Ursula leant forward and whispered in his ear, 'You like this?'

Poor Sir Hector, assuming Lady Sally had taken a turn for the worse managed to reply, 'No, not particularly you dotty old thing. Now get off.'

It was hardly the response Ursula had been expecting, so she tightened the noose a little more and gently writhed on top, again leaning forward to speak,

'Now don't you play hard to get with me lover boy. I saw the way you were looking at me earlier,' while she tightened the noose a little more.

Sir Hector was now struggling to breathe as he could feel his face becoming redder. The pain around his neck had become excruciating as he tried to raise himself up, onto his hands while Ursula grasped him, flexing her thighs tightly around his midriff. He was dribbling from the mouth with his eyes starting to glaze over and beginning to feel faint, Sir Hector managed to summon up from the depths of his lungs, what he thought would be his last words and in complete desperation managed to blurt out,

'Now get off me you silly old cow,' as the light switch was flicked on and Lady Sally entered the room, aghast to see Ursula, sitting half naked on her husband like a dominatrix.

The sudden illumination took Ursula by surprise, but, after a couple of blinks while her eyes re-adjusted, she looked down to see a mop of grey hair, sticking out of the top of some tatty old paisley pyjamas and then around at Lady Sally standing in the doorway. Realising her mistake, Ursula released the cheese wire and with Sir Hector coughing and spluttering while regaining his breath, she calmly slid off and out of the bed.

'Sorry, I thought this was Ranald's room,' said Ursula, before picking up her dressing gown and calmly walking passed Lady Sally into the corridor and back to her bedroom.

# Chapter 16 – Dear Fanny

Sir Hector hadn't slept very well after his ordeal with Ursula, so arose early at around six thirty and went to his study, a lovely oak lined room which had originally been the library. It had views to the west down Loch Fykle and a lovely cast iron Victorian fireplace in which a fire was kept lit during the winter months to fend off the cold. Walking over to the mirror above the mantelpiece, he examined his neck which revealed a narrow red mark where the cheese wire had perforated his skin. What on earth had that girl been up to? And as for Ranald, he would be having words with him later. Sir Hector didn't want Fykle Lodge tarnished with his sordid activities, particularly when they were with his friend's daughter. He tut tutted to himself while sitting down at his desk and looking out of the window, flicked on his laptop.

The study was the only room in the Lodge with internet access, something Sir Hector didn't advertise because he enjoyed his house parties without the interference of modern communications, where his guests spoke to one another rather than scroll their ipads and check their messages. It had been a monstrous job installing the connection and had involved placing a satellite on the hill which beamed a signal into the little black box, sat on the desk, which Sir Hector's laptop was linked to. Tapping the return button he waited for the screen to burst into life and contemplated the week so far.

It had been unusual, different to the norm. The ruddy Count had shot a Royal Stag which still irked him and Babek's daughter, Ursula, had caused a stir. He wondered if it had unsettled the party a little. She had certainly caught Ranald's eye and he didn't like the affection which Babek poured on her. It was well, unnatural, for a father and daughter to touch each other in the way they did. It gave him the creeps just thinking about it. And then there was the painting. Babek always bought unusual gifts, but this year, he seemed to have surpassed himself. The picture wasn't at all Fykle Lodge's style and didn't even have a surrounding frame. It mystified Sir Hector why Babek had given it to him and the more he thought about the painting, the more it played on his mind until, eventually, he got up and decided to get the artists name and try an internet search.

Up the stairs and along the landing trotted Sir Hector with his dressing gown swishing behind, while he fiddled with the pen and scrap piece of paper in his right hand as he walked towards the painting. The light was poor, so he squatted down, put on his glasses and strained his eyes, trying to read the signature. J seemed to be the first letter and then, something – mez....inger? It wasn't easy to decipher, but Sir Hector scribbled it down anyway and after reading it back to himself, felt he had enough for a google search to see what that would reveal.

The laptop was now up and running, so he typed in his password, launched explorer and then entered, J Mezinger and eagerly waited, watching the icon circle and circle, until suddenly the results flashed up on the screen in front of him. Mezinger gun dealers Idaho USA, Mezinger Circus Amsterdam, Mezinger dry cleaners Solihull Birmingham and so the list went on and on. Scrolling down the page, Sir Hector became a little dispirited until he looked back at the top of the search bar and saw.

*Did you mean J Metzinger?*

Clicking on the link, Sir Hector went through to the next page where he found in Wikipedia:

*Jean Dominique Antony Metzinger (June 24, 1883 – November 3, 1956) was a major 20th-century French painter, theorist, writer, critic and poet, who along with Albert Gleizes developed the theoretical foundations of Cubism.*

Surely that was his man! Very interesting he thought, but it hadn't help him identify the picture, so he re-entered;

*The works of J Metzinger,* which unhelpfully took him back to the same Wikipedia page. Not sure what to do next, Sir Hector looked out of the window and stared at the view while running a hand through his grey hair and then after a short pause, let his eyes wander back to the laptop as his right hand moved the mouse, until it hovered over – *images*. He right clicked!

Dozens of pictures flashed up in front of him, different colours, shapes and sizes, but there in the centre of the screen was – an exact match!

Again, Sir Hector clicked on the link and read the text.

*Jean Metzinger, 1913, En Canot (Im Boot), oil on canvas, 146m x 114 cm (57.5 in × 44.9 in), exhibited at Moderni Umeni, S.V.U. Mánes, Prague, 1914, acquired in 1916 by Georg Muche at the Galerie Der Sturm, sold to the Nationalgalerie, Berlin in 1936, confiscated by the Nazis and displayed at the Degenerate Art Show, Munich during 1937 and missing ever since.*

'CONFISCATED BY THE NAZIS!' Sir Hector repeated to himself in astonishment, while staring at the image in disbelief. Gobsmacked, lost for words and in a partial state of shock he made his way to the kitchen, to make a pot of tea and collect his thoughts together. It must surely be a copy, but nevertheless, it was a very odd discovery. Taking two cups of tea he returned to bed.

\*

Lady Sally was still asleep when he entered the room, although by the time Sir Hector had shuffled around, left a cup on her bedside table and returned to his side of the bed, she was beginning to stir.

'How did you sleep, Darling?'

There was no reply, so Sir Hector gave his wife a gentle kick as he slipped between the sheets. She moved her leg, then remained motionless, appearing to have had dozed off again, until at last, ever so slowly, she rolled over and sat up.

'Quite an evening last night,' said Sir Hector.

Lady Sally, with the beginnings of a thumping hangover, hadn't quite come around sufficiently to speak, so she had a sip of tea before replying,

'What on earth was that wretched girl doing in here?'

'Well you tell me, you could at least see what was going on. I was pinned down to the bed with my head in a pillow, being half strangled.'

'It was meant for Ranald you know and she was in the wrong room. I never thought he had it in him, the dirty sly dog. I am minded to have words with his mother.'

'Good heavens you can't do that,' spluttered Sir Hector through a mouthful of warm tea, 'she would probably drop off her peg, if she discovered innocent little Ranald had developed a penchant for asphyxiation and sadomasochistic practices.'

Lady Sally hesitated, still slightly impaired from the previous evening's excesses. Eventually she spoke. 'It's always the ones you least suspect.'

'True, but I doubt that will be much consolation to his mother. I wonder if I should mention something to Babek though.'

'You could, although it's a difficult subject to broach, after all, she's not a teenager. I'm not sure how you would go about opening up that conversation.'

'Umm,' they both sat in silence until finally, Lady Sally spoke some sense, 'Probably best to say nothing to the parents.'

Sir Hector remained quiet for a couple of moments, deep in thought before replying, 'Yes, I suppose you are right. It's the old family maxim – *in dubio, si nihil* – if in doubt do nothing. A mantra, which has served us Munro-Fordyce's well down the centuries.'

*

Ranald was awake in his little room, unaware of how events had unfolded last night and just how much havoc his throw away remark – *top of the stairs first room on the right* – had caused.

In any event his thoughts were elsewhere, planning his big escape with the painting.

Recalling, when he swapped them that they were quite heavy, Ranald had already decided that a pony would be needed and provided he didn't make a big fuss about what he was up to, he could delay his departure, until after everyone had left the Lodge for the morning and then quietly slip away. He reckoned it would take the whole day to reach Bridge of Orchy and then a couple of hours on the train to Glasgow, where he could hand the picture in, at the Police Station in the West End and be home by a reasonable time. He may even text Elspeth, to see if she would be interested in some supper. Clearly, he would need to let Sir Hector and Lady Sally know his whereabouts, but he could do that later, after the picture had been dealt with and make some lame excuse, although exactly what he was going to say, he was not yet clear on. Ranald realised his sudden departure wouldn't go down well with his Uncle and Aunt, but, he reasoned with himself that it would all be worth it in the end, when the painting was returned to its rightful owners, whoever they may be. Relishing the thought of an adventure and in anticipation of a long day on the hill, Ranald dragged himself out of bed and went to run a hot bath.

*

It was almost eight, when there was a knock on Ursula's door. She thought it was probably Babek, come for an update, but she wasn't totally sure and after the events of last night. Oh no. A cold shiver ran down her spine as she relived the torrid moment when the lights came on and she realised her mistake. There was another knock on the door.

'Psssst it's me. Babek.'

Ursula let him in.

'How did you get on last night?'

Ursula shook her head, 'not well.'

'What do you mean, not well?'

Ursula sat down on the bed with her head in her hands, before looking up at Babek.

'He gave me the wrong room. I never saw Ranald last night.'

'Damn that little man! I don't think he realises this is not a game we are playing,' replied Babek with a reddening face, and slamming a fist into his hand, started to pace around the room like a caged bear, as he could feel his blood pressure begin to rise.

'I was hoping you would get a lead out of him, a clue even, just something we could work on. The clock's ticking and we have made absolutely no progress whatsoever over the last twelve hours. The Count doesn't seem particularly bothered by it all and appears to think he can somehow slip out of the mess unscathed.'

After another tirade, Ursula looked again at Babek and sighed.

'So, what did happen last night, if you were led to the wrong room?'

There was a hesitation and another sigh.

'Ranald sent me to Sir Hector and Lady Sally's room.'

Babek quickly turned around and stared at Ursula, not sure whether to laugh or not.

'So, what happened?'

Again there was a pause, until Ursula managed to pluck up courage and blurt it all out.

'There is no easy way to explain. It was an innocent mistake really. But, I had the cheese wire wrapped around Sir Hector's neck when Lady Sally walked in.'

'You did what?'

'I panicked and thought I would try the cheese wire.'

'Oh my god, it was only meant as a last resort. You didn't kill him did you?'

'No, of course not.'

'Well, I suppose that is some consolation. In our current predicament it's probably the least of our worries,' continued Babek, while thinking that they were in for an interesting breakfast.

*

The Count rolled over in bed after what had been a disturbed night's sleep. The money which Babek had offered when he was first cut into the deal was significant, US$4 million and would help fund a new roof for his Bavarian Castle. In fact, it may go some way to paying off the Countess and the prospect of getting rid of her once and for all did appeal. However, the Count hadn't realised when he agreed to it all and arranged for the forged copy to be made, that there would be any risks. Even though he was still keen to get his share of the loot, the Count was now questioning if it had been such a good decision after all. For the last couple of hours he had laid in bed while Camille slept, mulling things over and had reached a decision. If they hadn't found the painting by four o'clock this afternoon, then it would be time to make a swift departure, homeward bound to his Bavarian castle. It had been the family seat for nearly five hundred years and he reasoned, that the steep walls and drawbridge would keep him well protected during his time of need. There seemed little point in hanging around waiting for the Black Widow to arrive.

*

Ranald descended the back stairs and made his way towards the dining room for breakfast. The smell of bacon frying, whetted his appetite and he made a mental note to eat well for what was likely be a demanding day in the hills. He met Lady Sally in the hallway,

'Good morning,' said Ranald in a brisk and friendly manner.

'I want a word with you,' replied Lady Sally pulling him to one side.

Slightly confused he asked, 'Why?'

'Don't you why me, Ranald Milngavie. You know fine well what I am talking about. Ursula visited our room last night thinking it was yours. Disgusting!'

'Disgusting? What was disgusting?'

'Now, don't you play the daft laddie with me. I know what sordid activities you had in mind. You must have planned it with her.'

Ranald looked at Lady Sally thoroughly confused, before asking.

'Planned what exactly?'

'You know. Adult sort of things.'

'Adult sort of things? What sort of, adult sort of things?'

'Do I really have to spell it out to you? Nudity, domination, cheese wire all that sort of adult sort of things. Poor Hector is still in a state of shock.'

'Oh,' said Ranald realising whose room was at the top of the stairs first on the right. He paused with connotations racing through his head. Perhaps he had been a bit hasty directing Ursula in the wrong direction after all!

'So that means I win the bet? Ten pounds I recall.'

Momentarily taken aback by Ranald's response, Lady Sally was for once lost for words, so he seized the initiative, stepped to one side and said, 'I will collect my winnings later in the week,' before disappearing into the dining room.

*

It was almost a full house. Noticeably, Max and Pippa were missing and Ranald wasn't surprised that they had decided to have a lie in. Otherwise, the atmosphere was sombre, Babek and the Count were understandably quiet and likewise Sir Hector seemed subdued after his encounter with Ursula last night. There was no sign of her at the table and when Ranald looked at Sir Hector, he struggled to contain a smirk.

Ewan arrived and without waiting to be asked, helped himself to a cup of tea from the pot on the sideboard, before walking to Sir Hector's end of the table.

'And have you decided what you would like to be doing today?'

Sir Hector remained silent, spooning his porridge around the bowl while his other hand rubbed his neck, until eventually he managed to pull himself together.

'Yes Ewan. I think we will take the boat down the loch, fish for a few slob trout and have a picnic on the sandy beach about halfway down on the left-hand side.'

Sir Hector looked around the room. 'Any takers?'

'We would like to join you,' replied Janet, prodding Hugh, who nodded approvingly while eating his toast.

'Babek, are you and Jacinta interested?'

He shook his head decisively.

'That's very kind of you, but Jacinta and I could do with a quiet day at the Lodge.'

'Me likewise,' said the Count, making sure he headed off the question.

Looking slightly deflated, Sir Hector glanced over at Ranald.

'I'll come.'

Although Ranald had no intention of going and would make his excuses later, he thought it would deflect Babek and the Count from their unwanted attention.

'Fine,' said Sir Hector, 'I am sure Mike and Heather will also join us, so that will make a nice little party.'

'What about Ursula?' piped up Ranald, 'she normally enjoys these sorts of trips?'

Sir Hector scowled, but before he could answer Babek intervened,

'Ursula has a migraine. She will probably spend the day in bed.'

'What a shame,' replied Ranald most insincerely.

'That will be good then,' said Ewan. 'We will launch the boat and collect everyone in the Land Rover at ten o'clock,' and then left to sort things out with Stuart.

*

Breakfast continued in a subdued manner and Ranald enjoyed his bacon and eggs before returning to his room to get ready for the day. After pulling on his plus fours and tweed shooting jacket, he then went to the boot room to collect his gaiters and walking boots.

There was no sign of Babek or the Count, so Ranald continued to the kitchen, where he found Fiona tidying up.

'Any chance of some leftovers for a sandwich?' he asked.

Fiona hadn't heard Ranald enter. She jumped before turning around.

'Oh! You gave me a fright sneaking up like that. But yes, by all means, help yourself,' waving her hand in the general direction of the large china serving dish and then went to retrieve some bread from the cupboard. Ranald wanted to make sure he had plenty of food for his trip, so he made four sumptuous bacon and egg sandwiches with generous helpings of tomato ketchup, which he wrapped in cellophane then stuffed into his pockets.

'You have a good day now,' said Fiona.

'Will do.'

She smiled. Fiona liked Ranald and was glad that the leftovers had not gone to waste.

*

Outside the Lodge, Ewan was waiting beside the Land Rover, chatting to Janet and Hugh.

'Morning.'

'Good morning Ranald,' he replied.

'Looks to be a good day, the sun's shining at least.'

'Aye, it will be nice for a trip down the Loch.'

Sir Hector bustled out of the game room along with Mike, Heather and the twins.

'Good, we all seem to be here. Lady Sally is bringing a picnic, so Ewan can you take Hugh, Janet, Mike, Heather and the girls and we'll follow on.'

Ranald was surprised to be held back, but, as Sir Hector walked over, he muttered under his breath, 'I want a word with you.'

The Land Rover left as Lady Sally arrived with a large wicker basket, which she placed in the back of the old Subaru and once they had climbed inside, Sir Hector started the engine, reversed out, before straightening up and setting off down the driveway.

'Now Ranald, about last night.' Sir Hector hesitated, not sure how to continue, until Lady Sally gave him a gentle nudge and he began again.

'Ursula came to our room. Mistakenly she was under the impression it was yours.'

'Yes, I know,' replied Ranald, 'Lady Sally mentioned it earlier.'

Sir Hector paused again, plainly not enjoying the conversation, but then after a couple of seconds fortified himself,

'I don't have anything against a bit of holiday romance between young adults. But it's just that; well it's not the sort of thing. Well not at Fykle Lodge,' he said clearly struggling with the discussion he had now got himself embroiled in. Lady Sally was becoming increasingly impatient and eventually became so exasperated that she decided to intervene.

'For God's sake, if you are not going to spit it out, I will. Ranald! Sir Hector and I are actually quite liberal-minded and we know you and Ursula are adults. But last night, I wasn't best pleased to find that young floozy half naked, straddling my husband and choking him with a cheese wire!'

There was momentarily silence in the car, until Ranald spoke, 'Oh, so that's what the cheese wire was for, I had been wondering.'

'I'm not sure what sorts of practices you youngsters get up to in Glasgow,' blathered Lady Sally, who was now in full flow, 'but in future can you leave them there and not bring your sordid activities to Fykle Lodge. I am minded to tell your mother.'

Ranald had no answers. The thought of being straddled by a half-naked Ursula was not totally without merit, but the cheese wire. Well that was just a step too far, even for him. There was silence in the Subaru while Ranald contemplated his mother's reaction.

*

On reaching the loch they saw that Stuart had already launched the boat, which was tied up alongside the pontoon. Mike, Heather and the twins were aboard and Ewan was helping Hugh and Janet climb in. Lady Sally collected the picnic basket and as they walked towards the boat, Ranald suddenly stopped.

'Damn, I've just remembered. I was supposed to contact Hutchinson's Gallery today about an exhibition. Blast, I had forgotten all about that.'

Sir Hector and Lady Sally stopped and looked around.

'So, what are you going to do?'

Not wishing for it all to look too pre-mediated, Ranald delved into his pocket and retrieved his smart phone, despite knowing there was no coverage.

'No reception. Urrrrr. I really ought to phone them though. Look if it's okay with you, I will skip the trip and return to the Lodge and make the call. Would it be all right if I used the landline in the study?'

'There is usually some mobile reception about halfway down the loch, but it depends on which network you are on,' replied Sir Hector.

Ranald paused, again to give the impression he was giving the idea some serious thought.

'It's an important call which I really need to make, so I think it would be best if I return to the Lodge and phone the gallery.'

'As you wish. Make sure you close the study door once you have finished though, I don't want all and sundry poking their noses in there.' Sir Hector was protective of his den.

Ranald waved the party goodbye from the pontoon, watching the little boat's outboard motor belching fumes from the manifold and then turned around and started on the short walk back to the Lodge. It was a beautiful morning and looking up towards Arragher he contemplated what the day would hold.

*

Diverting from the usual route up the drive, Ranald cut through a narrow overgrown path, which ran in between some rhododendron bushes towards the front garden and turned left just before the lawn so as to keep cover from the house. He managed to pick his way through the undergrowth towards the outbuildings at the rear. Beyond these was a small paddock where Duncan, a roan gelding and Fanny, a white mare grazed. They were friendly ponies and soon walked over to see if he had anything to feed them.

Gently taking hold of Fanny by the mane, Ranald led her into the stable and shut the lower door, before going through the second doorway into the tack room where he retrieved the halter and deer saddle. Fortunately, Fanny was docile and stood still while he fumbled with the straps and buckles, until finally, Ranald had managed to work out how it all fitted and secured it.

\*

In the Lodge, Babek was remonstrating with the Count, Ursula and Camille in his room.

'Look we really need to find the painting today or we are all toast. I can't impress on you all how important it is for us to retrieve it. The picture's a valuable piece and even on the Russian black market in Moscow is worth many US\$ millions. We can't just say to Belusha, whoops sorry, we lost it.'

Babek looked at his accomplices, they were silent, almost nonplussed by the disappearance of the picture and the situation they now found themselves in.

'Let's have another look around the house and see if we can find it, or at least a clue as to where the painting may be. There's hardly anyone around so we can be thorough, my gut feeling is that it is still here somewhere and my suspicions are with Ranald. Let's make sure we find his room and search it. If we still can't find any trace, I'm inclined to abduct him later and see what information we can extract out of him.'

With that they split up and started their search on the upper floors.

\*

Ranald was now in his room stripping a blanket off the bed to wrap the picture in, collect his rucksack and a few other essentials. He was quick and soon back at the stables without being seen. Leaving his luggage in a corner, he went to the game larder. The dead stags were still there waiting to be collected by the game dealer at the end of the week, but Ranald had no time to dwell. He hastily dragged the wooden box into the centre of the room, climbed on top, opened the hatch and put his hand through.

Groping to the left, he was unable to find the picture and becoming slightly alarmed, that the painting may have disappeared, he moved his hand to the right, where he reassuringly felt the canvas and the solid wooden frame on which it was mounted. Phew! The picture was still there. Ranald let out an audible sigh. Quickly retrieving the painting, he tucked it under his arm and scampered around to the stable where he wrapped it in the blanket and then started to work out how best to fix it to the saddle.

Not easy. Initially placing it one way and then another, until after a couple of attempts, with the canvas facing outwards, he began to fasten the unwieldy shape using the leather straps. It looked massive, enormous, strapped to the side of the pony and there was little doubt as to what it was, if they were to be seen.

'What are you doing?'

*'Flipping flamingo's'* – screeched Ranald, nearly leaping out of his skin and then letting out another little – '*shriekkkkkkkk.*' He turned around to see Stuart standing there.

'Christ, you made me jump.'

'I could see that. Are you going for a stalk?'

'Errrr. Yes. Ewan and Sir Hector said it would be okay for me to go on my own with Fanny.'

'That will be fine then. Where are you planning to go?'

'Umm. Arragher, that's what Ewan suggested.'

'And what's that on the saddle?'

Ranald paused, racking his brains and then calmly replied, 'It's a canvas. I might do some painting, if I don't find a stag.'

'Oh,' said Stuart, not really sure what to make of Ranald's response. He opened the stable door, allowing him to lead Fanny out.

'All set then,' said Ranald looking for reassurance.

'Are you not going to take your rifle?' enquired Stuart.

Ranald looked confused, completely caught out by the question.

'Yes of course, good point. Silly me, I must have had a dram too many last night. Yes my rifle, would you mind getting it for me and some rounds of ammunition? It's the Mannilcher .308 with full wooden stock in the gun cabinet.'

'Aye, I can do that for you, no problem,' replied Stuart, starting to wander towards the Lodge.

Ranald and Fanny were now standing in the paddock, ready to leave and fortunately screened from the house by the stable block and the other outbuildings. However, Ranald had not planned to take his rifle, because he had no intention of stalking a stag and he didn't want the extra weight and hassle it may cause him, when he would board the train at Bridge of Orchy. Neither was he best pleased to be kept waiting for Stuart and was on tenterhooks, afraid that he might bump into the Count or Babek and give the game away.

Looking at his watch, it was now ten thirty-five and Ranald was becoming increasingly agitated. The seconds seemed to pass slowly and he continuously watched the time, impatiently working himself up into a fervour. Ten thirty-seven, Ten thirty-eight, ten thirty-nine, ten-forty, it felt like waiting for eternity, for Stuart to return. Would his wait it ever end?

At last, he heard footsteps on the gravel to the rear of the Lodge, coming in his direction. Holding his breath, Ranald crossed his fingers, while they gradually became louder and louder, the steady crunch of gravel under foot and not sure who's they were, he instinctively ducked behind Fanny, before poking his head around the side, to see Stuart come into view when he entered the stable and walked through to the paddock with the rifle in its sleeve, casually slung over his shoulder. Ranald felt relief flood throughout his body.

'There you are now,' said Stuart in his slow west coast accent, taking the gun and handing it to Ranald along with a box of bullets.

'And I thought you might want to take this,' passing Ranald an estate radio.

'You can give me a call if you get a stag and need a hand, or get lost,' said Stuart, with a faint trace of a smile on his face.

'Thanks,' replied Ranald, slipping it into his bag'.

'Right, I think I'm ready,' and nodding to Stuart he began to lead Fanny away.

'Have a good day now and don't forget to give me a call if you need a hand.'

'Will do.'

*

The usual route was straight down the main drive and along the public road, although Ranald stayed in the field, which was partially obscured from the Lodge by a row of beech trees and then cut onto the drive as it meandered through the woods, where he would be screened. However, Ranald felt exposed as Fanny and he plodded along at a sedate walk.

Tugging at the halter, he tried to move her along a little faster, but, she was having none of it, simply stretching her head forward and keeping her short solid legs moving at the same monotonous gait. Fanny was not for rushing and Ranald soon realised it was pointless to try and hurry her along, so he let the leading rain go slack and resigned himself to their one-dimensional pace.

Without even the faintest hint of a breeze in the wood the midges began to circle and launch their ferocious attack. Fanny swished her tail and shook her mane to fend off the tiresome wee pests, while Ranald swiped them away from his face as best he could. However, despite the distraction there was inevitably an air of nervous tension, when without warning there was a squeak on the radio – which suddenly burst into life!

'Hello, come in, can you hear me?'

*Oh, my giddy aunt*, thought Ranald, what's Stuart up to now?

'Can you hear me?'

It was the last thing Ranald wanted, Stuart hanging around the Lodge blathering to him on the estate radio, so he quickly retrieved the rectangular black transceiver and then looked at it, not entirely sure how it worked.

'Hold the green button down to speak,' said Stuart, guessing his predicament.

Rotating the radio quickly through his hands Ranald saw the green button on the side which he pushed while he spoke.

'I can hear you Stuart.' There was a pause and then a crackle.

'Thanks Ranald. I just wanted to check you knew how to use it.'

'Okay, that's very good of you. Thanks for that.'

'You have a good day now,' replied Stuart, before hanging up.

Ranald took a deep breath, while beginning to wonder if he would really make it to Arragher without being found out. On they plodded, with the midges buzzing all around.

*

The day was sunny, birds were occasionally rustling through the trees and despite their tenuous situation, all was quiet, until there was the distant sound of a car approaching and then the unmistakable crunch of gravel under tyres, when a vehicle entered the drive. Ranald felt his body stiffen and heartbeat quicken, but was relieved to see the postman on his morning rounds. He nodded as the red van sped past and continued towards the Lodge.

Crikey, Ranald thought to himself, I am jumpy, looking around at Fanny who was completely oblivious to the significance of her precious cargo and the purpose of their journey, as she tossed her head to keep the midges in check. Oh, how they longed for a little breeze to blow them away.

On reaching the public road they were within five minutes of the track which leads to the bridge over the river Fykle and Arragher beyond. A pleasant stroll in normal circumstances, but Ranald's predicament was far from normal and he was all too aware, that if

Babek and the Count found out what he was up to, they could easily catch him in the Range Rover. In reality, he had put very little distance between himself and the Lodge.

Butterflies circled in the depths of his stomach as they plodded onwards, while in the background he heard an engine start and again the familiar sound of tyres on gravel.

There was nowhere to hide. Ranald and Fanny stood expectantly on the road side, waiting to see what the hand of fate was about to deliver and if a black Range Rover would appear from the driveway and cruelly dash Ranald's plan. His heart was in his mouth, the unbearable tension of being discovered on the rise, with adrenalin surging through his veins in readiness for what may come. Such a build up, such concern all for nothing, when he saw the little red van appear between the tall columns on the return trip. Ranald felt annoyance rather than relief, that an innocent act of delivering the mail, had put him through so much turmoil.

The postman tooted and waved as he passed and Ranald, despite being irritated, returned the gesture with a casual nod. On Fanny and he plodded until they reached the turn off onto the track leading towards the river and Arragher beyond. The gate was locked, but this mattered not a jot, because there was a gap in the fence which they walked through. Ranald was still just as edgy now as he had been when they had first set off and when he looked up at the majestic towering peaks of Arragher, he just longed to be in the hills, far away from the unwanted attention of Babek and the Count.

He reckoned it would take them at least three hours to reach the col near the summit, which they would pass over and then continue above Raick Forest in a south-easterly direction onto Mount Raick, owned by a wealthy brewing family, who were seldom there. Next, Tumult Lodge, a sizeable but run-down estate of nearly 15,000 acres, which the Count leased. Ranald had already decided to skirt along the west side of Raick Forest on the higher ground, well away from prying eyes at the Lodge House and then on towards Bridge of Orchy. It would be a little further, but he felt that the small excursion would be safer in the long run.

Onwards they plodded, making steady progress down the rough potholed track and eventually reached the small bridge over the river.

Just below was Big Pool and the fishing hut, where Ranald had caught Babek and Ursula in a lover's tryst and he recalled how it had both shocked and pained him at the time, while remembering the disappointment which had followed. But, how things had changed in the course of a few days. Keeping up his pursuit, to be rejected by Ursula on the hill and then for her to make the running when she sought to work her exquisite charms only last night. He knew her motives were not those of love, but it had nevertheless confused Ranald that when Ursula had presented herself, on the proverbial smorgasbord, he had rejected her advances. For some reason he couldn't quite bring himself to go through with it. The old adage of the chase being more fun than the kill sprang to mind, but deep down Ranald felt, that his plutonic relationship with Elspeth, was the root cause. He was, of course, stuck in a quandary. On the one hand a commitment-phobe, unable to do the obvious and make a go of it with Elspeth and on the other, his feelings for her were such that he couldn't bring himself to go out with anyone else. Ranald was sure it was the lingering thoughts of Elspeth, which had held him back. He would surely not have passed up on his chance with Ursula ten years ago, when he had been truly foot loose and fancy free! If any good was to come out of his encounter with her, then it was that it had pushed him in Elspeth's direction Aye, she really is a fine lassie indeed, he thought and with that pulled out his smart phone and sent her a text.

*'Hope this message finds you well and in good spirits. Currently making my escape with the painting, Luv R xxxxxxxxxxxx.'*

There was no reception at the lower altitude, but Ranald knew, when they ascended, he would pick up a signal and the message would be sent. Onwards Fanny and he plodded for another half hour until they reached the lip of the burn where they stopped to drink from the stream. It was now almost midday and on retrieving the first of his bacon and egg sandwiches, Ranald decided to have an early lunch, while he enjoyed the views back towards Fykle Lodge. He was now happier and his mood much improved since he had put some distance between himself and the Lodge. If they were to be chased, he would at least be able to see his pursuers coming, whom in any event would be confined to foot. Eating his sandwich he glanced at his phone to see that his text had been sent and he had received a reply.

*'I hope you know what you are doing! Take care Luv E xxxxxxxxxxxxxxxxx.'*

Ranald smiled and thought to himself, not a clue really, but boy he was enjoying his madcap escapade!

# Chapter 17 – The Chase Begins

Back at the Lodge, Babek, the Count, et all had scoured the house as best they could, but frustratingly to no avail. There had been an embarrassing moment when Ursula had burst in on Max and Pippa, when she attempted to enter their room. Whoops! Babek had discovered Ranald's lair up the back stairs and a whole host of other rooms which he also searched, but with no joy. Unable to find even a trace as to where the painting could be, he was beginning to fear that it had already left the Lodge, in which case it could be anywhere, even abroad. There was a general despondency about them, which was hardly surprising given the circumstances they found themselves in and with an air of defeat they decided to go in search of something they were more likely to find – lunch!

*

Fiona had left sandwiches in the kitchen and Ursula took a plate full into the dining room, while Camille put the kettle on to make a pot of tea.

'Let's face it,' said the Count, 'we now have only twenty-four hours to find the painting or we are in trouble and there is no point in us simply hanging around here, waiting for the Black Widow to arrive. It's time we started thinking about a plan B.'

For once Babek didn't react. He knew what the Count had said was true and he contemplated his words before eventually speaking.

'I suggest we give it until later this afternoon, by which time, Ranald should be back and I would like a proper word with him,' pulling out the type 54 pistol from the inside pocket of his jacket and placing it on the table, 'if you know what I mean!'

'I wish you would put that pistol away,' retorted the Count, 'It makes me nervous the way you continually flash it around.'

'I know,' replied Babek, lifting it upwards and pointing the barrel straight at him. Camille gave a little '*shriek*' when she walked into the room with the teapot. The Count stared, stony faced at Babek, wondering to himself, how on earth he had become involved with this mad, trigger happy Russian. Babek cocked the gun. And then after a few seconds, smiled as he lowered the pistol.

'Now you don't think I would shoot my dear friend, the Count, do you?'

'Now's not the time for your silly games,' he replied sternly, before helping himself to another sandwich and taking a bite.

*

There was a rattle of pans in the kitchen as Fiona returned to do some prep work for supper. Vegetables and potatoes had to be peeled, and she always preferred to get these chores completed in the afternoon, to relieve the pressure valve of cooking the main meal later. Popping her head around the door of the dining room she asked,

'I hope the sandwiches are okay?'

Ursula nodded, 'Yes, fine thanks.'

Fiona left them to it and went to find the potatoes in the larder and when making her way back to the kitchen, found Stuart sulkily ambling along the corridor.

'You coming for a cup of tea?'

'Aye, I am indeed. I saw your car pull up outside the Lodge and thought you would be making a brew.'

'Come on then, let's get the kettle on,' replied Fiona as they both walked into the kitchen. Making sure the door to the dining room was closed, so they wouldn't disturb the guests, Fiona collected some cups and saucers from the large wooden cupboard as the kettle began to whistle.

'What have you been up to this morning?' asked Stuart.

'The usual, clearing breakfast, cleaning the Lodge and then home for a quick bite of lunch.'

'And you? You didn't go with the party down the loch?'

'No, they didn't need me. Anyway, the boat was pretty full. Ewan will keep them all entertained, he's good at that sort of thing.'

'Yes, he is,' replied Fiona, 'in fact he enjoys chatting to the guests as much as the stalking and fishing.'

She was immensely proud of Ewan. He had been the under keeper at Glen Troch Estate in Caithness for five years, where they had both met. Fiona had been the cook and they soon found there was a spark between them, whereupon she moved into the idyllic whitewashed cottage which came with his job, to became a 'bidie in'. Halcyon days of long, dark, crisp winters, warmed by the log stove in the kitchen and open fireplace in the living room. Their romance flourished and they were married a year later.

Life moved on though, and Fiona was delighted when Ewan landed the Head Ghillies job at Fykle Lodge for Sir Hector, a position which came with a comfortable four-bedroom house. Fiona was employed to cook, from time to time, which she actually quite enjoyed. It kept her busy and she liked meeting the guests and the social interaction this bought. The tips were perhaps not as good as other estates, but Sir Hector and Lady Sally were good lairds and treated them well. In fact they very much felt like part of the family.

*

The door from the dining room opened and in walked Camille to replenish the teapot.

'Here let me do that,' said Fiona taking the pot from her and putting the kettle on again.

'You didn't fancy the trip down the loch then?'

'No. We thought we would have an easy morning in the Lodge.'

'And do you have any plans for this afternoon?'

'Not sure yet, it depends on what the Count wants to do.'

'I'm happy to take anyone fishing on the river, if they want,' piped up Stuart.

'I will ask, but I doubt there will be much interest. Everyone seems quite tired.'

'Okay, to be honest the waters down and it won't fish well. However, if you change your minds let me know. I don't have much on this afternoon until the boat gets back, unless of course, Ranald gets a stag and needs some help.'

Camille's ears picked up. She understood Ranald was supposed to have gone on the trip down the loch, so it seemed odd that there had been a change of plan. Fiona filled the tea pot.

'There you are now.'

'Thanks,' replied Camille, taking the pot and returning to the dining room.

'Anyone for more tea?'

The Count nodded and pushed his cup forward.

"You might be interested to know that Ranald, whom you all seem so interested in, has gone stalking.'

The Count looked up.

'He's done what?'

'Gone stalking, according to the Ghillie.'

Babek stood up and walked around the table looking at the Count.

'What do you make of that?'

'Not sure really. It may not mean anything.'

Continuing past the Count, Babek opened the door to the kitchen. Fiona looked around, surprised that they were being disturbed again so quickly.

'Hi.'

'Hello,' replied Babek, 'Camille mentioned that Ranald has gone stalking?'

There was silence. Stuart and Fiona looked at each other, surprised by the directness of Babek's approach.

'Aye that right, he's gone to the Arragher with a pony to see what he can spy.'

'The Arragher?'

'Aye the Arragher,' repeated Stuart stepping forward and pointing to the massive mountain, clearly visible through the kitchen window.

'I thought he was going with the picnic party. Do you know why he changed his mind?'

Stuart shrugged his shoulders as the Count also entered the kitchen. Babek turned to him.

'Ranald has gone stalking up there,' pointing out of the window towards Arragher. The Count stepped forward and lowered his head, stooping to look out.

'That's odd. It's a southerly wind and the wrong direction for Arragher,' turning around to look at Stuart. He shrugged his shoulders, before speaking.

'The Laird and Ewan let him stalk on his own, so it's up to Ranald where he goes. He's taken a canvas and his brushes, so he may just paint instead.'

Babek and the Count looked at each other. Canvas, was ringing in their ears. Alarm bells began to scream and their interest in what Ranald was up to, suddenly took on a new dimension. Turning back towards Stuart, Babek asked, 'Canvas? What do you mean by canvas?'

'Well.' Stuart hesitated. 'It was just a large rectangular shape wrapped in a blanket and fastened to the deer saddle on the pony. It seemed big to take to the hill and I did wonder why he hadn't taken a smaller one.'

Stuart shrugged his shoulders yet again, oblivious to the significance of the information he had just divulged. The Count tugged Babek's arm and pulled him back into the dining room and shut the door.

'What was that all about?' Fiona asked Stuart.

'Not sure really, although they seem pretty interested in what Ranald is up to.'

'Particularly the canvas,' replied Fiona, who had seen the surprise in both Babek and the Count's expressions.

\*

'Come with me,' said the Count, hastily leading Babek up the stairs to his bedroom with Ursula and Camille following on. Retrieving his telescope from its case, he opened the bedroom window and directed it towards Arragher. The Count had stalked there previously, on a number of occasions, knew the lie of the land well and followed the line of the path up to the lip of the burn. The usual way was to bear right, climb up and along the Arragher ridge and stalk stags in the corries below, so naturally, he traced the path along the route, but search as he did, he couldn't see Ranald anywhere. Oh, where was that pesky little artist, the Count mulled, continuing to scour the land and then with no joy, began racking his brains as to why he couldn't find him.

It made little sense to take a pony along the ridge path which was steep and exposed, in fact damn right dangerous, not at all suitable for a pony, even a Highland one. No, when he had previously stalked on Arragher, the pony had always stayed below the corries and the stags had been dragged down to meet them. Withdrawing the telescope back along the ridge, the Count directed it into the bowl.

'Seen anything yet?' asked Babek.

'No, not yet. Pass me my binoculars.'

The bowl was large and the Count realised he would do better with the wider field of vision his bino's would provide.

'Here you are,' said Camille helpfully, passing them to him.

Leaning the telescope against the radiator, the Count took the binoculars and began to scan the bowl, working methodically, looking from the left to right, gradually covering the ground up to the skyline, while all the time Babek fidgeted and fiddled becoming increasingly impatient. The tension eventually became too much for him,

'Found him?'

'No,' replied the Count with a faint trace of exasperation creeping into his voice. He was used to searching for stags on the hill and was all too aware, how easy it was to miss something, if one rushed. Silence returned and the suspense continued, until the Count pulled the binoculars away from his eyes and stared out of the window, while he thought.

'You can't find him, can you?' questioned Babek

'Not yet,' replied the Count tersely, putting his binoculars back to his eyes and starting again from the lip of the burn. He was now more convinced than ever, that Ranald would not have gone along the ridge with the pony and he was sure that he would be somewhere in the bowl.

The col at the far end, led over the ridge into the next glen and the Count recalled there was an old drover's track, which zig zagged to the pass. Systematically scanning the ground to see if he could pick up the route, he eventually found it beside the gulley where a small stream flowed. It was rocky ground and the path disappeared out of view in parts, but regardless, the Count diligently searched the area again to discover, nothing, nothing at all, not even a trace of where Ranald could be. Beginning to feel rather exasperated at the fruitlessness of his endeavours, the Count let his binoculars drop and hang around his neck, while shaking his head and letting out a sighhhhh.

'You can't find him can you?' questioned Babek, yet again.

'No, not at the moment,' retorted the Count, becoming increasingly vexed.

'Do you want me to have a look?'

'No, I don't want you to have a look. I know where he's likely to be,' riposted the Count firmly. He was riled by Babek's constant interjections. Again he pulled the binoculars to his eyes. Ranald must be somewhere between the lip of the burn and the col the Count reflected, as again he worked his way towards the skyline, and then without warning, his diligence was rewarded, 'Bingo. Gotcha!'

'Can you see him?'

'Oh yes,' replied the Count triumphantly, placing the binoculars to one side and picking up the telescope, which was much more powerful.

The track had been screened by some rocks and raised ground, which had shielded Ranald from view, but he was now in the open and clear to see.

'Has he got the painting with him?' asked Babek excitedly.

'I don't know, it's difficult to see from this distance. I can make out the pony and Ranald, but I just can't tell either way if the picture is with them or not.'

'It's got to be,' said Babek, 'why else would Stuart have mentioned the canvas. In any event, I don't know of any other artist who would lumber a ruddy great canvas up a hill on a pony just to paint a landscape.'

The Count had already put his telescope in its holder and was getting ready to depart.

'Let's go then, we've nothing to lose,' and after descending the stairs in haste, they went into the game room to put their boots on and collect jackets.

'We can drive down to the bridge and it's on foot from there. He's got a good start, but if we go along the Arrragher ridge we should be able to head him off before he reaches the col. It will be touch and go, but hopefully the pony will slow him down,' continued the Count, reaching inside the gun cabinet and retrieving his Carlos Gustafsson 30 06 and a box of shells.

'Why are you taking your gun?' asked Ursula, who still had a soft spot for Ranald, despite the mess he seemed to have got them all into.

'He'll have a rifle, so I see no reason not to go armed. In any event, if needs must, I can always shoot the pony. That will slow him down.'

Stuart walked into the game room to see what was going on.

'And are you all off to the hill to find Ranald?' he asked.

'Yes,' replied Babek.

'Oh,' said Stuart, not really sure why there was such urgency.

'He will be back at the end of the day, if you want to catch him then.'

'I doubt it,' continued Babek.

'Oh,' said Stuart again, now even more confused.

The Count interrupted.

'Stuart, can you let us have the key to the padlock on the gate, so we can drive down to the bridge?'

'Yes I suppose so,' he replied, fumbling through his pocket to retrieve the spare set which he handed over. He wasn't supposed to let guests have them, but it was clear from the body language and the tone of the Count's voice that he was not going to be trifled with.

'Why are you taking your gun?' asked Stuart.

'Never you mind about that,' snapped the Count as Babek and he marched out of the game room, towards the Range Rover with Ursula and Camille following. Within seconds they were all aboard and speeding down the drive, leaving a dust cloud behind them.

Stuart watched, mumbling to himself as Fiona came outside to join him.

'What was that all about?'

'No idea, but they seem determined to catch up with Ranald for some reason.'

'Strange. Do you think he's in trouble?'

'Don't know, I hope not. The Count has taken his rifle though.'

Fiona looked a little alarmed, which Stuart saw in her face.

'Don't worry, I let Ranald have an estate radio, so we can give him a buzz and let him know they are on their way.'

Retrieving the handset from the game room, Stuart clicked on to transmit.

'Ranald, Stuart here come in?' There was no reply.

'Ranald, come in?'

'Ranald are you there? Come in Ranald?'

On the hill, the estate radio in Ranald's bag remained silent. It had accidentally been switched off when he placed it inside.

*

Unaware that he had been spotted, Ranald was actually quite pleased with the way events had panned out so far. Fanny, like all good highland ponies had stamina, a good set of sturdy wee legs and had steadfastly kept plodding along the track towards the col, but she was slow, much slower than Ranald had anticipated and after recalibrating his timings he reckoned they would do well to reach Bridge of Orchy by sunset, which was far from ideal. Ranald knew he couldn't manage without Fanny's help, because in reality, the picture was too big and cumbersome for him to carry on his own, but Ranald was now concerned if he would make the last train to Glasgow. Without a clue of when that may be, he pulled out his smart phone and typed 'train times' into his browser before hitting return.

It was slow to react as the icon circled, but eventually it took him to rail enquiries where he managed to tap in Bridge of Orchy to Glasgow. The browser whirred yet again while Fanny and he continued plodding onwards, until eureka, the results flashed onto the screen! There were four trains per day and the last one was at half past six. Ranald sighed. At their current pace it was plain to see that there would be little prospect of them arriving in time to catch it.

Slightly dispirited Ranald stopped, pushed his shepherd crook into the ground and secured Fanny's leading rein and applied himself to coming up with an alternative plan. In any event the fresh air had made him hungry and he was happy to sit down, help himself to another bacon and egg sandwich and try and work out what he should do now.

Fanny was straining on the rein leaning towards the burn, clearly keen to have a drink, so Ranald untied the old mare and they both walked towards the stream to quench their thirst. Oh, how Fanny did slurp at the water's edge, sucking up big mouthful's, while Ranald lay down on his stomach and sipped from the highland stream, pausing to look at the clouds reflection in the clear water, as they drifted slowly overhead, blown along by a gentle breeze. He tried extra hard to come up with a new plan and the more he mulled matters over the more certain he was that there was little prospect of catching the last train from Bridge of Orchy. As he led Fanny away from the burn, Ranald pulled out his smart phone for inspiration. Flicking out of train times he ended up at his text's and Elspeth's message.

Of course, that was the answer. Obvious really, why hadn't he thought about it sooner. Plain as could be, the answer lay on the little screen in front of him. Ask Elspeth for a lift. Bridge of Orchy was only just over two hours from Glasgow and they could stop on the way home and have a romantic, candlelit dinner together. Ah, how surprised Ranald was to find himself suddenly longing for her company. It was now just after one, so a couple of hours to the col, then say five or six hours to Bridge of Orchy and he should easily be there by nine o'clock at the latest, leaving just enough time for dinner on the way home. Ranald clicked reply,

*'Any chance of a lift tonight from Bridge of Orchy 9 pm? Luv R xxxxxxxx.'*

\*

Elspeth was sitting in the Gallery, browsing a catalogue when the text arrived and when she read it, a smile came to her face, while she thought what on earth was Ranald up to now. Pushing reply, Elspeth quickly typed her response,

*'Not a chance! Luv E xxxxxxxxx'*

The doorbell rang and a tall gentleman entered the shop.

Ranald wasn't entirely surprised by the message, in fact he half expected it. Elspeth was no pushover, so he gave her a call to see if he could spin a yarn and work his charm.

The smart phone lit up, vibrating and flashing while it sat on Elspeth's desk. The gentleman who had walked in, asked, 'Do you want to take that?'

'It's okay, I know who it is. They will phone back later.'

Ranald went through to the answer service.

'Hi Elspeth it's me, just phoning to see how you are and of course as you can guess to ask for a wee favour. Now how about this lift from Bridge of Orchy tonight, say nine o'clock? I will take you for dinner somewhere nice. Crawford House Hotel? Give me a buzz when you get this message. Bye.'

It was time to get moving again. Ranald took hold of Fanny's rein and was just about to leave when he felt the phone vibrate in his pocket and was delighted to see it was Elspeth returning his call.

'Darling, how nice to hear from you. How's your day going?'

'Well not bad Ranald, although by the sounds of it, not as exciting as yours. What on earth are you up to?'

'It's a long story. I can't go into the details now, but can you pick me up from Bridge of Orchy tonight, at say nine o'clock?'

'Ranald, if you want me to trek all the way to Bridge of Orchy, then you had better start telling me why.'

He realised it would be futile to try and brush Elspeth off, so Ranald started to explain the events of the last couple of days as clearly and concisely as he could. Elspeth was gobsmacked on hearing his tale, but eventually, managed to pull herself together.

'Just so that I am clear Ranald, then you have found what you think is a painting looted by the Nazis, possibly worth US$ millions? You've pilfered it and you now want me to be your getaway driver?'

'Well I wouldn't put it quite like that. The picture is already stolen property and all I'm doing is returning it to the rightful owners. Whoever they may be.'

'But Ranald it's not yours to take. Why couldn't you just have notified the police and let them sort it out?'

'What, PC Plod from the Highlands? It would take them a week to get here. Look, I'll buy you dinner at the Crawford House Hotel on the way back. That's a pretty good offer.'

Elspeth sighed. The whole plan was ridiculous, completely absurd and she very much doubted the picture was the great work of art that Ranald claimed and for a moment she felt rather sorry for him, going to such great lengths to smuggle it out of the glen. The pity softened her normally steadfast resolve and in a moment of weakness Elspeth relented, and abandoned herself to whatever fate would throw at her in this madcap idea.

'Okay, Okay, Okay Ranald. I must be going completely bonkers, but I will come and collect you from Bridge of Orchy tonight, nine o'clock sharp and make sure you're not late. And! I expect the a la carte menu at Crawford House.' Elspeth hadn't completely lost her mojo.

'Thanks,' replied Ranald, 'I really do appreciate it.'

Elspeth reflected, shaking her head, not quite believing that she had agreed to Ranald's crazy plan. Ludicrous really, trying to console herself that it would at least make an interesting dinner party story, or so she thought.

*

Babek was struggling on the climb and although he knew the importance of catching Ranald, he was now questioning, if he really had the physical ability to do so. By the time he reached the lip of the burn the Count already had his telescope out and Ranald and Fanny firmly in his vision. He turned around to see Babek arrive all hot and sweaty.

'I'm pretty sure he's got the painting. It's not easy to see when they walk away, but on the side view, there's clearly something large and rectangular strapped to the side of the pony.'

'Good,' replied Babek breathlessly, while sitting down beside Ursula, who put a reassuring hand on his knee and smiled softly.

The Count looked at Babek and wondered how much further he would be able to go and after pondering for a short time, cleared his throat,

'Look, I think I need to go ahead and intercept Ranald, or at this rate we just won't catch him.'

Babek nodded. He fully understood he was holding up the group.

'Okay, but Ursula goes with you, Camille and I will follow on. Remember we need that picture back in one piece, so don't fill the pony with lead because the bullet's will pass through and damage the painting.'

'Fair point,' replied the Count, 'and what about Ranald?'

'Well, ideally not. We don't want a dead body on our hands. But,' Babek paused, 'if there's no alternative then it's his own fault. He shouldn't have taken the painting in the first place.'

Ursula looked alarmed, shocked actually, as her heart skipped a beat. It was one thing smuggling a picture on the black market, but murder. Well, that was something she would much prefer not to get involved with.

'I'll see what I can do without spilling blood,' replied the Count standing up and putting his telescope back in its case, before setting off on the climb towards the ridge, closely followed by Ursula. Poor old Babek remained seated for a couple more minutes, continuing to perspire while sipping some water. Camille looked at him pitifully.

*

On Mischief, Lieu Chang sat blissfully on the top deck enjoying the sun while he sipped Pol Roger Champagne and watched his two wives playing deck quoits in the nude, not a stitch or a thread to be seen anywhere, as they daintily tiptoed around, collecting their pieces! Odd as it may have seemed, Suki and Mor were used to such nonsense and like the rest of Lieu Chang's wives frequently stripped at his behest for their communal yoga sessions within the ornate gardens of his Beijing home, while he simply watched in silence, taking in the scene and admiring the view. However, it was one thing cavorting around naked in the warmer climes of a Beijing summer, but playing deck quoits in the buff on the west coast of Scotland as the autumnal westerly winds rolled in off the Atlantic, was an altogether different proposition. Not that this seemed to bother Lieu Chang, who had almost been rocked to sleep by the gentle roll of the boat on the swell. It was becoming a bit breezy and with a faint chill in the wind, goose pimples started to appear on Suki and Mor, as the colour drained from their cheeks. They persevered with the silly game a little longer, until eventually the shivers set in, whereupon they walked over to stand either side of Lieu Chang to explain their predicament. Quite frankly, if he didn't let them go indoors soon, get dressed and warm up, then he would end up with two hypothermic wives on his hands! Lieu Chang listened and then stared out to sea in silence, appearing to be in a world of his own, almost oblivious to his wives, before eventually coming back down to earth and nodding his head to dismiss them.

*

Below deck, Wran Chin was busy in the office dealing with the administrative work to keep the yacht and Lieu Chang's life in order, when the Black Widow walked in.

'Have you heard if our Russian friend has found the painting yet?

Wran Chin shook his head. He didn't like the Black Widow and tended to avoid anything other than the bare minimum of conversation with her.

'Forty-eight hours will be up tomorrow at midday,' she continued. 'And if there is no sign of the picture. Well. I suppose, I will have to pay them a little visit?'

Wran Chin knew only too well what this meant. It would be curtains for Ursula and Camille and then in due course, Babek and the Count. He didn't approve of her methods and couldn't understand why she didn't simply get on with the job and kill her victims without delay, rather than flounce around with her distasteful little games.

Suddenly without warning, Lieu Chang opened the door. Entering the room, his enormous bulk almost became wedged in the doorway as he pushed and shoved until, after a final surge, he managed to slip through. Grunting to both Wran Chin and the Black Widow, who stood up as if to attention, Lieu Chang continued to waddle into the centre of the office where he sat down on a chair with his thighs and buttocks spilling over the sides and hanging downwards. His grotesque stomach was resting on his legs and looking at Wran Chin he asked, 'Any news from the Russian?'

'No, not yet. Would you like me to call him?'

Lieu Chang nodded.

Wran Chin shuffled some papers, before picking up his phone and dialling Babek's number. It rang and rang and rang until finally, he answered.

'Hello, Wran Chin, how are you?'

'Okay thanks. Lieu Chang wanted to know if you have recovered the painting yet?'

'Not quite, but we are hot on the trail and all being well we should have it back in our possession shortly.'

Wran Chin was surprised. He hadn't expected them to deliver and when he conveyed the news to Lieu Chang, he smiled contently and nodded.

'And where did you find it?' asked Wran Chin.

'It's a long story. I will let you know all when we deliver it.'

'And when might that be?'

'All in good time my friend, all in good time. I'm confident we will make the deadline though,' and with that Babek hung up. Christ, he thought to himself, we really do need to get hold of that picture and soon.

*

Without Babek, the Count and Ursula were making much better progress and soon ascended the steep climb at the start and were on the ridge. They stopped intermittently to spy Ranald who was still plodding along with Fanny, gradually making his way towards the col. Fortunately, the ridge route was much shorter than the drovers track through the bowl and now they had closed the gap, the Count could clearly spy a large rectangular shape wrapped in a blanket and attached to the side of the pony. Looking around at Ursula,

'He's definitely got the painting.'

'Good,' she replied and then reaching inside her pocket, retrieved her smart phone to text Babek the news.

'It's just a question of how we go about getting it back,' said the Count.

He paused, looking again at Ursula and then continued, 'They're still around five hundred yards away, which is a bit far to get a shot in, so if we keep off the skyline he won't see us while we scramble around to the next corrie, which will bring us much closer to the path.'

Now they had the scent of the picture in their nostrils, they moved quickly to the far side of the ridge and travelled as fast as they could on the uneven ground.

*

Babek was delighted to hear the news from Ursula. They may yet save the day. He texted Wran Chin with an update, 'Closing in on the painting, Babek.'

Wran Chin smiled while climbing the stairs to the large reception room on the fourth floor where Lieu Chang had retired to. He had been re-joined by Suki and Mor, who had taken a hot shower and were now warmed and dressed in silk camisoles, casually lounging with him on the soft seats. At being disturbed, Lieu Chang looked unamused, in fact slightly annoyed, but this all seemed to dissipate on hearing the news. Eventually he managed a smile and nodded approvingly.

*

The Count and Ursula crawled to the edge of the corrie and peered over the side. They were within about three hundred and fifty yards of the path and they could see Ranald and Fanny approaching at a leisurely gait, appearing to have not a care in the world. Turning to look at Ursula the Count raised a finger to his lips, indicating silence and then carefully withdrew his Carlos Gustafsson from its sleeve. Ursula, who was lying on the ground behind him tugged at his trousers and when he looked around she shook her head and mouthed, 'No.'

Ignoring her protestations, the Count, filled the magazine as quietly as possible, before loading the barrel and then clicking the safety switch on. Pulling the gun to his shoulder he started to search for Ranald and Fanny through the scope of his rifle.

He felt another tug, this time on the arm of his jacket. Ursula had crawled forward and shaking her head whispered, 'Don't shoot him.'

The Count was irritated at having his preparation disturbed and lowered the rifle as Ursula drew alongside.

'I'm not going to kill him,' he whispered, remounting the gun to his shoulder and the scope to his eye.

'What are you going to shoot then?'

'The pony, if I get a clean shot. Otherwise, I will just fire a warning round over their heads. We need to stop them before they disappear over the col.'

'Okay, but no mistakes. I don't want blood on my hands.'

The Count dropped the gun from his shoulder yet again and looked around at Ursula, 'you quite like our friend Ranald, don't you?'

Ursula found herself momentarily blushing, before she pulled herself together.

'No, not particularly. But. I just don't think he deserves to die over the painting.'

The Count remounted his rifle for the third time and picked up Ranald and Fanny in the scope, where he could clearly see the picture strapped to the far side of the pony. A chest shot was out of the question, so he looked towards Fanny's head to see if there were other possibilities. Ranald was almost a foot in front holding the leading rein, which left a clear gap between him and the picture and the chance of a neck or head shot. Neither would be easy, but after a few seconds of wavering, the Count settled his cross hairs on the pony's head.

He knew his chances of hitting the target were distinctly average, no better than fifty/fifty at best, but flicking the safety catch off, the Count tried to settle his breathing down while taking aim.

\*

Ranald was relaxed as Fanny and he approached the col. What a lovely day. If he could just make it into the next glen without being seen, he was beginning to think that his chances of success would greatly improve and he may yet pull off his great escape. To clear the Arragher mountains was mentally a significant hurdle and Ranald felt, that once they were behind him, he would be on the homeward stretch, even though in reality, there was still a long way to go. At least it would be mainly downhill beyond the pass to Bridge of Orchy he reasoned, while looking up to the skyline and watching the clouds gently drift past with their shadows rippling over the mountainsides.

*

The Count squeezed the trigger and there was a mighty – *'kerrboom'* – as the Carlos Gustafsson unleashed its toxic load.

Ranald, found his feet transfixed to the ground, as the shot reverberated around the hills. He was all too familiar with the sound of a rifle being discharged and a split second later, he heard the ricochet of the bullet bouncing off a rock behind them. Fortunately it had sailed clean over Fanny's head. They both looked around, not sure where the shot had come from, as the Count hastily withdrew the bolt to expel the spend cartridge and then slammed it forward to put another bullet into the barrel. This was his chance. He knew full well, that he would only have a few seconds, with both Ranald and Fanny standing still, broadside on, facing towards him, while they were momentarily confused.

Lowering the cross hairs to the centre of Fanny's head, the Count gently applied pressure to the trigger, but, on increasing the tension, felt a tug on his jacket and flinched as the gun let out another round. *'Kerrbang'* – ringing around the mountains and again the bullet flew well above Fanny's head and ricocheted behind.

The surprise of the first shot had now been replaced by the realisation that they were under fire and as quick as he could move, Ranald sprang into action, pulling the leading rein and dragging Fanny in the direction of the gulley, which was close by and the only place they could possibly seek cover.

'Drat, you made me miss my shot,' exclaimed the Count, turning around to look at Ursula.

'Sorry.'

The Count reloaded the rifle and mounted it to his shoulder yet again and looking through the scope at Ranald and Fanny scrambling downwards, he was presented with the back end of the pony and a moving target. He instinctively placed the cross hairs on Fanny's rear and contemplated bringing her down with a shot up the derriere, but it was dangerously close to the picture, which was still hanging from one side. Out of frustration, he lifted the barrel and sent another bullet above their heads and then quickly reloaded again in case he got the chance of another shot. But, by the time he had the scope back to his eye, Ranald and Fanny were almost out of sight, as they dropped into the gulley.

'Damn it, he's found cover!

# Chapter 18 – Fanny Plays her Part

Ranald was slightly breathless after his short but energetic burst with Fanny and his heart was pounding as adrenalin raced through his body. His predicament was suddenly becoming quite precarious, now that he was being shot at, so wisely, he removed his trusty Mannlicher from the sleeve and loaded it. Tying Fanny to the stick, which he had managed to push into the soft ground close to the stream, Ranald moved down the gulley a short distance, crawled up to the edge and slowly pushed his rifle forwards, between some hillocky tufts of grass. Up to the scope he moved and ever so slowly directed the gun around the corrie, moving the barrel systematically back and forth, left to right, gradually working his way to the skyline, but nothing, nothing at all, not even a clue as to where his pursuers may be. They were well concealed.

*

Babek had heard the shots and was running along the ridge, so as to find out what was going on with Camille in tow. But, unaccustomed to stalking, they briskly jogged along the top, in full view and Ranald soon spotted them out of the corner of his eye. Taking a closer look through his scope, he instantly recognised the rotund shape of Babek, with his stubby little legs propelling him forward. Fine he thought, they will at least lead me to their accomplices. Ranald had already guessed that it was likely to be the Count.

Babek got to within thirty yards of Ursula, before he called out. 'What's happened?'

Turning around the Count started waving frantically, signalling to Babek to get down off the skyline, but it was too late. Ranald saw and marked their position; directly up from the large brown rock which sits on the grassy knoll at the base of the corrie. Good, he thought, at least I know where they are.

'For Christ's sake,' hissed the Count 'get off the ridge, you've probably given our position away.'

Babek realising his folly was silent, while he and Camille crouched, shuffling forwards until they joined the Count and Ursula in a hollow.

'What's happening?'

'He's holed up in the gulley, like a filthy rat.'

'Yes, but what about the painting?'

'He's certainly got it. Strapped to the side of the pony, that was clear to see.'

'Well that's good news. We just need to work out how to flush the filthy little rat out and get our picture back. Do we know if he is armed?'

'Yes, for sure, he had a rifle over his shoulder.'

'Okay,' said Babek, beginning to contemplate what to do next, while he looked at the gulley and started to work out, how best to go about retrieving the picture without being shot. They had the upper hand on the high ground, but the safest way to approach was not particularly clear.

*

Meanwhile, Ranald had moved back towards Fanny and likewise was in a quandary as to what his next move should be. He could of course wait until nightfall, before playing his hand, but it was only half past two and there was sometime to go. In any event, he didn't fancy leading Fanny in the dark and he questioned how easy it would be for them to slip away without being caught.

Ranald started to take stock of his situation. He was cornered in a gulley by a trigger-happy Kraut while trying to smuggle a painting, which didn't even belong to him, out of the glen just so he could hand it into the authorities with absolutely no material gain for himself. It was a lovely romantic idea, made perfect sense when he had first hatched the plan, but now that he was being shot at, Ranald was starting to question if it really had been such a sensible decision after all. However, the more he thought about the circumstances he found himself in the more certain he was that he couldn't simply surrender, because there was no guarantee Babek and the Count would spare his life once they had the painting back. Alas, in many ways the die had been cast for poor old Ranald, who now felt committed to his venture with no obvious exit routes from his madcap plan. He crawled up to the edge of the gulley to see if there was any movement on top of the corrie.

*

Babek and the Count had withdrawn from the edge of the ridge to a position where they could at least sit up and discuss what they should do.

'I've been thinking,' said Babek, 'we can't simply just hang around here waiting for Ranald to hand the picture back. Somehow, we need to get down there and negotiate with him.'

'Well he's got a high-powered rifle and by all accounts he's a decent shot, so if you think I'm going to walk down there to ask him for the painting you are living in cloud cuckoo land,' riposted the Count firmly.

'Well. I wasn't really thinking about you. No. It would have to be someone who errrr… has some charm and whom Ranald quite likes,' looking around at Ursula.

'You must be joking,' she retorted.

'Why not? He isn't going to hurt you.'

'How do you know? He's got a gun. Anyway, how will he recognise its me from this distance?'

'He'll see you clearly through his scope,' interjected the Count, who didn't think it was such a bad idea at all.

'Exactly,' continued Babek. 'You're our best chance of negotiating something with Ranald, otherwise it will just be a shootout. Look, we are up against the forty-eight hour deadline and if we don't get that picture to Lieu Chang soon, then it will be our blood which is spilled!'

'I don't care, I'm not doing it,' snapped Ursula defiantly.

Babek sighed. There was silence. No one spoke. There was nothing to say. Ursula appeared to have made up her mind and

Babek's plan looked to be in tatters. Surprisingly, he reached out to Ursula and put a comforting hand on her knee and gently stroked her to sooth the angst away. She offered no resistance, while gazing across the hills into the distance.

Ursula was fully aware that she was coming under pressure to lead the negotiations and as much as she was reluctant to do so, she knew full well that Babek had a point. They really did need to get hold of the painting or there would be trouble and she was as much in the firing line as anyone else. Oh, it was tortuous, the position she now found herself in, because deep down she knew that she was best placed to deal with Ranald. After a further prolonged period of silence Ursula let out a long sighhhhhhhh.

'Okay, okay then, so what do you want me to do?'

*

Ranald was busy re-adjusting the picture on Fanny's saddle and pulling the blanket straight. He didn't fancy waiting for nightfall and had decided to roll the dice. Untying the leading rein, he pulled Fanny further down the gulley and up to a small track which led over the side, towards the path they had ascended on, back to the lip of the burn, the bridge and Fykle Lodge beyond. Fanny knew the way home and Ranald reckoned if he gave her an encouraging – *giddy up* – and good slap on the derriere, she would trot on back and hopefully the Count and Babek would follow, allowing him to escape.

Securing the leading rein around her neck, Ranald gave the old mare a fond pat on the mane. They had been on many stalking trips together over the years and she had never let him down, never once; always reliable and dependable was Fanny. Momentarily, he recalled their trips with an air of nostalgia and then letting go of the rein ran his hand along her back and over her rump. She stood still, turning her head to look at Ranald while he returned her stare. The moment was poignant, for Ranald realised he now needed Fanny to play her part more than ever before and then without warning hissed, '*giddy up*,' slapped her on the rear and raised his arms to shoo Fanny along as best he could.

\*

Ursula nodded her head while the Count explained the best way to descend the corrie.

'Okay, I will keep the white hanky raised in my left hand and hope he doesn't shoot me.'

'That's my girl,' said Babek squeezing her knee and giving her a peck on the cheek.

'Here goes then,' replied Ursula, tentatively standing up to start the descent.

\*

Ranald had crept up the side of the gulley and had his Mannichler pointed towards the ridge to spy the skyline through his scope. Pulling back from the gun he looked down the path to see that Fanny had now slowed and was proceeding at her usual ambling gait. Damn, he thought. Ranald had wanted her to briskly trot on home and not be caught, so as to allow him more time to escape. Muttering inaudibly to himself, he re-mounted the gun and started to search the skyline above the corrie – *jalloping jalapenos*! There at the side was someone standing up waving their arm!

\*

Ursula had walked out on to the top of the ridge with her hanky raised, while looking for the easiest route down. She had been so busy concentrating on where to place her feet that she hadn't really looked up, but gaining in confidence on the rough terrain, Ursula eventually stopped to peer around and check she was heading in the right direction. The gulley was straight ahead and as she allowed her peripheral vision to scan further afield, she suddenly saw Fanny, walking down the path back towards the Lodge. No Ranald? What was going on? Quickly retracing her steps Ursula shouted out in Babek and the Count's direction.

'The pony is on the move.'

Babek heard her call and instantly stood up, clearly visible on the skyline.

'Get down,' shouted the Count, eager not to give their position away again.

'Ursula what's up?'

'The pony is walking back down the path on its own.'

Babek stepped forward, so he could see for himself what the furore was about and sure enough there was Fanny ambling along.

*

Ranald had been watching events unfold on the skyline and realised the sight of Fanny had caused some confusion. However, he was keen they didn't catch her soon, so aiming at some gravel about six feet to Babek's right in between him and Ursula, he squeezed the trigger and – 'kerrboom.' The deafening sound of the rifle echoed throughout the corrie as shale was kicked up and scattered all around.

'Christ, he's shooting at us,' exclaimed Babek, stating the obvious.

Ursula started to move quickly towards him and the ridge beyond.

'Come on, get a move on,' she shouted at Babek as they both began retreating as fast as they could on the rough ground.

'Kerrboom!' – Ranald fired again into the same area of shale, scattering more stones and earth. Ursula and Babek put on a final spurt and within a few seconds made it over the ridge and dropped into the hollow, where the Count and Camille were seated.

'Did you see that? He shot at us,' said Babek.

'No, I didn't see it,' replied the Count in a matter of fact manner, 'but, I heard it. I suspect, he was just scaring you off. Anyway, it doesn't look like he is in a mood to negotiate.'

'Yes, but he's let the pony go. Its walking back down the path.'

'He's done what?'

'The pony, he's let it go.'

'And is the painting still on?'

'Yes, I think so.'

The Count crawled further along the ridge so he could spy the pony through the scope on his rifle. Taking cover behind a good-sized rock, he slowly pushed the Carlos Gustafsson between a gap, put his shoulder to the stock and picked up Fanny. She had trotted on a little after hearing the shots, but had now reverted to walking pace, ambling down the path. Even though she was around seven hundred yards distant, the Count could clearly see the picture strapped to her side. It must have got a bit hot in the kitchen for dear old Ranald he thought and then smiled. Aha! They would get that painting back after all and complete the deal, he wistfully mused.

*

Ranald had watched the Count crawl behind the rock and was concerned he might try and bring Fanny down with a well-aimed shot. He wanted to keep them on the ridge for as long as possible, so aiming at a grassy patch around six feet to his right, squeezed the trigger and – 'kerrboom' – echoed around the corrie with turf being scattered into the air. The Count, instinctively lowered his head. Quickly shuffling backwards, he slid into the hollow where Babek, Ursula and Camille were waiting.

'What did you see?' asked Babek.

'The painting, it's definitely on the pony. We just need to scramble around, catch her and collect our prize.'

'Why has he done it?' asked Babek.

'I guess he is surrendering. He knows we will follow the picture and leave him to make his escape.'

'Yes, I suppose that makes sense.'

*

The gun fire spurred Fanny along and she had again broken out into a trot which pleased Ranald. If he could just hold them up on the ridge for a bit longer there was a good chance she would make it back to the Lodge before being caught. Again, he aimed at the patch of turf and let off another round – '*kerrboom.*'

'Why's he still firing at us?' questioned Ursula.

The Count shrugged his shoulders,

'I don't know. I guess he wants to keep us pinned down, so it takes us longer to catch the pony and gives him more time to escape. Who knows? He may be worried that we will come after him once we have the painting.'

'Oh,' said Ursula, 'I didn't him have down as a trigger-happy type.'

'I don't think he's trying to shoot us,' replied the Count, 'the shots have been wide of the mark by a good distance. It looks like he is deliberately missing.'

'Well you may be right,' said Babek, 'but I've no wish to test your theory, so how do you propose we go after the pony?'

'We'll have to crawl to the far side of the ridge and make our way down out of sight. The terrain is rougher there, so it will take a little longer, but at least we should be safe.'

\*

Ranald let off a final round for good measure, scattering more turf and helping to gee old Fanny along, before sliding down the bank into the gulley and then started to make his way towards the col.

\*

Meanwhile, the Count had crawled to the distant side of the ridge, where at least they could all stand up, without being seen. Typically, Babek was last to arrive, all hot and grubby and the Count wondered whatever had attracted Ursula to him in the first place. Money he supposed, that was usually the answer. Looking at Camille he pondered, were his own circumstances so different?

Babek got to his feet, stretching his stubby little legs and flexing his back, plainly not used to the exertions he was being put through, while the Count, who was becoming impatient to leave, started the hike towards the lip of the burn, which he reckoned was likely to take them the best part of an hour with Babek in tow.

*

Ranald had ascended as far as he dare along the gulley and then climbed up the side and peered down the path towards Fanny. She had travelled well and as she neared home her pace seemed to be quickening. Ranald decided that once she reached the lip of the burn and disappeared out of sight, he would make his final move from the safety of the gulley towards the col and continue over the pass, in the direction of Bridge of Orchy. It was still sunny with a warm, gentle breeze and Ranald actually felt at peace with himself. Reaching inside his pocket he pulled out another bacon and egg sandwich to boost his reserves and replace the nervous energy he had lost over the last hour or so. Intermittently he spied Fanny through his scope. Within another twenty minutes she would be over the lip and it would be safe for him to move on.

*

Despite the rougher ground on the side of the ridge, the Count was striding out with purpose and with gravity on their side they were making better progress than expected. He was just so keen to catch Fanny and retrieve the painting, that after half an hour, he decided it should be safe to walk along the well-trodden path on the ridge, which would help them descend much quicker.

*

Ranald was delighted when he saw them on the skyline in the distance, following Fanny. Since she had almost reached the lip he saw no reason not to make his move now, leave the gulley and head to the col. Slipping his rifle back into its cover Ranald had a drink from the stream and climbed back onto the path. The col was not far and without Babek and the Count in pursuit, he felt an air of relief and liberation, no longer fettered by their attentions, while he started to contemplate dinner with Elspeth at the Crawford House Hotel. Deep fried whitebait to start, ribeye steak, cooked rare of course, all washed down with a decent Argentinean Malbec. Naturally, Elspeth would be driving!

\*

The route off the ridge became steeper, closer to the lip of the burn and the Count who was out in front could see Fanny pass below, around five hundred yards in front, continuing along the path towards the flat marshes and the bridge over the river Fykle beyond. He doubted they would catch her before she reached the Lodge, but regardless, he was relentless in his pursuit and within twenty minutes they made the lip. Fanny was still some distance ahead, although now she had reached the marshes, her pace had slowed while she occasionally stopped to nibble on grasses as she gently ambled along. Everyone was exhausted, particularly Babek who was flushed red and perspiring, but, the Count sensed they may just catch Fanny sooner than he had thought and continued to push on.

'Come on everyone, let's keep going, the pony has slowed and we are closing the gap.'

The encouraging words were met with silence. On they trudged, poker faced with dogged determination and soon they reached the marshy area.

\*

Fanny had virtually slowed to a standstill, grazing on the rich lowland grasses and with the Count still leading the chase, they were now within three hundred yards and closing in fast, on the large rotund white rear and their cherished prize. Self-driven, they marched onwards, until she was no more than two hundred yards, then one hundred, then fifty and suddenly, there she stood, a little over twenty-five yards away.

Raising his hand, the Count brought everyone to a halt and then turning around to the group lifted his index finger to his lips for quiet. Lovely unadulterated silence, but for an occasional crow squawking in the distance, such was the peace they could almost hear Fanny chewing while she grazed, swishing her tail and shaking her mane to keep the bedevilling midges in check.

The Count's moment had come. Carefully placing his feet, like a well-trained cat burglar, he stealthily approached, hardly daring to breath as the midges also turned their attention to him, congregating around his face to launch their ferocious attacks. He was oblivious, focussed on the job in hand. The Count slowly progressed, teetering on the balls of his feet, ensuring he made no noise and soon he was within ten yards. Oh, how so close he was, within striking distance of the painting, he could almost smell it. When suddenly, without warning, Fanny became spooked, jumped, looked around at the Count and momentarily stood still, staring at the strange looking German aristocrat who had got so close. Until, with a neigh and a whiny she jumped again, bucked and cantered off towards the bridge.

'*Kerfuddling cupcakes*' – swore the Count slinging his rifle off his shoulder and taking aim at Fanny, who was now trotting briskly over the bridge with her head held high.

Babek put a hand on his shoulder.

'It's not worth the risk of hitting the picture.'

The Count hesitated and the chance of a shot disappeared. Lowering his gun he watched Fanny reach the other side and become partially obscured by some alder trees.

'Come on let's keep going,' encouraged Babek, surprisingly breaking out into a jog and within a couple of minutes they had crossed the bridge and climbed into the Range Rover.

\*

Fanny, bless her, now had the bit between her teeth and was merrily cantering along the track with Babek and the Count closing the gap as the Range Rover sped after her, kicking up gravel and stirring the dust as it went. With the gate onto the public highway still open, Fanny briskly trotted out, continuing along the road and still held the lead when she passed the tall columns on the entrance drive to the Lodge.

'Slow down, slow down,' shouted the Count, 'we don't want to chase the pony through a fence and damage the painting.'

Babek sensibly backed off and allowed Fanny to trot up the drive in her own time and on reaching the gravel area at the rear of the Lodge, which adjoined the outbuildings, she came to a halt beside the stable door.

Quickly jumping out of the Range Rover, the Count strode towards Fanny with conviction while he strangely raised his right hand to catch the pony's attention and most peculiarly this seemed to work. Fanny stood still, almost hypnotised, flattening her ears backwards, as the Count approached and took hold of her halter.

Babek was – *cock a hoop* – that they had at last caught the pony, ecstatic and almost in a frenzy at the prospect of getting the picture back. He wrestled and fumbled with the leather straps and buckles trying to free the prize, as his little rotund fingers strained at the joints. With his knuckles becoming whiter, he eventually released the last strap and removed the painting still wrapped in the blanket and placed it against the stable wall. The Count let Fanny go.

Such impatience led to frustration at the wretched string holding it all together, which proved no less troublesome. Tied in unrecognisable knots, pulled tight, almost impossible to undo, until the Count removed his penknife to cut the painting free, allowing the blanket to fall to the ground.

The excitement, the suspense, the tension was shockingly replaced with – *blawbluff*! Babek and the Count stood there, open mouthed, hardly able to comprehend what they saw... an empty frame! The canvas had been removed.

# Chapter 19 – A Change of Tactic

Ranald summited the col at around four o'clock. With the sun still shining and a gentle breeze it was perfect weather for walking in the hills and without Fanny in tow he could travel much faster. The views were spectacular and Ranald felt rather pleased with himself, in the way he had shaken off Babek and the Count and still kept the picture, carefully rolled up and resting on his shoulder. It must be worth a fortune he thought. Not that he would make anything from handing it in, other than the satisfaction of ensuring the painting was returned to the rightful owners. Buoyed on by his own self-congratulation, Ranald stopped to text Elspeth and have a drink from a clear highland spring.

'Hi Darling, making good progress and looking forward to seeing you later R xxxxxxxxx.'

It had been a strange week at Fykle Lodge this year, the painting, the guests and the predicament he currently found himself in. Ursula had caused him a bit of consternation, initially he was drawn drawn to her seductive looks and aloof manner; she was exotic, glamorous, intriguing and to cap it all ran an art gallery in Moscow. However, as the days had passed his candle for her had waned. Elspeth had constantly been at the back of his mind and his heart had been pulled in her direction. Less seductive perhaps, but nevertheless a good-looking girl with a sensible head on her shoulders and plenty of fire in her belly. Ranald suddenly found himself longing for her jovial company and easy nature. He was very much looking forward to seeing her later.

\*

Elspeth was packing up the gallery early when Ranald's text came through. She continued to put the better pictures in the large safe at the rear of the shop and re-adjust the display in the front window, where she left some of the less valuable works, before pulling down the metal chain link shutters. It had been a reasonable day. She had sold a Mora McBeggs painting at lunchtime; a bright seascape of a beach on the Isle of Lewis with a solitary boat pulled up on the shore. A pretty little painting set in a decent distressed white frame.

After locking the shop door, she glanced up at the window to see Ranald's Glasgow skyline take centre stage, sitting on the easel, proud as could be, with a spotlight shining over its vibrant colours. She smiled. He would be delighted to know his painting was on the main display in the front window.

While reading his text, Elspeth thought it was utter madness to drive all the way to Bridge of Orchy tonight and collect him, all for a dinner at the Crawford House Hotel. As for the painting, she really hoped that he knew what he was doing.

*

Ewan thought he had heard some rifle shots during the afternoon and mentioned this to Sir Hector.

'Probably Ranald practising on the range.'

Ewan shrugged his shoulders and let it go.

They had managed to catch a few slob trout for lunch on their way down the loch to the sandy beach and Ewan had made a small fire in which they cooked the fish, wrapped in foil and placed neatly around the edges within the hot ashes. It was a simple meal, almost biblical, trout in well buttered bread rolls with some salad which Lady Sally had provided along with a couple of bottles of white wine, which they drank from plastic cups. Fully satiated, the party sat on tartan travel rugs, looking out across the loch, while Flora and Lilly amused themselves making sandcastles and playing games. The wine had slipped down rather nicely and all in all, everyone was content and enjoying themselves

'This is the life,' said Hugh lying back and letting the sun's rays warm his face.

'Yes, you're right. It's not so bad on a day like today,' replied Sir Hector, looking aimlessly across the loch, with little on his mind.

'Sir Hector, I've been meaning to ask you. What do you think of the painting which Babek gave you?' enquired Janet.

'It's unusual. I mean typical of Babek to bring a gift like that. To be frank, I am not sure what to make of it. I did a google search this morning and found that the original had been looted by the Nazis during the Second World War.'

'LOOTED BY THE NAZIS?' spluttered Lady Sally, through a mouthful of wine. 'You never told me that.'

'Well, I didn't want to bother you my dear, not after the shenanigans we had with, errr… you know who last night'

'What shenanigans with "you know who" last night?' asked Heather, seizing on the comment.

There was an uncomfortable silence as everyone turned around, looking expectantly for more details.

'Well,' said Lady Sally. 'Ursula mistakenly came to our bedroom, thinking it was Ranald's. It was all rather distressing really.'

'Distressing? What was distressing?'

Lady Sally hesitated, not sure whether to go on or not, although the wine had loosened her tongue and increased her bravado. After a moment's pause, she continued.

'It was dark, the poor girl can't have realised it was our room and not Ranald's, when she jumped into bed with your father.'

'She did what?'

'Climbed into bed with Sir Hector. I burst in on them.'

Heather sniggered.

'Don't laugh, it wasn't funny.'

'Come on Mum, you have got to see the amusing side of it. A fairly harmless mistake after all.'

Lady Sally wasn't smiling and now found herself slightly regretting that she had ever embarked on the tale.

'I promise you, it wasn't amusing in anyway. You see by the time I arrived she was… well, sitting on Sir Hector, with a cheese wire wrapped around his neck.'

Heather suddenly looked a little shocked, while staring at her mother in disbelief.

'Cheese wire?' she repeated.

'Yes, cheese wire,' replied Sir Hector, gently rubbing his neck, 'and it wasn't an experience I would want to repeat. I have no idea what Ranald and Ursula had in mind, in fact, it makes me go weak at the knees just recalling it.'

'I'll remind Ranald about it at dinner tonight,' said Heather, recovering her composure.

'I think the less said about it the better,' replied Sir Hector, standing up and looking at his watch. 'Come on. It's time we made our way back to the Lodge to see what delights Fiona has baked for tea.'

Ewan followed Sir Hector's lead and began to clear up and get the boat ready.

*

Initially the Count and Babek were in a state of shock by the way that Ranald had duped them and managed to continue on his way with the painting, but as the reality of their predicament began to sink in, it soon turned to anger. Oh how they fumed, livid that he had given them the slip.

Babek marched into his room, walked over to the window and opened the curtains. Jacinta who had been asleep began to stir and on hearing Babek stomping around promptly sat up. She could sense something was bothering him.

'Come on, get out of bed and pack up, we're leaving!'

Jacinta knew not to question Babek when he was in one of his moods and instead watched him drag the suitcases out from under the bed in silence, before eventually she asked, 'Any particular reason why we are departing in such a rush?'

'It's complicated, it will take me too long to explain just now, but believe me, we have to get out of here and go into hiding. I'm in trouble.'

Babek had got himself into scrapes before and Jacinta didn't reply as she wondered what on earth he had done this time.

The Count and Camille were likewise packing and soon all of them gathered in the hallway with their luggage, which they began to carry out to the Range Rover.

Fiona, who had been in the kitchen, sorting out scones and cake for tea, walked through to find out what all the toing and froing was about.

'Are you leaving?' she asked Ursula, who was carrying her bags towards the door.

'Yes, as it happens,' she calmly replied, continuing to walk out of the hallway and across the gravel parking area. Babek came back into the hall to collect some more bags and on seeing Fiona walked up to her.

'Look, something important has just cropped up and we all have to leave in a hurry. Can you let Sir Hector know and thank him for our stay. Tell him, I will be in touch when it's all settled down.'

Fiona was lost for words, watching Babek abruptly walk out and then hearing the Range Rover start and the gravel crunch under its tyres as it sped off down the drive. Walking back into the kitchen she caught Stuart sampling one of her scones.

He smiled, 'Quality control.'

'You'll never believe it but, Babek, the Count and the rest of that crowd have just left with not so much as a by your leave or good bye to Sir Hector and Lady Sally. I can't believe they have just upped sticks and gone.'

Stuart hesitated with his mouth full of scone and jam, digesting the news before he spoke, 'I don't suppose they left a tip?'

'No, they didn't leave a tip. Those sorts rarely do, even when they stay the whole week.'

'Oh,' said Stuart, unable to hide his disappointment, while he thought a little longer about their sudden departure.

'I hope Ranald's alright.'

'Ranald's alright?' questioned Fiona. 'Why do you say that?'

'Well, it's just that they all went after him, when I told them, that he had gone to the hill and I did hear a few shots earlier. I just assumed that Ranald had shot something or was practising. However, now I come to think of it. The Count took his rifle.'

'That's odd, because I thought I heard some shots as well. Crickey, do you think Ranald is okay?'

'I'll try again to get hold of him on the estate radio,' replied Stuart nonchalantly, plainly not too concerned. Walking into the game room he picked up the handset, made sure it was switched on, before firmly pushing the button down to speak.

'Ranald. Stuart here, come in Ranald.' There was no reply.

'Stuart here Ranald, come in.'

'Try it outside. Ewan always reckons the reception is much better outdoors.'

Stuart walked onto the gravel parking area with Fiona.

'Ranald come in. Do you read me?'

He looked around and there partially obscured by the stables, he saw the rear end of Fanny sticking out from behind the building, while she grazed in the paddock.

'Crumbs, what's Fanny doing back,' he exclaimed, striding over to investigate, to find that she still had the saddle on and appeared to have been deserted.

'What's going on?' asked Fiona.

'I don't know, but Ranald took Fanny to the hill, so it does seem odd that she is back with no sign of him.'

Fiona looked alarmed.

'Something's happened to Ranald hasn't it?'

*

The Estate Land Rover swept up the drive and pulled onto the gravel parking area quickly followed by Sir Hector's battered old Subaru. Ewan got out and was surprised to see Stuart and Fiona standing beside the stables and when they walked over to meet him, he could see the concern in Fiona's face.

'What's up?'

'We are not sure. Babek and the Count have suddenly departed and Ranald appears to be lost on the hill.'

Ewan looked at Stuart, not sure why Ranald should have been on the hill, as Sir Hector strode over to see what they were all discussing.

'Sir Hector,' blurted out Fiona. 'Babek and the Count have left, apparently something important has cropped up and...' Fiona hesitated, 'and we think Ranald might be in trouble on the hill.'

'Well, we're not sure about Ranald,' interrupted Ewan.

'Aye, but it's odd that Fanny should be back without him,' said Stuart.

Sir Hector was now thoroughly confused.

'Stop, please stop. I haven't a clue what you are all talking about with everyone giving me snippets of information. Fiona, can you go and fetch a pot of tea and some cake and bring it to my study. We can sit down, while you explain to me what has happened.'

'Okay, Sir Hector, I'll do that.'

'Ewan and Stuart, please can you get that saddle off Fanny and then come and join us.'

It was rare for Sir Hector to convene a meeting like this, although within ten minutes Fiona had managed to set up afternoon tea in the drawing room and take the small teapot and some scones to the study.

'Would you like me to pour the tea?' she asked politely.

'That would be good of you,' Sir Hector replied, helping himself to a scone and jam before motioning to Ewan and Stuart to do likewise and as they all sat down with their tea in hand, Sir Hector began to speak again,

'Now who's going to tell me what has happened? I suggest you start Fiona. Tell me about Babek and the Count.'

'Well, there was a commotion in the hallway, just before you returned, so I went through to see what was going on and found them, with their bags packed, ready to leave. Babek explained that something urgent had come up and that they had to depart in a hurry.'

'And the Count, he went as well?'

'Yes all of them, including the women.'

Sir Hector wasn't particularly surprised that Babek should have left in a rush. He always had his fingers in a few pies and on previous stays had left abruptly to sort out problems. However, never quite so suddenly and it did seem odd that the Count should have gone as well.

'And what about Ranald then? Where is he?'

'Tell Sir Hector all you know Stuart,' said Ewan.

Stuart hesitated and stared at the floor, before speaking.

'Well, Ranald set off to Arragher this morning with Fanny. He told me, you and Ewan had said it was all right for him to go stalking on his own.'

Ewan shook his head, 'he never mentioned anything to me.'

'Nor me,' said Sir Hector, 'which seems odd, as we have let him stalk by himself before and I don't think we would have had any objections.'

He looked at Ewan, who nodded in agreement.

'Babek and the Count went after him,' continued Stuart. 'They seemed desperate to catch up with him for some reason and I did hear quite a few rifle shots earlier.'

Sir Hector was silent, clearly in thought.

'Well Babek and the Count are back safely, so I don't think the shots mean anything. It could just have been Ranald practising.'

Stuart paused again, not really enjoying the gentle interrogation he was receiving from Sir Hector. After another silent spell, he continued,

'Aye, but the Count took his rifle.'

'Oh,' replied Sir Hector, absorbing the information.

The small half-moon clock, which sat on the mantelpiece, could be heard ticking, until eventually Sir Hector spoke again,

'Well it doesn't necessarily follow that some harm has come to Ranald. Let me give him a call on his mobile.' However, reception in the hills is always hit and miss and he went straight through to the answer service.

'No reply,' said Sir Hector putting down the phone. 'I suppose we ought to go and check though. Ewan, can you and Stuart go and climb to the lip of the burn and spy around Arragher to see if you can find him. Take an estate radio so you can keep me informed.'

Sir Hector looked at his watch. It was now almost five o'clock and it would be dark in a couple of hours or so. However, he thought they should give Ewan and Stuart a chance to find Ranald and if no luck he could contact the Mountain Rescue and ask for help. Sir Hector knew the local Team Leader, Jim McAllister his GP and if need be, he could call him direct.

'Right, we have a plan, crack on and make sure you keep me updated.'

'Aye we will do,' replied Ewan, as Stuart and he stood up and moved towards the doorway.

*

Ranald was walking briskly on the high tops which led in the direction of Bridge of Orchy. He was now around half a mile above Riack Forest which stretched for miles in front of him and was enjoying the splendid scenery and pleasure of being in such a wild, beautiful place. He was still chuffed, in the way he had shaken off Babek and the Count and was convinced that surely, they would not catch up with him now.

*

Babek was driving with haste up the single track road out of the glen, when the Count spoke,

'Do we know where we are headed for?'

'No, not really, so long as it is a long way from the Black Widow and for that matter Belusha as well. He's not going to be happy when he realises we have lost his painting.'

'I've been thinking,' said the Count. 'We know roughly where Ranald is and it's wide open country up there. Why don't we get Lieu Chang to send the Black Widow in the helicopter. She can deal with him and collect the picture?'

'Helicopter?'

'Yes, there was one parked on the stern of the yacht.'

Babek was quiet while the idea sunk in.

'Why not? I suppose we have nothing to lose, but, I still don't have any phone reception and I have absolutely no intention, whatsoever, of climbing any more mountains to pick it up.'

'That's not a problem. Tumult Lodge is only a few miles further up the glen, we can pop in there and use the landline.'

'Okay, let me know when we reach the turn off.'

*

Elspeth had just stepped out of the shower, dried herself and was in a dilemma on what to wear. The prospect of driving to Bridge of Orchy to collect Ranald and a stolen painting, now seemed more ludicrous than ever, but despite the ridiculousness of the whole charade, she was actually quite looking forward to seeing him and dinner together at the Crawford House Hotel. Perhaps they would stay the night, she wondered, contemplating if to pack an overnight bag and a spare set of clothes. Elspeth didn't want to appear too keen, but, it was always best to be prepared she thought, pulling out a holdall from under the bed and going to her wardrobe to pick somethings to wear.

Black was her colour, always flattering and elegant. No girl could go wrong in black, particularly with her dark eyes and sultry look. Pulling out a black sequined top she held it up in front of the mirror to check the look while she twisted to the left and then the right, cocking her head to one side and enjoying the reflection which sat before her. Sequined top it was, with of course, what else, but her favourite designer label – *gag ga grachia* – black skinny jeans, which she proceeded to squeeze into, before pulling the top down over her head and flicking her hair out behind. Utterly irresistible, thought Elspeth, smiling at herself in the mirror, with a mischievous sparkle in her eyes, before spinning around for one last admiring glance. After slapping on a little make up and throwing a few spare clothes into her bag, Elspeth was ready to leave for her long-haul date!

*

Ewan and Stuart left the Land Rover parked at the bridge and were now on foot. Quickly crossing the marshy area, they were ready for the ascent to the lip of the burn which would only take half an hour, at most.

'Do you think anything has happened to Ranald?' asked Stuart inquisitively.

'I just don't know, haven't a clue. It all seems odd though, him going to the hill on his own, Fanny coming back without him and Babek and the Count suddenly leaving. God knows what has been going on, but, I suspect that by the time we reach the lip of the burn we will find him, walking home without a care in the world, unaware of all the bother he has caused.'

'Well let's hope so,' replied Stuart.

*

'First turning on the right just ahead.'

Babek slowed as he approached and once on the apex of the small stone bridge, he could clearly see the entrance to Tumult Lodge, delineated by the poorly maintained, tatty post and rail fence.

'Run out of money?' he asked, turning momentarily to look at the Count.

'The estates not mine. I just rent it.'

They sped up the potholed drive and within a couple of minutes arrived at the front of the shabby Victorian Lodge, which looked in desperate need of some care and attention. Babek abruptly bought the Range Rover to a stop, leaving tyre marks in what little gravel there was.

'Come on, follow me,' said the Count, jumping out and walking towards the large stone front porch, opening the door and stepping inside.

Unexpectedly, there was jazz music coming from the drawing room, Ella Fitzgerald delicately plying her trade to a sparky rendition of Mac the Knife. The Count, who was surprisingly upbeat, found himself being drawn along the hallway, humming in tune, until he stopped at the drawing room to put his head around the corner and see what was going on.

'Hello darling, are you having fun?'

There was the Countess, dressed in an elegant chiffon dress with a lovely ostrich feather boa casually draped around her neck, clutching a gin and tonic, moving and swaying to the seductive music, in a world of her own, oblivious to all, until she twirled around to find her husband standing in the doorway. Ah, how disappointment and vengeance flooded her persona as she was suddenly dragged back into her own tawdry life. There was the Count and no doubt his trollop of a mistress, zee bitch, would not be far behind and the Countess was not pleased, not pleased at all to be disturbed from her musings.

'What are you doing here?' she demanded with distaste.

'Well, it is my home darling.'

'Get out. Get out, get out and leave me alone,' she screamed throwing the remnants of her gin in his direction. The Count hastily withdrew firmly shutting the door behind him.

'The Countess seems pre-occupied,' he said looking around at Babek and raising his eyebrows, before continuing down the hallway to the phone which sat on a small antique table beside the stairs.

'Help yourself.'

Babek looked up Wran Chin's number on his smart phone, picked up the receiver and started to dial. There were four rings before he answered.

'Hello.'

'Hi, it's me Babek.'

Wran Chin hesitated, caught slightly off guard because he hadn't recognised the number.

'Babek, thanks for the call. What a nice surprise, now can you tell me. Do you have good news for us yet? I mean have you got the painting?'

There was a pause from Babek.

'Almost,' he replied, trying to sound upbeat.

'What do you mean almost?' riposted Wran Chin abruptly, while leaving his office and starting to climb up the stairs to the main reception room on the fourth deck where he had last seen Lieu Chang.

'Actually, the thief's still got it, but we know where he is.'

'Well, why don't you go and retrieve it then?'

'It's not that easy, he's up a mountain. We thought that perhaps... you and the Black Widow could take the helicopter and collect it?'

Wran Chin reached the door to the large reception room, he knocked and waited to be called in. There was no reply so he knocked again and within a few seconds, he saw the door handle turn and Suki's head appear around the side. She turned away and spoke in Mandarin and then withdrew, opening the door.

Wran Chin entered and bowed to Lieu Chang, who was sitting in a loosely tied silk dressing gown on the curved couch fitted alongside the circular window. He nodded politely to acknowledge Wran Chin and then released Mor from his overbearing grasp, so he could take a sip of Pol Roger champagne.

'Babek wants some help to retrieve the painting. It's been stolen by a thief who is trying to escape across the mountains. He knows where they are and has asked if we can collect it in the helicopter?'

Lieu Chang sat motionless, like a beached whale cast up on the shore, unable to move. He was clearly not amused, in fact, slightly cross to have been interrupted with his wives, just to be told the picture had still not been recovered. His face was solemn, expressionless with no sign as to how he might react, while he continued to contemplate matters. Wran Chin looked on expectantly, until eventually the whale stirred, stood up and pressed the panic alarm!

Sirens screamed within the room and a red flashing light could be seen through the window on the deck outside, lighting up the surrounds intermittently and within a few seconds the Black Widow arrived, with a Walther 45 pistol to hand and her two lackeys, Fee and Foo who were clutching AK47 assault rifles. Oh, how their eyes prowled the room looking for danger, ready to pounce and unleash whatever firepower was needed to protect their master. But, as they surveyed all before them, the Black Widow soon realised that there was no attack, no threat, nothing at all to be concerned about. They had simply been summoned. Lieu Chang nodded towards Wran Chin, who cleared his throat ready to speak.

'Babek still hasn't recovered the painting, it's been taken by a thief who is escaping over the mountains and Lieu Chang wants us to take the helicopter and collect it.'

The Black Widow nodded accepting her orders while Lieu Chang sat back down on the couch, as Suki and Mor came in like the tide to re-join him. Ah, how pleasurable it was to be back on the beach with the warmth of his wives at his side.

Babek had been hanging on the phone for what felt like eternity, when at last, Wran Chin came back onto the line.

'Babek, are you still there?'

'Yes' he replied tentatively.

'Lieu Chang has agreed to your idea; now can you tell me exactly where the thief is?'

Babek felt a surge of relief flow through his body, thankful that Lieu Chang had accepted his suggestion. There was absolutely no chance of the Count and him retrieving the painting now, but, the Black Widow with the aid of a helicopter? Well, that was an altogether much better proposition.

'Come straight down the loch towards the pontoon where you collected us in the boat and there on your right is a large mountain. We are sure he is on the far side somewhere. Its open ground so you should easily spot him.'

'Do you know if he has a cell phone?'

'Not sure, possibly. Why do you ask?'

'We have a phone tracker, so if his phone is on we will soon find him.'

'Okay, that sounds good.'

'Where are you?' asked Wran Chin.

Babek didn't want to answer the question and blow his cover.

'Still at the Lodge, the bottom of the Glen. You can call on this number if you want to get hold of me.'

Wran Chin hung up, collected his jacket and headed for the helicopter on the stern of the boat, where the pilot was already in the cockpit awaiting his orders.

On reaching the helipad, he was joined by the Black Widow, Fee and Foo, laden with their guns and rounds and rounds of ammunition, well-armed for whatever lay ahead. Up the steps scrambled Wran Chin, taking a seat beside the pilot and putting his headset on, while the rest of the merry band settled into the rear hold and fastened their seat belts.

Round and round the rotor blades began to turn, slowly at first, but with an ever increasing whine, all the time picking up speed and within a couple of minutes they were airborne and flying in the direction of Loch Fykle.

\*

It was almost six o'clock and Elspeth was in her old Renault, negotiating rush hour on the outskirts of Glasgow, bumper to bumper with nowhere to go. Through pursed lips she cursed herself for not leaving earlier, as the river of traffic slowly edged down Great Western Road and it was not until she neared the Erskine Bridge, that the congestion began to clear and her mood started to improve. Switching on Radio Clyde, Elspeth began to enjoy the lively banter, interspersed with a smattering of good music. Beautiful, beautiful was the sunset, lying low in the sky, casting intoxicating colours, flittering over the Campsie Hills and dancing with the mountains. At last she could start to make some meaningful progress and begin to enjoy the journey.

\*

Ewan and Stuart had reached the lip of the burn, but there was no trace of Ranald anywhere and they had, not an inkling, as to where he may be. Surprised that they could not see him, they continued to scour the mountains, but, after a further ten minutes aimlessly shook their heads, not sure of what to do next. Without warning the estate radio crackled into life.

'Hello Ewan, any sign of Ranald yet?' asked Sir Hector hopefully.

'No, nowhere to be seen I'm afraid.'

'That's strange. He's experienced in the hills. It seems odd that he appears to have vanished without trace.'

'Aye, it's odd for sure. I suppose he might have injured himself and be stuck somewhere.'

'Yes, that's beginning to look like a distinct possibility. Let's give it another twenty minutes and if he still hasn't turned up, I suppose, I ought to phone Jim McAllister at the Mountain Rescue and report him missing.'

'Aye, I think that's the only thing you can do,' replied Ewan as they broke off the call.

*

The Augusta 109 helicopter swept gracefully down the Loch, gliding a couple of hundred feet above the water with the downforce disturbing the calm, sending out ripples below. Slowing, when it neared the landing pontoon, it began to hover. Wran Chin turned on the cell phone tracker and the wee device bleeped, its little lights flashing and then settled down to a blank screen. Nothing was showing, not a phone signal to be seen anywhere. They advanced slowly, gradually ascending and contouring the side of the mountain. Wran Chin looked expectantly at the tracker and then away, enjoying the fine highland scenery, craggy outcrops and steep precipices all around, but, he was starting to become a little impatient, continually glancing at the tracker. Alas, there with no hint of a signal. On they went, climbing ever higher and higher, around the side of the hill, until suddenly, their perseverance was rewarded when the little device vibrated and a flashing red light appeared on the screen.

Glancing around at the Pilot, Wran Chin nodded as he tapped the screen with his left index finger and the little red light turned green, indicating they were locked onto the signal. Looking over his shoulder, he began to speak into his head set.

'We have a trace on a cell phone, so get ready for the assault.' Turning back to face the pilot he indicated the direction they should go, pointing towards Arragher and pulling the joystick to the right, the pilot continued following the mountain line below the summit. Wran Chin swivelled around again to catch the Black Widows attention and continued to speak.

'The plan is to surprise the thief by bursting over the ridge, laying down some fire power and hopefully they will surrender. However, make sure you don't damage the painting. It won't be worth much riddled with bullet holes and don't forget, Lieu Chang has already paid a substantial deposit of US$5 million. He will not be happy if you shoot up his investment. With a bit of luck the thief will simply hold up his hands and give up.'

The Black Widow looked unusually pensive, continually fidgeting as she sat in between the lumbering figures of Fee and Foo, who cocked their AK 47's and placed their hands on the doors handles ready to slide them open when the time came.

'Just one thing' added Wran Chin, 'assuming we do get the picture back, it's probably best not to shoot the thief in cold blood. We'll just have the authorities after us and it will create more hassle than its worth. Remember our primary objective is to retrieve the painting.'

\*

Ranald was striding out close to the top of the Arragher Ridge. He had climbed higher, moving away from the low lying wet areas and was now almost a mile from Raick Forest, just under the skyline on firm dry ground, perfect for walking on. Looking forward to seeing Elspeth later, he was engulfed by a warm, carefree and contented mood, fuelled on by the excitement of his adventure.

Initially, he seemed unaware of the helicopters thumping rotor blades as it approached. But it was there in the background, in his sub consciousness the constant thud, until eventually he stopped and looked around. Confusion reigned and played with his little mind, because his eyes could not confirm what his hearing was telling him. Where was the helicopter? Where indeed he thought spinning around, totally perplexed as to why he couldn't see it. But, it was a conundrum which was soon resolved, when suddenly without warning, the Augusta 109 burst over the ridge, exploding into Ranald's view and heading in his direction!

*Holy flying mackerel!* – Ranald was spellbound, not sure as to what was happening, caught up in something he knew not what, when at two hundred yards the side doors were flung open and from either side Fee and Foo leaned out of the hold. With their AK 47 assault rifles in one hand they started to empty their magazines, spraying bullets into the ground either side of Ranald, tearing up the earth and scattering debris in all directions. The noise was deafening as the helicopter, in a whirlwind of terror, roared overhead no more than fifty feet above and began to climb, arching to the right to come back for another run.

Another run! Ranald now knew full well what that meant. Glancing at the rolled-up canvas, he instantly realised why he had come under attack.

Momentarily deafened by the noise and shocked by the ferocity of the gunfire launched at him, Ranald was stranded in open ground, with no obvious places to hide. With the helicopter completing its manoeuvre and straightening up in his direction, it was time to decide if it would be flight or fight. His survival instincts took hold. Quickly removing the rifle from its sleeve, Ranald withdrew the bolt and slammed a bullet into the barrel, while raising the gun to his shoulder and scope to his eye. He could clearly see the pilot and Wran Chin, sat smugly in the cockpit and instantly decided to wipe the smiles off their chirpy little faces.

'He's got a gun!' screamed Wran Chin, covering his face with his hands, while the pilot started veering to the right as panic suddenly pervaded the cabin. Fee and Foo were committed, hanging out of the side and yet again, began unloading their magazines, ripping up the earth around Ranald. But, he stood his ground and with the cockpit firmly in his sights as the helicopter climbed and climbed, at no more than one hundred yards, Ranald flexed his right index finger, squeezing the trigger of his faithful old Mannlicher and sent a round through the top of the cabin, shattering the glass windscreen. Missing both Wran Chin and the pilot, the bullet continued out of the back without causing any significant damage.

Acting quickly the pilot leant forward, knocking out part of the screen so he could at least see where they were going and then turned around to Wran Chin and pointed downwards. It was time to land.

Now, was Ranald's moment and he wasted no time in seizing his opportunity and started to run – *hell for leather* – downhill off the ridge towards Raick Forest way below. On he ran, bounding over the rough, uneven ground with determination and grit, but, why on earth he should have stopped after a couple of hundred yards was a mystery, but stop he did, pulling up behind a rock to catch his breath and to see where the helicopter had gone.

# Chapter 20 – Ranald's Dash

Ewan and Stuart both stared at each other in bewilderment. They had seen the helicopter approach down the loch and the sound of distant gun fire was unmistakable, short bursts of what sounded like a machine gun. It was now six o'clock and without warning the estate radio crackled into life.

'Ewan come in, Sir Hector here.'

'Aye, we hear you all right.'

'Good Ewan, is there any sight of Ranald yet?'

'No, nothing, nowhere to be seen.'

'Right. That is strange, it looks like I will have to call the Mountain Rescue.'

'Sir Hector, there been a lot of noise up here, a helicopter flew down the loch earlier and we've just heard gunfire.'

Sir Hector was silent for a few seconds.

'Gunfire? Gunfire you say?'

'Yes, rapid fire, to be frank it sounded a bit like a machine gun.'

'A machine gun?'

'Well, yes, that's what it sounded like.'

'Oh,' replied Sir Hector, contemplating what to do next.

'Look, I don't think there is anything more you can do up there, why don't you come back down and I will phone Jim McAllister and see what he suggests.'

'Aye, okay Sir Hector, we'll do just that.'

\*

The helicopter pilot managed to land on the top of the Arragher ridge where Wran Chin et all quickly jumped out and followed the Black Widow, who took cover behind some rocks. Ranald had watched the manoeuvre through the scope of his rifle and then decided to make another dash. Getting up he started running downhill towards the forest again as fast as he could on the rough terrain, with his rifle hanging from his shoulder and holding the picture in both hands. After forty yards the familiar sound of an AK 47 exploding into life started to reverberate around the hills as bullets tore up the ground to his left throwing up shale, earth and small lumps of turf. Ranald dived for cover, managing to scramble into a hollow just under a small landslip and keep his head down while the gunfire continued all around. Eventually, it stopped. Fee turned towards Foo and grinned.

'What do you suggest now?' asked Wran Chin.

The Black Widow looked back towards the helicopter. It was an open target on the skyline and if anyone came looking for them it could easily be seen and would give them away.

'Take the helicopter back to the boat. We'll continue on foot and once we have the painting you can return to collect us.'

'Is that going to be safe?' asked Wran Chin, 'I mean it's sitting right on top of the ridge in full view and the thief has a gun.'

The Black Widow gave him a deathly look. Her eyes narrowed as she stared at him with contempt, wondering why Lieu Chang employed such a pathetic, wet, little man to help run his affairs.

'Don't fret, we will give you some covering fire. The thief won't even get his head up let alone his rifle. Now go and don't waste any more of our time with your spineless deliberations.'

Turning towards Foo, she asked,

'Do you have him located?'

Foo nodded, pointing to Ranald's position around three hundred yards below. The Black Widow pulled the AK47 up to her shoulder and let off a couple of rounds, just to his right and then gave the pilot and Wran Chin the nod. Steeled by the Black Widows withering remarks, they moved quickly, running with purpose across the rocky ground towards the helicopter, not wholly convinced that the cover fire would work. But, with Fee now also shooting wildly over Ranald's head, keeping him pinned down, they made it in one piece, climbed inside and started the engine.

Ranald carefully spied around the side of the landslip to see the rotor blades begin to turn as the whoop, whoop sound began to gather momentum and eventually, the helicopter took off and disappeared out of sight, much to Wran Chin's relief.

*

The phone rang in the hallway of 34 Leander Gardens, the Old Manse in Glencoe. Jim McAllister left his tea sitting on the kitchen table and followed by Jess, the faithful family collie, wandered through and took the call.

'Hello.'

'Hello, is that Jim?'

'Yes,' he replied, not instantly recognising the voice.

'Ah Jim, I'm glad I've caught you. It's Sir Hector from Fykle Lodge.'

The penny dropped.

'Sir Hector, nice to hear from you. I haven't seen you for some time. Hopefully you are keeping well and in good health?'

'Yes, thank you. I am as it happens, fit as a fiddle. But, I am not phoning for medical advice. No, the reason for my call, is that my nephew has gone missing and appears to be lost on the hill.'

'Oh,' replied Jim, looking at his watch.

'Well, he left this morning to go stalking and hasn't returned. I've sent the Ghillies to look, but no sign of him anywhere.'

'It's quite late. It will be starting to get dark by the time we get to you.'

'I know, but you have head torches and I can lend you the Ghillies to help out. My sister would never forgive me, if we didn't at least try and find him.'

'Okay, fine. I will gather some of the team together and we should be with you in half an hour, forty minutes at the most.'

'Thanks. Just one small matter though. The Ghillies. They said they heard shots being fired when they looked earlier.'

'Right. I suspect they have been on the whisky. That's the usual explanation when strange goings on are reported around here.'

'Yes possibly,' replied Sir Hector, not wholly convinced by Jim's theory. 'See you in half an hour or so.'

*

Ranald was pinned down under the landslip. He had just over an hour to wait for nightfall and the cover of darkness, but he didn't fancy his chances of holding out until then. Yet again surrendering crossed his mind. Hoist the white flag, hold up his arms and let whoever was giving chase, take the wretched picture and leave him be. But, for some reason Ranald couldn't quite let go, even though realistically, he was in a dire situation with his life in peril. In any event, a bullet may just come his way once he handed over the painting. It was time for a plan.

*

Ranald surveyed the lie of the land below; a wild inhospitable moonscape of rocks, heather, grassy hillocks and the occasional peaty puddle of dark standing water. Nowhere obvious to hide and with little cover he looked around forlornly, struggling to come up with any clever ideas. Oh, what was he to do? But then, he looked again and looked closer at the contours, shape and undulations and noticed there was a small gulley, within about fifty yards, which led in the direction of Raick Forest. If he could just reach that, it would at least give him some cover and at this particular juncture, it appeared to be his best chance of survival. Ranald was confident that if he could make it to the forest, he should be able shake off, whoever was pursuing him once he was amongst the trees.

Reflecting on recent events, while his plan started to take shape, Ranald stared at a tuft of grass on the edge of the landslip and there amongst the long stems he saw some movement. Unsure what it was, he poked his hand in, to see a small frog leap out and hop off. Delicate wee creature. How could something so small and fragile survive in such a wild inhospitable environment? Ranald realised, he too was vulnerable. But, if he was to reach the forest and give himself a half decent chance of escape, like the little frog, he would have to be bold and brave.

Inspired by the wee amphibian, Ranald crawled to his left and pushed his gun forward so he could spy the skyline through his scope. There was no obvious sign of his pursuers, so he picked up a stone and threw it under arm to the side and waited to hear it land. A split second later, he heard the clatter of the stone hitting the ground and then, the unmistakable, 'rattle and rat, a tat, tat,' of an AK47, as Foo opened up, firing wildly at where the stone had landed.

'I thought you said he was over there?' hissed the Black Widow pointing to the top of the landslip.' Foo shrugged his shoulders and looked unconcerned.

Ranald had seen the flash of muzzle fire, beside the big rock and now had a marker. Pulling the bolt of his rifle back, he loaded a bullet into the barrel, took aim and gently squeezed the trigger – 'kerrboom.' A split second later the bullet could be heard ricocheting off the ground.

The touch-paper had been lit. Fee and Foo opened up, returning fire sporadically and when this died down, Ranald sent another shell at the rock to set them off again as Fee and Foo continued to empty their magazines.

Sliding back down into the hollow of the landslip, Ranald started to work out exactly what to do. The painting was lying close by on the deep purple heather and letting his hand wander over, to drag it closer, Ranald started to unroll the picture, glancing admiringly at the wonderful shapes and subtle colours. Ah, to have such beauty with him in this treacherous place. Wrapping the canvas over his rucksack and then sliding it onto his back, he managed to secure the picture, which was now wedged in between and exposed for all to see. Precariously it hung there while Ranald rehearsed his plan, crawled forward and retrieved the magazine from his rifle, which he loaded with five bullets. Taking aim at the rock, he squeezed the trigger – 'kerrboom.' And a split second later the bullet could be heard ricocheting. Yet again, Fee and Foo responded in the only way they knew how, wildly returning fire. Oh, how Ranald goaded them on by continuing to shoot in their direction until finally, he shot his last round and suddenly, there was complete and utter silence. Not so much as a scuffle or a dink to be heard, while Fee and Foo reloaded their magazines.

Like the brave little frog, Ranald leapt up. Now was the time for him to take his chance! With bristling determination and real conviction, he began his dash towards the gulley. As he guessed, the cumbersome Fee and Foo were too busy re-loading their rifles to notice, but not the Black Widow, who had simply been watching events unfold. Guessing what Ranald was up to, she swung her AK47 in his direction, aiming directly at the middle of his back. Now was her moment, her opportunity, her destiny as she psyched herself up, ready to extinguish the thief's tender hold on life with a single decisive shot. The cross hairs wavered on the moving target. She breathed in, held her breath, ready to complete the deed and squeeze the trigger, but hesitated, because there hanging from the rucksack – was the painting!

Boy, was Ranald pumped up. Adrenalin coursing through his body, all too aware of the great risk he was taking and half expecting to be brought down at any moment by a barrage of fire. It was a do or die act and committed to give it his best shot, Ranald ran as if he were Tam O'Shanter with a wanton witch in a cutty sark, breathing down his neck. Large bounds, leaping over rocks, stretching his sinews, pounding his muscles as he desperately threw himself onwards, with gravity helping to push him forwards. A trip, tumble, slip or a twisted ankle and he would be down, prostrate on the ground, little more than a sitting duck. But, by the grace of God, his strong legs and stout walking boots didn't let him down and on he clattered, with scree and rocks rolling alongside him.

The Black Widow had lifted the cross hairs which were now trained on the back of Ranald's head with his brown wavy hair, bobbling in her sights – '*kerrboom.*' A bullet whizzed past Ranald's right ear and spurned him on for one final dash for glory. Leaping over the top of a couple of boulders as the Black Widow fired again; there before him was the gulley, his haven, his hiding place, his refuge. Two more strides, a leap of faith and Ranald slid down on his side, amongst a tumble of stones and heather into the relative safety of the hollow. '*Rowwww'* – spat the Black Widow firing in frustration over Ranald's head and then silence returned. The danger had passed and on realising this, Ranald sighed with relief, thankful for his narrow escape, before reloading his rifle and climbing back up the side of the gulley to see what was going on.

There was some movement on the skyline. Fee and Foo had left their hiding place and started to descend after him. Ranald fired close to them, within a couple of feet of Foo who dived for cover behind a rock quickly followed by Fee.

*

It was around six thirty when Jim McAllister and a couple of colleagues, Patrick and Joan arrived at the bottom of the glen, where Sir Hector met them beside the track which leads towards the footbridge over the river Fykle and to Arragher beyond.

'Evening Jim. It's much appreciated you coming out at this time of night. I'm not sure what has happened to the boy, he's normally quite sensible on the hill.'

Jim nodded, as Sir Hector continued,

'Anyway, come on. Follow us down to the river,' before jumping into the estate Land Rover with Ewan and Stuart.

At the bridge Jim, Patrick and Joanna quickly changed into their walking boots and with their head torches secured and rucksacks on their backs they were ready for the climb.

'I'll send Ewan and Stuart with you. They know the mountains well and have an estate radio. They can call for assistance, if it's needed.'

'Thanks,' replied Jim who let Jess out of the boot of his car and gathered everyone around.

'Patrick, Joanna you know what you are doing, so I suggest you bring up the rear and Ewan and Stuart can accompany me at the front and lead us into the mountains.' He looked at Ewan and Stuart and paused, before continuing,

'Sir Hector mentioned that you heard some gun shots earlier?'

'Yes,' replied Ewan. 'Unlikely though it seems, we definitely heard shots being fired. Rapid a bit like a machine gun going off.'

Jim raised his eyebrows. Ewan looked a sensible chap, but machine gun fire in the hills? Well, he had never come across that before.

'Okay Ewan, bring a rifle just in case.'

'Good luck and Ewan, keep me informed,' said Sir Hector as they all set off.

*

Ranald was holed up in the gulley and had Fee and Foo pinned down behind a rock in open ground. He wasn't entirely sure how many people were chasing him and the single shots which were fired, when he made his desperate lunge for cover, caused Ranald to suspect there may be a third person.

*

The Black Widow had stealthy moved off the ridge without being seen and was now behind the skyline, out of sight and able to take stock of the situation. She had seen another gulley around a hundred yards to the right from where she could stalk her victim and with Fee and Foo keeping Ranald distracted, she wasted no time in making her way towards it. Ranald was too pre-occupied, to notice the Black Widow climb over the ridge and drop into the second gulley, undetected.

*

Babek and the Count were pacing around the kitchen, while Camille served tea and Ursula went to the pantry to find something to eat.

'How long do you think it will be before we hear any news?' asked the Count.

'Not sure,' replied Babek, 'It's been quite a long time since we last spoke with Wran Chin. I suppose I could give him another call.'

'Okay, I'll come with you.'

Babek dialled the number and waited while it rang out. There were almost half a dozen rings before finally, Wran Chin picked up.

'Hello, is that you Babek?'

'Yes, I was just phoning to see how you were getting on. And if you have managed to retrieve the painting yet?'

'No, not yet. But the Black Widow is in hot pursuit.'

'Good, presumably she will do the business, one way or another?'

'We hope so. But your friend, what do you call him? Ranald? Well he's not proving a pushover. He shot the windscreen out of the helicopter and was showing no signs of giving up, when I left.'

'Yes, but surely the Black Widow will sort him out?'

'As I said, she is on the case, we hope so.'

Wran Chin was short with Babek and soon hung up.

'They still haven't retrieved the picture,' said Babek, looking at the Count despondently.

'I can't believe it. That hapless house guest of Fykle Lodge has caused us so much bother. The picture is worth US$50 million and there he is cavorting around the hills with it, as if it's all a silly little game.'

'I know, sickening,' replied Babek.

The Countess, who had gone upstairs to get changed, was standing above them on the landing and was shocked, in fact stunned, to learn how much the picture was actually worth. What on earth was that scheming husband of hers up to, she thought.

\*

Ranald was totally unaware that the Black Widow was in another gulley stalking him. He had stayed put, keeping Fee and Foo pinned down and since it was now approaching seven o'clock, the light was starting to fade and it would be dusk in just under half an hour. Eating the remnants of his last bacon and egg sandwich, Ranald contemplated waiting until night fall and escaping in the dark, but, he only had a couple of bullets left and he doubted he could keep Fee and Foo at bay that long.

\*

Riled to have missed Ranald earlier, the Black Widow became more measured and calculated in her approach while descending the second gulley. Scenting blood she was now more determined than ever that he would not escape her clutches for a second time, as she quietly climbed up the side and peeped over the top; it was clear. With the AK47 now over her shoulder, the Black Widow reached for the Walther 45 pistol, cocked it and ever so slowly started to crawl towards where she had last seen him.

Gripping rocks to pull herself forward, sliding over heather and hillocky tufts of grass, delicately crabbing over the ground, onwards she went, quietly manoeuvring her lithe frame across the rough terrain and all the time closing the gap on dear old Ranald. Ten minutes of perseverance and the Black Widow was within a few yards of the gulley, where she stopped, remaining motionless and listening. But, no scuffle of a boot, rustle of a jacket, snuffle, cough or sneeze could be heard. Just stony cold silence. With the pistol clutched in her right hand, ready to fire, the Black Widow slowly advanced until she was now within a yard of the gulley's edge, where again she ground to a halt with a pounding heart, the palpable tension of the stalk continuing to build, yet more. Again she listened for any clues as to exactly where Ranald may be. But, as much as she strained her ears, the Black Widow heard nothing which gave him away. Her eyes narrowed and holding the pistol in both hands, on she edged, ever so tentatively, ever so quietly, until she was within inches of the gulley edge with her legs coiled beneath like a spring. The Black Widow's heart pounded yet faster, her pulse raced and then without warning, she launched herself over the lip with the pistol pointing forward, ready to take the shot. But, while perching on the side, there was nothing to shoot at. Ranald was nowhere to be seen. He had moved on, descending further down the gulley.

'*Torranachi,*' – cursed the Black Widow – '*torranachi.*'

*

Ranald was pleased that he had moved without being seen. However, despite managing to widen the gap with his pursuers, he could see that ahead, the gulley flattened out, where the small stream which ran during wet times spilled out onto a boggy area, from where there was still around five hundred yards of flat land to cross before the safety of the forest.

'*Kerrboom, kerrbang*' – out of frustration the Black Widow fired a couple of shots in Ranald's direction.

*

Jim and his team were walking briskly, making good progress and had passed the lip of the burn. They were following the zig zag path towards the col, when they heard the shots being fired in the distance.

'Did you hear that?' exclaimed Stuart excitedly.

Jim stopped and stood motionless. He was all too familiar with the sound of rifle fire in the hills and there was no mistaking it.

'It's quite distant,' he replied, 'It could be another ghillie shooting foxes. I think we should get a move on to the col and make a decision on what to do once we are there.'

'It's usually an hour from here,' said Ewan, 'and it will be dark soon.'

'I know,' replied Jim, 'but we have head torches and if we keep our pace up we should reach the col sooner than that.

*

Ranald felt cornered. He had glimpsed the dark outline of the Black Widow approaching down the gulley. She had taken a few shots to slow him down and on hearing this Fee and Foo had started to recklessly empty their guns, spraying bullets aimlessly in his direction.

Ranald slipped his last two shells into the magazine and cocked his rifle. Although he knew the Black Widow was behind him, he didn't know exactly where, so he lobbed a stone to his right to see if that drew fire, but, to no avail. It was now around ten past seven and within twenty minutes it would almost be dark which would help his plight considerably, if of course, he could somehow hold out until then.

*

The Black Widow had texted Fee and Foo and told them to move down the mountain to join her. She reckoned to be able to keep Ranald pinned down in the meantime and if there was to be a shootout some extra fire power would do no harm.

Fee and Foo were trudging downhill, but they were not entirely sure where the Black Widow was and in which direction they should go as they haphazardly strode on.

*

Ranald was concealed on the right-hand side of the gulley. If he strayed into the centre he would present himself like a fairground duck for the Black Widow, who was not very far behind, so instead he crawled further to the side and from behind a rock popped his head up to take a look. The light was fading, although he could just make out the shadowy figures of Fee and Foo walking in his direction. Ranald knew the Black Widow was somewhere in between, so he instantly decided that his only chance of escape would be to crawl out onto the open ground to his left and see if he could find some cover elsewhere. It was bold, almost reckless, to chance his luck in this way, but regardless Ranald moved decisively and after crawling for around thirty yards found a little hollow behind some rocks.

*

The Black Widow had remained in situ waiting for Fee and Foo to arrive, but when she crawled to the side and put her head up, saw they had veered off line and were now wandering in the wrong direction. 'Idiots,' she cursed, reaching inside her pocket and retrieving her smart phone to send them a text.

After a little head scratching, Fee and Foo corrected their route, but it had lost them valuable time and it was now nearing half past seven. The daylight was almost gone and the Black Widow, realising events were slipping away from her, began to crawl down the gulley towards where she had last seen Ranald.

*

Fee and Foo were within two hundred yards of the gulley when Ranald aimed his rifle in their direction and gently squeezed the trigger, firing a round into the ground beside them. The effect was spectacular. They opened up, shooting wildly over the gulley, lighting up the night with muzzle fire as their rifles flickered in the twilight. Instinctively ducking, the Black Widow hit the ground, fearing she would be caught in the crossfire and as soon as the shooting died down, Ranald crawled further to his right dropping into another hollow. Remarkably, he had managed to put a reasonable distance between himself and the Black Widow, but when he looked up, he saw that Fee and Foo were closing in fast. They were within a hundred yards of the gulley and would soon be reunited with their master. Firing his last round into the ground near their feet, Fee and Foo replied, firing randomly across the gulley. It was now almost dark and once the shooting had died down, Ranald decided to move again.

Huddled over, in a crouched position, he started descending towards the forest and the cover of the trees. Oh, how he longed to be amongst the shadowy depths that the tall pines would provide, where he was sure he would be much safer. It was daring, a gamble that he wouldn't be seen in the disappearing light, but regardless, Ranald wafted along in a ghost like manner, carefully picking his footholds and making sure he didn't make a clatter.

*

Fee and Foo arrived at the gulley to join the Black Widow who pointed then downwards to where she had last seen Ranald, spurring them on with her ever threatening looks. Fee and Foo continued descending in their bumbling way with the Black Widow following from a safe distance. On they went, hardly bothering to conceal themselves, clumsily stumbling forwards, until they arrived at the point where the gulley opened out onto the flat boggy area. There was no sign of Ranald anywhere.

'*Rowwwwww* – he's given us the slip,' remonstrated the Black Widow, pressing her forehead into the palm of her hands and promptly sitting down.

# Chapter 21 – Declaring Love

Ranald entered the forest where he instantly felt a lot safer. His eyes had become accustomed to the dark and with his compass to hand, he felt confident he could navigate his way eastwards, towards Bridge of Orchy. There was little point carrying his beloved Mannlicher without any ammunition, so reluctantly, he left it propped up against a tree with a tinge of regret and then set off through the forest with haste.

*

The Black Widow was despondent and with little idea what she should do next, pulled out her smart phone and called Wran Chin.

'Hi, it's me.'

'Hello. Do you have the painting yet?'

'No, he's given us the slip.'

'He's done what? I mean how? You had Fee and Foo to help you.'

'Yes, and fat lot of good they were.'

'Well, what do you suggest?' asked Wran Chin.

'I don't know. I thought you may have some ideas.'

'Well, where's the thief gone?'

'We think he made it into the forest, but it's difficult to know. We can't see much now, it's dark.'

'Why don't you locate him on the tracker?'

There was silence while the Black Widow fumbled through her pockets. Wran Chin spoke again,

'The tracker, I gave it to you before I left. If he's still got his phone on you will be able to pick up the signal and follow him. It's locked onto the number.'

Pulling out the small black device the Black Widow looked down to see the screen lit up with a couple of red flashes and then a lone green flashing light, some distance away in the forest.

'Okay I've got it. I can see some lights, mainly red and a single green one.'

'Well he's the green flash. I locked the device onto his signal when we first tracked him in the helicopter. If you follow that it will lead you to the thief.'

'Okay, we should be able to manage that.'

'Good. Now make sure he doesn't get away and you retrieve the picture,' replied Wran Chin, before he hung up.

\*

Ranald was moving quickly, following an open ride in an eastwards direction and with a clear sky and bright moon overhead, he could see remarkably well. It was now almost eight o'clock, when he felt his smart phone vibrating in his pocket and on retrieving it, saw Elspeth's name flash up on the screen. He took the call and in whispered tones started to speak.

'Hi darling, how are you?'

'I'm fine Ranald and you?'

'Okay, making progress. Whereabouts are you?'

'I've made good time. No delays, so I should be at Bridge of Orchy within the next forty minutes, may be a bit longer.'

Ranald hesitated, 'Good that's excellent. I'm running a little late.'

Elspeth felt her heart thud and her whole body deflate, 'Well how late exactly?'

'To be honest, I'm not sure. A couple of hours, possibly longer.'

'What,' riposted Elspeth vehemently, as she could instantly feel her blood pressure begin to rise. 'I've just spent two hours rushing to reach Bridge of Orchy on time and you now tell me you are going to be a few hours late!'

'Look I'm being chased, I've been fired at and all sorts.'

'Well it's your damn own fault. I'm not sure why you took that wretched painting in the first place, it's not yours anyway.'

'I know,' replied Ranald, beginning to question his own sanity.

'But I did, and I can hardly just leave it in the forest now.'

Elspeth was silent while considering if she should simply turn around and drive straight back to Glasgow. Arghh! Why had it not worked out with Jeremy Brown she sadly reflected. Dear Jeremy, he was never late, mechanical in his timings just the like the computers he programmed.

'Elspeth, look I know it's not quite how we planned things, but realistically, I'm in a bit of bother and I need you to wait for me. Why don't you book into the Railway Hotel when you arrive and I will get there as soon as I can.'

Elspeth was fuming inside, livid that she had been dragged on some wild goose chase on little more than a whim. So annoyed, she could barely speak as words deserted her. What was she to do?

'Elspeth are you still there?' asked Ranald.

Silence continued as Elspeth held the phone to her ear, unable to reply. A tear trickled down her cheek, she felt let down and neglected. This wasn't how it was meant to be, a ruddy long drive to be virtually stood up, left on her own to while away time at the Railway Hotel and all, so annoyingly after she had gone to such great efforts to glam up. Suddenly, the sequined top seemed to lose its sparkle.

'Elspeth are you okay?' repeated Ranald.

'Yes, Ranald I'm here,' she replied, still deflated and hurt in the way she had been led astray, but gradually, ever so slowly recovering her resolve. Elspeth was now beyond caring so fed up with the predicament she found herself in, that she finally relented,

'Okay then Ranald, I will wait at the Railway Hotel, but I'm not best pleased and for heaven's sake, can you just get rid of that painting. It was a crazy idea taking it in the first place.'

'Thanks, I really do appreciate it.'

Elspeth was left hanging on the line. Looking up at the rear-view mirror, she wiped away the smudged mascara, remnants of a dashed hope and a wasted evening.

\*

The Black Widow, Fee and Foo made it through the wet area and to the forest edge where they squelched around in their deck shoes with damp feet and socks. Ill prepared for the hill, onwards they trudged. The tracking device was proving remarkably easy to operate and the Black Widow cursed herself for not using it sooner, when they had first been on the mountain. They soon found the open ride through the trees and once on this, they started to close the gap between themselves and the little green flashing light in front of them.

*

Ranald was oblivious to being followed, but spurred on by Elspeth's sharp words he was walking briskly to cover the ground as fast as possible. He was now confident that he had left his pursuers on the hill and had little concern if he made a noise, splashing through puddles and rustling through the undergrowth. But unfortunately Ranald had misjudged the situation, because all the while the Black Widow, Fee and Foo were catching him and suddenly, where the ride went over a small hillock, they could see his silhouette against the star filled sky.

*

It was after eight when Jim and all finally made the col. They had heard the gunshots earlier and were unsure what they would find when they looked into the next glen. As it happens, nothing, other than the vague outline of the hills under the beautiful moonlit sky.

'What do you suggest now Jim?' asked Patrick.

'Not sure really. I don't think there is much point in us going on,' he replied reaching down to give Jess a biscuit. She appreciatively wagged her tail.

'And what about the gunshots?' asked Ewan.

'Yes, I've been thinking about that. I suppose we ought to report it.'

*

The Black Widow tapped Foo on the arm and pointed at Ranald's silhouette and then up towards the starry sky, indicating where he should shoot.

With a gleeful smile, Foo mounted the AK47 into his shoulder and let off a quick burst – *'rat a tat tat.'*

Ranald felt his whole body stiffen uncontrollably. He was momentarily paralysed with fear at the sudden shock of coming under attack, until the adrenalin started to course through his veins and he took flight, diving off the ride to his left and frantically running between the trees.

*

The sound of gun fire could clearly be heard on the col and the AK47 muzzle, flashing briefly in the distance was clear for all to see. There was a stunned silence, while everyone looked at each other in disbelief and without a word being said, Jim pulled out his phone, called the emergency services and was eventually put through to Argyll and West Dunbartonshire Police Force.

'You say you can hear gunfire,' repeated the duty officer, not really sure what she should do, while Jim explained in clear and concise terms the events of the evening so far.

'Okay, let me have a word with the Station Commander,' she replied, leaving Jim hanging on the line to go and seek some guidance. After a few moments a new voice came onto the phone.

'Hello, Mark Greg, Station Commander. It's Jim is it from the Glencoe Mountain Rescue?'

'Yes, that's me.'

'And you have definitely heard and seen gunfire?'

'Yes, there's no mistaking it.'

'Well, I hope this is not an elaborate hoax?'

'No, certainly not. It is simply what we have seen and heard.'

'Okay, I will refer it to the Chief Constable. Stay where you are and we will phone back in five minutes.'

Jim waited for what felt like ages. A little stifled conversation flowed between the group until at last his phone rang,

'Hello is that Argyll and West Dunbartonshire Police?' he asked.

'Yes, it's Station Commander, Mark Greg again. The incident has been referred to the Defence and Scotland Secretary. They have authorised the deployment of 45 Commandos who are in the area on training. If you stay where you are on the hill, a rescue helicopter should arrive within forty-five minutes with a small unit of armed marines.'

'Okay,' said Jim, stunned by the response. Patrick looked at him questioningly.

'They're sending a helicopter full of armed marines!'

*

Sir Hector was helping serve the main course to his depleted party of guests when he heard the estate radio crackle on the sideboard in the dining room. Abandoning his duties he picked it up and pushed the receive button

'Hello Ewan, any news of Ranald yet?'

'No nothing, we've made the col and Jim has sent for help.'

'Help, what sort of help?'

Ewan cleared his throat, before speaking

'A helicopter full of armed marines.'

'Armed marines?' repeated Sir Hector, not sure it he had heard Ewan correctly.

'Yes, armed marines. There have been gunshots up here and all sorts, so Jim called the police who organised it. We have to stay on the col to help guide the helicopter in, when it arrives.'

'Oh,' replied Sir Hector, not entirely sure what to say. He finished the call and with his mind racing, contemplated how he was going to break the news to Ranald's mother.

'What's happened?' asked Lady Sally.

'I'll tell you in a minute,' replied Sir Hector, retiring to his study to make the call. It was a conversation he was not particularly looking forward to.

*

Ranald had paused briefly behind a tree for a short time while taking stock of the situation and then with his compass to hand, continued to move quickly through the forest in an easterly direction. The Black Widow simply smiled, while watching his progress on her little screen, knowing it was futile to run. It was easy to follow him with the help of the tracker and as soon as he stopped for a rest, she would tap either Fee or Foo on the arm and they would promptly let off a couple of rounds to gee poor old Ranald along. Oh, how she was really beginning to enjoy the chase, as the flashing green light would start to move.

*

Ranald had the rolled-up canvas tucked under his arm. He was moving between the trees as best he could in the dark, but he had now been on the hill for around ten hours, his legs were weary and he really began to question, why he had ever embarked on his crazy, romantic idea, to smuggle the painting out of the glen. It puzzled him that gunshots were fired whenever he stopped and with fatigue beginning to set in, his legs were starting to cramp. Ranald felt the tide was turning against him and under the moonlit sky he suddenly became melancholic. If this was to be his end, it was perhaps not a bad place to die, in the midst of the highlands under a beautiful starry moonlit night with an exquisite work of art wrapped in his arms.

It had been a good life, enjoyable, carefree, a pleasure to live and he had few regrets, other than never managing to find true love, a soul mate, someone to share with and care for. It was his own fault of course, no one was to blame other than himself for flitting around with little direction, but it saddened Ranald and as he looked down at his mobile phone, he decided to give Elspeth a call.

*

Sitting in the bar of the Railway Hotel with a glass of white wine, Elspeth jumped when her smart phone began to vibrate with Ranald's name flashing on her screen. Her anger had mellowed and she was now genuinely concerned for his well-being.

'Hello Elspeth it's me,' he whispered into the hand set.

'Ranald are you okay?'

'Well, I'm still alive... just!'

'Where are you?'

'Lost in the Forest and being closely pursued.'

'Who by?'

'Well I don't know exactly, I guess whoever wants the painting back. I thought I had lost them, but somehow, they seem to be able to pick up my trail and keep following me.'

'Christ Ranald, I wish you had simply left that picture alone. Whatever possessed you to take it in the first place?'

\*

The flashing green light had been stationary for a short while. The Black Widow withdrew the Walther 45 from her jacket and continued in Ranald's direction, moving quietly between the trees. She sensed that he had holed up and felt now was the time to strike at her prey. The tracker showed they were within a hundred and fifty yards and closing fast.

\*

'You see Elspeth, if by chance I don't get out of this fix in one piece, then I just wanted to let you know that I have been thinking about you all week and deep down, I have realised that... I love you!'

Elspeth was momentarily stunned by the sudden revelation.

'Oh, Ranald you are a funny one. Why have you left it to this stage to let me know? I love you too and I'm sure you will pull through tonight. However, can I just make one suggestion?'

'What?'

'Turn your smart phone off. Whoever is chasing you is probably following your signal. Love you, bye.'

Ranald looked down at his phone and pressed the off key.

\*

The Black widow stopped in her tracks when the flashing green light disappeared from the screen.

# Chapter 22 – Events Escalate

Major George McCulloch gathered his best half dozen marines together in the hangar at RAF Lossiemouth while the flight crew checked the Sea King helicopter and filled it with fuel. 45 Commando Regiment – Royal Marines had been on exercise in the area and although they didn't usually get involved in civil unrest matters, the Defence and Scotland Secretary, had personally sanctioned the deployment, following a heated conversation with the Chief Constable of Argyll and West Dunbartonshire Police Force.

The wiry, ginger haired Major was pretty hacked off, in fact, damn right annoyed at being called out at this time on a Thursday evening after two days in the field, for what he was sure would prove to be little more than a hoax. McCulloch led his soldiers onto the tarmac as the pilot started the engines and the rotor blades began to turn.

'Right lads all aboard. Let's go and find out what some time wasting, drunken highlander has dragged us out for.'

Within five minutes they were airborne for the forty-five minute journey to Argyllshire and their rendezvous with the Mountain Rescue.

\*

After switching off his phone Ranald had remained put while listening and trying to hear his pursuers approaching. Standing up he held on to the nearest tree, scanned all around and then slowly set off, carefully moving through the forest. But, it was dark amongst the shadows and murky undergrowth, when suddenly without warning he stood on an old branch, tripped and – *'trubssttle!'* Went crashing into some bushes.

The Black Widow's ears pricked up when she heard the commotion. She was within fifty yards of Ranald and looking around at Fee and Foo, signalled for them to follow as they carefully moved off after him.

Ranald lay distraught on the ground, realising that he may have given his position away, while again he listened. He heard nothing, nothing but stony cold silence within the depths of the forest. Very slowly he stood up and clasped a nearby tree, unsure whether to make a run for it or hold his nerve and stay put. Hesitating, while he deliberated, the Black Widow was getting ever closer and closer and then, Ranald caught a glimpse of some movement in the shadows, no more than thirty yards in front of him. He gulped knowing his end may not be far away. It was too late to run, so he pressed his body into the thick trunk of the scots pine he was clutching and began to pray to a higher being.

His thoughts returned to his childhood and the Free Church of Scotland service he attended nearly every Sunday without fail. With impending doom almost upon him, Ranald wondered if his diligence would be repaid on the other side, when he would finally meet his maker. And then there was Elspeth lingering in his thoughts. Oh, why had he been such a fool and not made a go of it with her. She was perfect, beautiful, sassy, wonderful in all facets, but, he had been the curmudgeon, too afraid to face up to the fact that deep down he really loved her. Reality returned and his whimsical musings were banished. He could now hear footsteps moving ever closer, the death march of the executor, come to dispatch their duties and surely finish him off and collect the painting. Ranald's heart pounded yet faster and his brow perspired. Death was almost upon the doorstep and it was not a particularly attractive thought.

*

But above in the starry moonlight sky, detached from the gruesome, tawdry events which looked likely to unfold on the ground below, flew a tawny owl, gliding serenely, effortlessly through the forest tops, occasionally flapping while manoeuvring and darting in between the trees, continuing on its hunt. A vole would do, yes a nice tasty little vole, caught out in open ground on their night time excursion would more than suffice for the time being. But, no little mammal could be seen and instead the owl suddenly came across three rather large bodies all stood upright, creeping through the forest – *rackadoodle do* – what was an owl to do?

Veering left to avoid the soiree, the owl purposefully flapped its wings to escape the intrusion and when passing above the Black Widow et al, let out a raucous – *'sssssssssssssscccccc rrrrrrrrrrrrrhhhhhhhhhhhheech.'*

Fee and Foo leapt out of their skins, startled as to what was happening and started shooting wildly all around, lighting up the woods with muzzle fire, while Ranald crouched in fear of being shot. But, fortunately, no bullet arrived. The Gods had been kindly to him, as there amongst the disturbance was just a glimmer of hope, the faintest whiff of a chance of survival and with all the ker-fuffle going on around him now was Ranald's chance to escape. Holding the rolled-up canvas, he seized the opportunity and moved quickly to another Scots pine about ten yards further away.

'Idiots,' screamed the Black Widow, looking around at Fee and Foo in disgust.

They shrugged their shoulders and after a couple of minutes of heated debate, continued to search the immediate area, but all to no avail. Because, by now Ranald had quietly slipped away between the trees.

\*

Ranald was now confident that he was no longer being followed, so he stopped and looked at his watch to check the time. It was around ten thirty, he was exhausted, hungry and the toils of the day had taken their toll. His earlier call with Elspeth had shaken him up and he now realised his plan had been folly; it was time to quit and seek some safety.

Contemplating whether or not to leave the painting in the forest, he wisely reckoned that it would be best to keep it for the time being.

If, by chance he was caught, the picture at least gave him something to bargain with. However, a change of plan required a change in direction and Ranald quickly decided to head north out of the forest, towards Tumult Lodge where he would leave the painting and escape via the road to Bridge of Orchy, the relative safety of the Railway Hotel and the warmth of Elspeth. Oh, how he was longing to see her.

Alas, Ranald felt slightly deflated to be throwing in the towel, but, he nevertheless felt he had made a good run of it and on reflection, it was clearly time to bail out and let whoever wanted the picture so badly take it. Within twenty minutes of following his compass northwards he reached the edge of Raick Forest and there only a couple of miles away stood Tumult Lodge with it lights on, shinning like a beacon in the darkness.

*

The Sea King helicopter managed to pick up Jim's phone signal with its tracking device and hovered overhead, shining a light downwards and illuminating the tired craggy faces. Jim pointed in the direction of Raick Forest. Major McCulloch, who was hanging out of the side, waved, pulled himself back into the hold and returned to the cockpit to direct the pilot in the right direction.

*

Babek and the Count had waited patiently all evening for news from Wran Chin about the painting, but had heard nothing.

'What do you think?' asked the Count.

'About what?' snapped Babek.

'Well the painting of course, do you think the Black Widow will have retrieved it yet?'

'I don't know, hopefully she will have.'

'Why haven't they called and let us know? Do you think they may just take it and leave us to hang out to dry?'

It was a good point and one which Babek hadn't really considered. What was to stop them simply scarpering off with the prize they so desperately wanted?

'I'll give Wran Chin a phone and see if there is any news,' he replied.

\*

As the Sea King approached the forest the pilot tapped Major McCulloch on the arm and pointed at the screen in the cockpit, showing a couple of small red flashing lights in the view finder. They had picked up the Black Widows and Fee's cell phones. McCulloch returned to the hold.

'Listen men, we're getting a signal from the forest where the Mountain Rescue thought they heard gunshots. It's probably just a lost hiker, but you never know so load up and be alert.'

\*

The Black Widow heard the drumming beat of the helicopters rotor blades approaching, gradually getting louder and louder and wondered what the implications were, while Fee and Foo shook their heads aimlessly, not sure as to what was going on. There seemed little point in running, so they stood still, huddled amongst the trees to wait and see what would unfold.

\*

The Sea King was moving ever so slowly while the Pilot homed in on the red flashing lights until eventually, he turned around to Major McCulloch and gave him the thumbs up, indicating they were above the target.

'Search light,' barked McCulloch, as one of his men held the powerful torch out of the hold and started to scour the ground below.

The downforce from the helicopter was buffeting the Black Widow, Fee and Foo while it hovered above, but, they held their nerve standing motionless, watching the beam of light move systematically back and forth, while Fee and Foo clutched their AK47's, poised for action.

'Nothing sir,' shouted the squaddie. McCulloch turned around and looking at the pilot, shrugged his shoulders. Glancing at the screen to check they were still above the target, the pilot nodded his head and again pointed downwards to confirm. The wiry Major sighed, not sure what he should do next, but, after a short pause, stepped back into the centre of the hold, retrieved a couple of flash flares from his rucksack and signalled for his soldiers to withdraw the search light and gather around to peer out. They knew the drill well enough – *all eyes open* – and readied themselves while McCulloch, casually tossed the lit flares out, letting gravity drag them downwards. Hissing and fuzzling they fell for a few seconds and then exploded into life, showering bright light, fanning out all across the forest.

'There!' shouted a squaddie, pointing at the startled, illuminated faces of the Black Widow, Fee and Foo standing below.

The beating sound of the helicopter overhead, buffeting down force, search light and now the exploding flares all proved too much for Fee and Foo, who panicked and responded in the only way they knew how, firing wildly in the general direction of the bright lights above. A couple of bullets, dinked and ricocheted off the side of the helicopter and instantly Major McCulloch sprang into action screaming,

'Engage, engage, engage,' as his soldiers pulled out their weapons to return fire.

But, it took them a split second to thrust their guns out of the hold to take aim and it was a split second too long for them to fix their targets. The Black Widow, Fee and Foo were already running through the trees, when a cacophony of bullets rained down from the helicopter, before it quickly pulled away.

McCulloch, who had seen active service in Afghanistan, had nevertheless been surprised, in fact shocked, by the attack. However, he was an old hand, familiar with encounters against insurgents and knew exactly what to do. He got on to the radio and phoned RAF Lossiemouth.

'Major McCulloch here, we've engaged the enemy and I need back up. Can you send me a couple of dozen or so more of my men?'

Within ten minutes two more Sea Kings were scrambled and on their way to Argyllshire.

*

Babek put the phone down after speaking to Wran Chin,

'No news on the painting yet, the Black Widow is still in pursuit.'

It was now after eleven o'clock. Jacinta had already retired to bed and Babek was feeling tired, after his strenuous day on the hill. Ursula yawned and looked at the Count.

'Where can I sleep?'

'Up the stairs take any room on the left.'

'I think I'm also going to turn in,' said Babek, making his way towards the staircase and soon afterwards the Count and Camille followed, leaving the Countess downstairs, slumbered on the chaise lounge in a corner of the drawing room.

*

Ranald had seen the battle in the forest illuminated by the flares and heard the helicopter and exchange of fire, which did little more than reassert that he had made the right decision to throw in the towel, be rid of the painting and get out of the area as fast as possible. Despite his tired, leaden legs, he had walked quickly across the open ground and was now within a mile of Tumult Lodge, where he would leave the picture before continuing on his way to Bridge of Orchy.

*

The Black Widow, Fee and Foo were lost. They had followed the tracker religiously and now without anything to guide them, had no idea in which direction they should go. All too aware that they could be followed on their own phone signals, they had turned these off and didn't feel they could even call Wran Chin to ask for help. Ill equipped with no compass to guide them, their only prospect of travelling in a straight line was to follow the stars, if only they knew which direction the constellations indicated. Deflated, the Black Widow sat down with Fee and Foo to consider what they should do next.

*

Apart from the odd dent the Sea King escaped unharmed and after retreating to the far side of the forest, hovered above an open area to allow McCulloch and his men to abseil to the ground, before returning to RAF Lossiemouth. Major McCulloch was in his element, plotting on the GPS, where they had engaged the insurgents and their route back towards them. Reinforcements should arrive within twenty minutes and as soon as they did, he and his men would go back and tackle, whoever had the audacity to attack 45 Commando's.

*

Elspeth had retired to bed in a double room at the Railway Hotel and not surprisingly was struggling to sleep, while she tossed and turned, worrying herself sick about Ranald.

*

The evening at Fykle Lodge had been subdued, while they waited for news of Ranald. Sir Hector had managed a difficult conversation with his sister about the boy's disappearance and following his earlier conversation with Ewan, he had little optimism that Ranald would be found soon. Only Pippa and Max seemed in good spirits and after a single nightcap of whisky, they all retired to bed sometime after eleven to wait and see what the morning would bring.

*

The two Sea King helicopters picked up Major McCulloch's beacon emitting from the hillside, just above the forest and within five minutes the soldiers had abseiled to the ground and the helicopters were on their way back to Lossiemouth. The Defence and Scotland Secretary had been surprised that more soldiers were required, but eventually agreed to the request, on condition he was kept informed of developments.

\*

Meanwhile, Ranald had continued walking towards Tumult Lodge while watching the upstairs lights go out. He knew that the Count rented the property, although had no idea that he was staying there with Babek and Ursula; the exhaustion had perhaps clouded his judgement. Ranald kept striding on with little concern as to who was inside and soon he was within a few hundred yards of the Lodge.

On reaching the ha-ha to the front, he followed it around towards the house. Some downstairs lights were still on and while approaching the side entrance, Ranald hesitated, deliberating if to simply leave the picture on the doorstep or take it inside. Overcome by fatigue and without thinking clearly, he placed his hand on the door knob and slowly turned it anti-clockwise. The doors were never locked and after poking his head through the entrance, he was drawn inside the shabby hallway, illuminated by the wall pendants lining the corridor. Otherwise, the house was quiet. Not a soul to be seen and for some unfathomable reason, Ranald kept walking until he reached a doorway on his left leading into the drawing room. He entered, where he found the room lit by a couple of sidelights and the fire still glowing.

Situated in between matching sofas, set opposite each other, was a large mahogany coffee table which looked to be the ideal place to leave the picture.

Ranald paused, looking around at the scruffy interior and then unrolled the canvas and laid it on top of the table, before stepping back to admire the painting for one last time. Ah, how the picture had grown on him and he was in many ways sad to be saying goodbye, to what now felt like an old friend. Running his fingers over the paintwork one more time, he was melancholic, at what he was sure would be their last encounter and then managing to pull himself together, took his smart phone out of his pocket, switched it back on and placed it under the table. That would surely lead his pursuers to the prize they so desperately coveted. Retracing his steps back along the corridor, Ranald stepped outside, quietly closing the door behind him.

*

The Countess had been lying on the chaise lounge, situated in a corner of the drawing room, with a rug draped over her and half obscured by a free-standing screen. She had heard Ranald enter, but not entirely sure who it was or what they were up to, remained silent not wishing to give her presence away. As it happened, the Countess had been struggling to sleep and after hearing the side door close, raised herself off the chaise lounge to see what the mystery visitor had been up to.

Arriving at the table, she stood rigidly still, shocked and in awe of what she saw, as there before her was the picture, lying loosely off its frame. Leaning forwards the Countess stared in bewilderment, questioning why someone should leave it here, in the midst of the night. Baffled, she peered over the painting taking a closer look, while confusion whirled through her head, as to why the picture should suddenly have turned up at Tumult Lodge, without warning. With the strange turn of events, she ambled through to the kitchen and put the kettle on, while mulling over her find. What was it Babek had said the painting was worth? US$50 million she recalled?

Back to the drawing room wandered the Countess with her tea in hand and sitting down on one of the sofas she looked at the picture, captivated by its beauty and intoxicating charm. US$50 million was a lot of money and even with a fraction of that she could leave Egbert, once and for all, and make a fresh start, a new life for herself, elsewhere. Suddenly, taking the picture and leaving didn't seem like a silly idea at all. It was just a question of how to do so.

A cunning plan was required to outwit that dullard of an aristocratic husband of hers. If she could just somehow find a way to fake the picture's disappearance she would be home and dry and free of the Count once and for all. Returning to the kitchen to make another cup of tea, the Countess's thought process began to stir.

*

Major McCulloch had assembled his reinforcements and with night vision goggles on they were making their way through the forest towards where they had previously engaged the insurgents. He had received orders from the Defence and Scotland Secretary, 'Apprehend using reasonable force and only engage as a last resort,' although McCulloch, a veteran of Afghanistan, simply smiled when he saw these come through onto his little screen. Last resort, last resort indeed he thought. Who on earth was going to prove otherwise! His heckles were up, after his earlier encounter and he was most certainly going to ensure they 'engaged,' come what may.

*

The Black Widow was sat on a log with Fee and Foo prowling close by, when she became aware of the acrid smell of smoke and on looking around she could just make out the flicker of burning undergrowth in the dark. Of course, the flares. The breeze was blowing in their direction and with the wind fanning the flames, it wouldn't be long before the fire would be coming towards them. In any event, it was time to get moving. There seemed little point in waiting for whoever had been in the helicopter to return on foot. With no idea in which direction to go, the Black Widow casually glanced at the tracker for inspiration, and – *hallelujah!* – was elated, ecstatic, to see the green flashing light back on the screen.

The thief must have turned their phone back on! Tapping Fee and Foo on the arm she showed them the signal and then, they started to pick their way through the forest in the direction of Tumult Lodge.

\*

The Countess returned from the kitchen with a pair of scissors in her hand and hovered over the canvas, before she picked up the bottom left hand corner and took a deep breath. It was barbaric, criminal really what she was about to do, as she then carefully cut off a small triangle with the artist's name on. The Countess knew it was wrong and fully aware, that in this act of vandalism, she had probably devalued the work by US$25 million, perhaps even more, but reasoned to herself that it would all be worth it in the end if her plan was successful. Taking the small corner towards the fireplace, she very carefully singed the edges in the dying flames and left the damaged signature on the hearth. Burnt and destroyed, yes burnt and destroyed was surely the logical conclusion which would be arrived at on finding the charred remains. Satisfied with her work the Countess finished her cup of tea, rolled up the canvas and collected her jacket from the hallway, before walking out of the side entrance, jumping into her Range Rover and within a couple of minutes, she was on the single track lane leading out of the glen.

\*

Ranald heard the Countess approaching and quickly jumped off the road and hid in some bushes, peering out as he watched her speed past. He was also travelling in the same direction, towards Bridge of Orchy and the Railway Hotel.

\*

The Black Widow, Fee and Foo arrived at the edge of the forest and were pleased to be out, in open ground and away from the trees.

The moon was still bright and they could see the ground floor lights of Tumult Lodge a couple of miles away, towards which, the tracker was directing them. Buoyed on by their change in fortunes and with the prospect that they may yet recover the painting, they continued walking with haste, towards the Lodge with a little hope in their hearts and spring in their steps, that all was not lost.

*

Major McCulloch and his men were moving through the forest with aplomb, reminiscent of the jungle warfare training they had completed in Malaysia. But, as they approached the area where they'd previously come under fire, they were concerned to see the trees were a blaze, with flames leaping upwards through the branches. The fire had begun to pick up a head of steam as the dry tinder burned ferociously, encouraged by a gentle breeze.

Without any air support McCulloch was left to think on his feet. Quickly he decided to split his troops, sending half around the fire to the right and the other half he led to the left, reckoning the insurgents would have gone one way or the other. Keeping in radio contact with his men McCulloch made sure they carefully avoided the flames and continued through the forest.

*

Babek had heard the Range Rover depart and was struggling to get back to sleep. He assumed the Countess had left and was slightly puzzled, why she should have waited until almost midnight to leave the Lodge and go elsewhere. However, with her now out of the way, he decided to visit the kitchen and get something to eat.

There was cheese and ham in the fridge and with a leftover croissant, Babek made himself a sandwich, while the kettle boiled. With a cup of tea in hand, he wandered around the downstairs and into the drawing room, where he sat down on one of the sofas to enjoy his night-time snack.

*

The Black Widow et all had travelled well and were only half a mile from the Lodge when McCulloch led his men out of the forest. The fire had continued to gather momentum and he reckoned it was best to be in open ground and away from the burning mass. Briefly pausing, he radioed to the rest of his troops,

'McCulloch here, come in?'

'Aye, we read you loud and clear Sir.'

'Seen anything?'

'No Sir, nothing. Not a dickie bird.'

'Okay, are you out of the forest yet?'

'Nearly Sir, nearly. A couple of minutes and we will be through.'

Looking back, McCulloch saw the fire was now roaring and with the wind fuelling the flames it would soon reach the forest edge.

'Come on boys, let's go and collect the others.'

McCulloch suddenly felt a firm hand on his arm,

'Just a minute Sir, I think I have got something,' said one of his squaddies, pointing towards Tumult Lodge.

'Look there Sir. Can you make it out? A couple, possibly three bodies may be a mile or so ahead of us. McCulloch strained his eyes through his night goggles and then after a few seconds said, 'Gotcha,' before he spoke into the radio again.

'McCulloch here, come in.'

'Yes, we read you Sir,' came the reply.

'Positive ID of insurgents around a mile in front of us. They're heading directly towards the house. We are proceeding to engage, join us on route.'

'Aye, we will do Sir. Be there in a jiffy.'

McCulloch and his men set off at double quick time while the fire continued to blaze behind them.

*

The Black Widow, Fee and Foo had reached the ha-ha which they climbed over and under the cover of some shadows from a line of mature fir trees, made their way to the side door of the Lodge. They were now virtually on top of the green flashing light.

Withdrawing the Walther 45, the Black Widow placed her hand on the knob and slowly turning it anti-clockwise opened the door. Yet again, they were tantalisingly close to the prize they so yearned for and looking around at Fee and Fo, she raised a finger to her lips as they quietly stepped inside.

Aware that the thief was likely be armed they were on tenterhooks, making their way, ever so slowly, down the corridor all too aware they could be walking into a trap. But on, they delicately tiptoed until they came to the drawing room door on the left-hand side. Taking a deep breath and cocking the pistol ready to fire, the Black Widow tentatively pushed her head around the doorway and peered through the murky light. She froze, completely dumfounded to see Babek, with his bald head in his hands, sitting motionless and staring at the coffee table in front of him. Holding the gun with outstretched arms and aiming directly at the shiny bald patch on the back of his head, the Black Widow advanced until eventually, she pushed the cold steel of the barrel into the rear of Babek's skull. He didn't flinch, staying seated, almost oblivious to the fact that he was no longer alone. At last he spoke.

'There's the painting.'

With Fee and Foo now in the room the Black Widow withdrew the pistol and stepped around the side of the sofa, not entirely sure what Babek meant, until she leaned forward and looked down at the coffee table, to see the charred remains of the corner with the signature of Jean Metzinger. Picking up the fragment to examine it closer the Black Widow then looked at Babek and shook her head, 'Oh dear, Lieu Chang will not be very happy!'

*

McCulloch and his men raced, hell for leather towards the Lodge, determined to catch up with the insurgents. On reaching the ha-ha they peered over the top and clearly saw Fee and Foo through the drawing room window with their AK47's to hand. They were staring outwards, looking at the fire raging in the forest behind them, throwing spirals of sparks billowing upwards into the sky. Decisively, McCulloch sent a third of his men around the ha-ha to the left, a third to the right and kept the remainder with him, spread along the full length of the wall, so as to encircle the house. Now was the time to seek orders to engage, but the war hardy veteran was having none of it. He had been in plenty of skirmishes before and rather enjoyed them and knew all too well that command would buckle and keep him at bay.

Gripped by the moment, the excitement, the trepidations of what he was about to do, McCulloch raised his head above the ha-ha, pulled the SA80 assault rifle to his shoulder and squeezed the trigger –'*rat a tat tat tat*' – letting some rounds fly towards the house and ricochet off the stone work.

The impact was explosive! Fee and Foo pointed their guns at the large bay windows and shot out the glass, returning fire. Babek was now flat on the floor and starting to crawl towards the doorway with the Black Widow sensibly following, leaving Fee and Foo to defend their position.

*

Upstairs the Count had been jolted awake and was sat bolt upright in bed, not really believing that he could hear the exchange of gun fire below. Wondering what on earth was going on, he leapt out and went to look from the window, where he saw the fire raging within the Forest and then was staggered to see the flash of gun muzzles below and the deafening noise of 45 Commando's opening up and returning fire. '*Galloping catfish*' – he shouted above the din, not really sure what this all meant and then, still in his pyjamas, fled downstairs with Jacinta, Camille and Ursula following on behind. He met Babek and the Black Widow in the hallway, still crawling along the floor.

'What's happening?' he shouted above the racket of gunshots, while Foo also retreated to join them.

'Haven't a clue,' replied Babek, 'but there are some fairly inhospitable natives outside who seem intent on shooting us up. Do you get on well with your neighbours?'

Ignoring the jibe, the Count said, 'quick, follow me,' and hastily moved through to the gunroom, where he armed Babek and himself with sporting rifles and plenty of ammunition. Two years in the German Second Armoured Cavalry Regiment had not been completely wasted on the Count, who was assembling his troops in the hallway, ready to give them their orders.

'Right. You,' pointing to Foo, 'into the dining room and help cover the front of the house.'

Stationing the Black Widow at the side door, Babek and Jacinta in the kitchen, he kept Ursula and Camille in the hallway, from where he could direct operations and cover the corridors. But, as the gunfire from 45 Commandos rained down on the house, the Count sensed they were in desperate need of some help, so he scurried down the hallway to the phone on the little mahogany table and dialled 999.

'Emergencies, which service do you require?'

'This is Count Von Kelheim of Tumult Lodge, Argyllshire. I am being attacked by some lunatics with guns, send help quickly.'

A bullet whizzed down the corridor and shattered a mirror close by, as the Count instinctively ducked.

'Sorry, I didn't quite catch that, which service do you require?'

'All of them!' screamed the Count, 'Police, Ambulance, Fire Brigade the lot,' while all the time the sound of window panes being smashed could be heard in the background. Another bullet ricocheted in the corridor as he dropped the phone and left the receiver hanging. It was time to defend their position. Crawling through to the kitchen, the Count, began to help Babek and Jacinta at the rear of the house.

\*

The young receptionist wasn't entirely sure what to make of the call, so had a word with the Operations Manager who put his newspaper down, looked up from behind his desk and starred at her blankly, before raising his eyebrows and shaking his head,

'Count Von Kelheim, whoever next?' he replied with a big grin. The Operations Manager looked at his watch and continued,

'Typical, an hour or so after closing time and we get them all phoning up. We had Donald Trump last night, Mother Teresa the week before, Sir Billy Connolly only last month and so it goes on week in week out, and as sure as God made little green apples, I can almost guarantee it will be a timewaster. But, as you know, we can't ignore our procedures, so you had better send the local bobby along to take a look. Give them a call will you.'

'Count Von Kelheim,' the Operation Manager mumbled to himself while walking back along the corridor towards the kitchen to make another cup of tea.

*

Within ten minutes, Sergeant Ken McGubbins had locked up the Glencoe Police Station, jumped into his Ford Fiesta and with the siren on and blue light flashing, set off towards Glen Fykle and Tumult Lodge.

*

It was now after midnight and Ranald was still trekking along the public road to Bridge of Orchy. He could see the fire ranging on the hillside and was sure he had heard the sound of gunfire, as he wondered what was happening at Tumult Lodge. Ranald was glad to be rid of the painting and all he really wanted to do now, was see Elspeth and give her a big hug. On he trudged, Bridge of Orchy was still some miles away.

*

Major McCulloch was in his element directing operations around Tumult Lodge. They had shot out all of the window panes and had the insurgents, well and truly pinned down in their lair. He contemplated storming the building, but the enemy, was clearly well armed and he knew from bitter experience of his urban warfare training, that there was a much higher chance of casualties, if they entered the house. Not wanting his men to come to any harm, for once, McCulloch sensibly decided to play the long game. There was no way they could possibly escape and in any case, he was rather enjoying shooting up the old Victorian Lodge and drawing fire. Surely, they would soon run out of ammunition and surrender.

*

Sergeant Ken McGubbins had driven quickly in the Ford Fiesta and was now sat in his car at the top of Glen Fykle, observing the Forest Fire and listening to the exchanges of gunfire below. He had switched off the blue flashing light and killed the siren, so as not to draw attention to himself while he phoned the emergency number at Argyll and West Dunbartonshire Police Force.

'Hello,' the receptionist said.

'Sergeant Ken McGubbins here. You sent me to investigate a disturbance at Tumult Lodge, Glen Fykle, Argyllshire.'

'Yes, I remember that.'

'You mentioned that some Count said they wanted all the emergency services.'

'Yes'

'Well you had better get them. It sounds like the Battle of the Somme here, listen to that,' said McGubbin, thrusting the radio receiver out of the car window.

'Okay,' replied the receptionist and for the second time that night went off to find the Operations Manager.

*

Inside Tumult Lodge the Count was taking stock of the situation. They had not fared well in the exchanges and it was blatantly clear to him, that they were considerably outnumbered and outgunned.

Pulling Ursula and Camille into the kitchen, where Babek and Jacinta were stationed, he then started rummaging around under the kitchen sink, until eventually, he found what he was looking for, firelighters.

'I have a plan,' announced the Count above the noise, 'There's a secret passage from the pantry to the ice house, which is about two hundred yards north of the Lodge and has an external door, leading into the woods. We should be able to slip away without being seen.'

'So, what are the firelighters for?' asked Babek.

'Well, we don't want to be followed, so we may as well torch the old house to keep them at bay,' replied the Count, leaving the kitchen and going back into the hallway. He crawled into the drawing room and put some of the lighters on the old sofas, lit then while signalling to Fee, to retreat and follow him out. Repeating the process in the dining room, lighting the curtains, he collected Foo and then likewise he did the same in the study, library, and finally the downstairs bathroom, before picking up the Black Widow and gathering everyone together in the kitchen. With all the windows shot out and a gentle breeze swirling around the house, the fires soon started to take hold. Smoke billowed around the hallway and began seeping under the kitchen door. Lighting the final firelighter, the Count placed it in the laundry basket beside the wooden kitchen units and then said, 'Right, follow me,' walking into the pantry and opening the thick oak door which led down some steps to the passage and the ice house beyond. This was it, the Great Escape! The Count was buoyed on by his clever plan and making sure the door was firmly shut behind them, he locked it, lit a match and led everyone along the passage. Within a minute they arrived at the cavernous ice house with steps to the door leading into the woods. They paused to collect themselves together.

*

Major McCulloch was surprised by the turn of events. He hadn't expected the insurgents to set the house alight, while they were still inside. The gunfire had dried up and he was curious, in fact perplexed as to what was going on. Again McCulloch was tempted to enter, but without any breathing equipment it seemed a fool hardy idea and in any event the house may be booby-trapped. The fire had now truly taken hold, roaring viciously in the front rooms and on quiet reflection, the wiry ginger haired Major, saw no harm in firing the odd grenade in, to see if that drew a response.

*

'For Christ sake, get McCulloch out and quickly before he does any more damage,' were the orders given by the Defence and Scotland Secretary, as the three Sea King helicopters were once again dispatched from RAF Lossiemouth.

*

Ever so quietly, the Count opened the external door, slowly poking his head out and listening. The gunfire now seemed to have been replaced by intermittent explosions. McCulloch had become increasingly exasperated by the lack of a response, so given orders to, 'fire grenades at will,' as the house began to crumble and collapse into a pile of molten rubble.

Beckoning for the others to follow, the Count quietly led them away from the burning wreck, through the woods and within forty minutes they had managed to put a good distance between themselves and Tumult Lodge, while all the time they climbed up onto higher ground. The burning fires could clearly be seen below and they became aware of the distant sound of helicopters approaching. Within five minutes they saw the Sea Kings land in quick succession to collect Major McCulloch and his men. Phew! They breathed a collective sigh of relief, not really sure how they had managed to survive the ferocious attack.

*

It was around three o'clock in the morning when Ranald stumbled into the reception of the Railway Hotel. It was never locked; there was a nightlight in the hallway, illuminating the corridor which Ranald staggered along until he found a small collection of seats beside the main desk, where he lay down and promptly fell asleep. Poor old Ranald was completely exhausted!

# Chapter 23 – Serenity Returns

<hr>

Ranald felt a hand gently rocking his shoulder and managing to open his eyes, saw a heavily moustached porter in a tartan waistcoat and tie,

'Wake up laddie you canny be sleeping here now.'

Ranald slowly sat up. He felt stiff from the previous day's excursions.

'Sorry, I arrived late. I am with Elspeth McLoughlin, she booked in last night'.

The porter stood up and walked behind the reception desk, to find the register and search last night's bookings and notes. There she was, in room 14a. Reaching behind the desk to retrieve the spare key, he hesitated, not sure if to hand it to Ranald or not.

'Can I have some ID, credit card, driving licence, perhaps?'

Ranald was stumped, unable to reply, staring back at the porter with a vacant look on his face.

'I'll tell you what, why don't you take your walking boots off and come through to the dining room. We can sort you out some breakfast while you wait for your friend to arrive.'

*

The Count had led his group over the mountain range to the north of Tumult lodge and descended into Glencoe during the early hours of the morning. Their progress had been slow, but they had managed to trudge on and make the small village before sunrise, where the party promptly split. The Black Widow, Fee and Foo going in one direction while the rest went in another. Fortunately, there was mobile phone reception, so between them they started to plan their escape from the Scottish Highlands, homeward bound to familiar surrounds. Babek had received an email from Belusha,

'Have you done the deal yet? No money has arrived in the account.'

He shuddered, at the thought of how he was going to explain what had happened.

*

Major McCulloch was marched into the Commander in Chief's office for a debrief. The overweight, greying Brigadier peered over his half-rimmed glasses while picking up the piece of paper in front of him and starting to read.

'Three thousand six hundred and eighty-seven rounds of ammunition, thirty four grenades fired, one Sea King helicopter with bullet damage. He paused skimming over the rest of the report.

'And yet you say no causalities?'

'No sir, none that I am aware of.'

'And the so-called insurgents, what about them?'

'I don't know, Sir, we were pulled out before we had chance to assess collateral damage.'

'COLLAERAL DAMAGE?' shouted the Brigadier, managing to raise his overburdened chassis and stand up with a flushed red face. 'You emptied half the ruddy armoury into the house. We know you caused collateral damage, but it's the people who were inside whom we are most concerned about.'

'They had fired at us earlier Sir,' replied McCulloch, looking straight ahead, staring into the distance.

The Brigadier glared at McCulloch, as his brow furrowed and face turned yet redder.

'I have a call with the Defence and Scotland Secretary at eight o'clock this morning and if it transpires that you and your men have killed innocent victims, then mark my word you will be for the high jump. Do I make myself clear?'

'Yes Sir,' replied McCulloch. Saluting, he left.

*

When Elspeth entered the dining room at around half past eight, she instantly saw Ranald slumped on the small table in the far corner fast asleep. She hadn't slept well herself and although she was relieved to see he was alive and kicking she was slightly irritated, actually annoyed with him for putting her through so much worry and turmoil. Walking slowly Elspeth arrived at the table and prodded his shoulder. Ranald stirred, moving his head to one side and then snuggled back down into his arms, so Elspeth picked up a table spoon and gave him a firm crack on the head – ouch! Instinctively running a soothing hand through his hair Ranald slowly came round and eventually looked up to see Elspeth staring into his tired, dirty face.

'You haven't shaved.'

He smiled, delighted to see that Elspeth had not lost her sense of humour, as she sat down at the table with him.

'Christ, I have been worried sick about you. Now promise me, you haven't still got that wretched painting, have you?'

'No, of course not. I took your advice and left it where it would easily be found, so that is the end of my little adventure. Quite something though. Missing for over seventy years no doubt worth millions. I had it in my hands – but now it's gone!'

'No one will ever believe you.'

'Probably not, but it's still an incredible story. I wonder where it will end up.'

The waitress arrived and took their orders and within ten minutes Ranald was enjoying a bowl of porridge, quickly followed by bacon and eggs.

\*

Sir Hector had not slept well, he had been up for most of the night tossing and turning while worrying about the well-being of his nephew. Ranald and he had always enjoyed a good rapport and although he didn't approve of his slightly bohemian lifestyle as an artist, he was nevertheless fond of the boy. Sir Hector felt a sense of responsibility and was upset that Ranald had gone missing on his watch.

The mood over breakfast within the large dining room was solemn, with little conversation other than the usual pleasantries, until suddenly the quiet was disturbed when the phone started ringing in the study. With a sense of foreboding, Sir Hector got up to take the call.

'Fykle Lodge.'

'Sir Hector, good to speak to you. Now tell me, how are you this bright sunny morning?'

'Sorry, I am not wishing to be rude, but who is this?'

'Do you not recognise my voice?'

'No, not really, I am not particularly sure. I mean, is that you Ranald?'

'Well done, it is indeed, your favourite artist no less.'

Sir Hector was momentarily speechless, taken by surprise, until at last he regained his composure.

'Well – *ballihugh* – Ranald'. Where on earth have you been? We were worried senseless about you. I never slept a wink last night and as for your mother. Well perhaps not surprisingly, she is in a bit of a state.'

'I've had quite an adventure, but don't worry, I survived unscathed.'

'Well what happened?'

'I'm exhausted. It will take me too long to explain just now, but we can chat soon.'

As Sir Hector came to terms with the news, he was again lost for words.

'Oh, and can you let Mum and Dad know that I am okay?' Said Ranald before he hung up.

When Sir Hector ambled back into the dining room Lady Sally looked at him questioningly, 'And who was that?'

Sir Hector kept walking in silence, until he reached the head of the table and sat down,

'I'm pleased to say, I have just spoken with Ranald and he is okay,' with a broad grin appearing on his face. There was stunned silence while the news sank in. Max stood up. 'Well thank goodness for that,' he said raising his tea cup as if to propose a toast. Max remained on his feet. 'There's something else I would like to announce.' He paused, looking down at Pippa and grabbing her hand. 'We would have told you sooner, but with Ranald missing and all that, we felt it was perhaps not the right time.' Max hesitated. Everyone looked on in silence. He continued. 'Yesterday afternoon, when everyone was out, Pippa and I went for a walk to the top of the Drum.' Max paused, gazing into Pippa's eyes. 'I was feeling romantic, and I had the audacity to ask Pippa to marry me. To my great happiness, Pippa accepted!'

It was almost too much for everyone to take in with the silence continuing, but regardless Max raised his tea cup and proposed a toast, 'To the next Mrs Munro-Fordyce.'

There was at last a little cheer as Sir Hector slowly got to his feet.

'Good heavens, we can do better than tea. Now let me get a few bottles of champagne from the cellar and we can have a proper drink to celebrate.'

Lady Sally smiled.

*

Elspeth's mood thawed while sitting in the reception area, enjoying a cup of coffee with Ranald. There were now plenty of smiles and giggles, as at last, the conversation flowed. She had decided to leave the gallery shut for the day and remain with Ranald, who would have to return to Fykle Lodge at some point to collect his belongings. He was plainly exhausted, so Elspeth took him to her room and put him to bed. She planned to visit Oban to have a look around Finnian's Gallery.

By the time Elspeth arrived, Mischief had already set sail and was being waved off from the harbour side by a host of onlookers. The Black Widow, Fee and Foo had made it back and were on board busy explaining themselves to Lieu Chang, while Wran Chin looked on, interested to hear what they had to say.

\*

Babek had already returned the US$5 million deposit and was now making his way south in a hire car with Jacinta and Ursula, while pondering how best to deal with Belusha. The Count and Camille were on a Glasgow bound train, heading for the airport so they could catch a flight to Bavaria and then onto the safety of the castle.

\*

Ranald slept and slept and slept, until eventually at around four o'clock he awoke. There was no sign of Elspeth anywhere, apart from a bag of new clothes which she had bought for him in Oban and left at the end of the bed. After taking a shower and changing he went downstairs to the bar, where he found Elspeth reading a book.

She looked up and smiled, 'Feeling refreshed?'

'Yes,' replied Ranald, leaning over and giving her a gentle kiss on the cheek and returning her smile.

'I've been thinking.' Elspeth looked expectantly.

'It's Friday evening, let's go for dinner at the fish restaurant in Ballahulish and stay another night.'

'Elspeth's grin widened, 'that sounds like a good idea.'

\*

At Fykle Lodge the champagne was flowing at the pre-dinner drinks and Lady Sally was gushing euphorically, pleased with her new daughter-in-law and that there was a wedding on the horizon. Sir Hector was tickled pink at the prospect of Max settling down and the potential of an heir to the estate and when the landline in his study rang, he wandered through the hall to take the call, with a champagne flute in his hand and a big smile on his face.

'Sir Hector Munro-Fordyce, Fykle Lodge, at your service.'

'Sir Hector. It sounds as if you have been drinking?'

'Well that is most certainly correct, as indeed I have. Is that you Ranald?'

'Yes, and in a slightly more sober state than you, by the sounds of it.'

'That is also probably true, but tonight we are celebrating at Fykle Lodge, as indeed we have good reason to. Max and Pippa have got engaged!'

Ranald was initially, a little taken back by the news, not sure what to say...

'Fabulous Sir Hector. Please do pass on my sincere congratulations to them both. Lady Sally and you must be delighted.'

'Very much so Ranald, very much so and to mark the occasion we are having an engagement party tomorrow night. We've hired the local ceilidh band and invited the neighbours, so you better make sure you are here, otherwise the happy couple will be disappointed.'

'Well, I will be. In fact, I was planning to drop in anyway, to collect my bags and thank Lady Sally and you for an excellent week.'

'Good that's settled then. The party starts at six but come earlier. Your room hasn't gone anywhere and you can of course stay the night.'

'I will Sir Hector, definitely. It will be a pleasure. I am looking forward to it already. Just one thing though.'

'Yes, and what is that?'

'Would it be okay, if I bring a friend?'

'A friend? What sort of friend?'

'Well you know, a girlfriend!'

'A girlfriend. Well, you kept that quiet, but, by all means, please do bring your girlfriend. We will be delighted to meet her.'

Sir Hector hung up and walked back into the drawing room.

'Who was that?' asked Lady Sally.

'Ranald. He's coming tomorrow night and you will never guess what?'

'What?'

'He's bringing a girlfriend.'

'Good heavens,' said Lady Sally, 'whatever next?'

# Chapter 24 – An Engagement Party

Ranald and Elspeth enjoyed a leisurely breakfast in the Hotel dining room, overlooking the pretty garden to the rear which was flooded with russets, reds and yellow autumnal colours. Neither of them had a particular agenda so they took their time, Elspeth spooning her muesli while Ranald poured the tea as they looked at each other over the table and smiled. They were smitten, in love and delighted that their simmering affection had at last come to the boil. Oh to be young, to be joyous, in the dramatic scenery of the Higlands and most importantly together. Ranald had never felt like this before, completely content, at peace with himself, totally relaxed with his belle and likewise, Elspeth was delighted with the change in her circumstances.

Time moved on, and after checking out of the Hotel they drove to Fort William so Elspeth could buy a dress for the ceilidh and some postcards to send to her family and friends.

McGuigan's cafe was busy with weekend shoppers, but Ranald managed to find a quiet corner and a free table where Elspeth could write her cards and he could enjoy a coffee. Pushing the plunger of the cafetiere downwards he glanced towards Elspeth,

'So, are you ready to meet some of my eccentric family?'

Elspeth, stopped writing and smiled, returning Ranald's look, 'No time like the present. I'm sure I will hold my own. Now, I hope your dancing is up to muster?'

'Don't worry, I won't disappoint. I know my polkas; *heel toe, heel toe, heel toe* and, I'll be making sure I put you through your paces, Miss McLoughlin!'

'Well, we will see about that,' replied Elspeth raising her eyebrows, before going back to writing her cards.

\*

Argyll and West Dunbartonshire Police Force had started their investigation of Tumult Lodge late on Friday afternoon, when the fires had stopped burning and the place had cooled down sufficiently for them to get on site. The forensic team were meticulous in the way they sifted through the ash and the surroundings, but no bodies were found. The tunnel to the ice house was discovered and under duress from the Defence and Scotland Secretary, the cause of the fire was put down as unsubstantiated. By the time the police had finished tidying up on Saturday morning, they were happy to let the insurers on site to survey the damage.

*

McCulloch was summoned to see the portly Brigadier.

'Sit down.'

'Yes Sir.'

'Forensics have been through the house you attacked. Remarkably there were no casualties. It appears there was a tunnel to the garden and that looks to have been the likely escape route of whoever you were chasing.'

McCulloch was rather disappointed that the insurgents had given him and his men the slip, although deep down he knew it was for the best.

'Will that be all Sir?'

'Yes, McCulloch. Now go back to the barracks.'

*

It was after lunch by the time Ranald and Elspeth drove down the single track road towards the bottom of the glen and Fykle Lodge. They stopped on route and pulled over to look at Raick Forest which was charred and still smouldering with faint wisps of smoke, rising from the ashes and drifting in the breeze.

'Good heavens Ranald, you've left a trail of destruction behind you.'

'It seems so,' he replied nonchalantly.

Onwards they continued, down the narrow twisting road, enjoying the towering mountains and splendid scenery, until again, they stopped to see Tumult Lodge, a shadow of its former Victorian splendour, now a burnt-out shell, surrounded by police tape with the insurers poking all over it.

'Was the painting really worth all of this?' mumbled Elspeth, as Ranald took in the ruin which sat before them.

However, they didn't linger and within twenty minutes they were motoring up the potholed drive to Fykle Lodge and crunching to a halt on the gravel parking area beside the east entrance.

Lady Sally bounded out to meet them, with Pinot and Grigio following and it was reminiscent of the scene almost a week earlier, when he had first arrived.

'Ranald dear, delighted you have made it back in one piece. Now please, you must introduce me to your delightful young lady.'

Without waiting Elspeth stepped forward,

'Nice to meet you,' she said leaning to peck Lady Sally on the cheek.

'Come in the pair of you. We have finished lunch, but we can get you a cup of tea, or perhaps even something a little stronger, if you like? As you know we've good news to celebrate, now Max and Pippa have decided to tie the knot,' continued Lady Sally striding across the gravel and into the hallway.

On hearing them arrive, Sir Hector dragged himself out of his study.

'Ranald, you little scallywag,' he boomed, 'pleased to see you fit and well. I must say you had us worried as sick as parrots the other night. Your mother was beside herself, in a real fret and not surprising really, all things considered. But anyway, we're delighted that you're back safe and sound.'

Sir Hector looked at Ranald's innocent, almost puritan smile spread over his face and all he saw before him was the angelic little boy he had known since birth. Most untypically he stepped forward and gave him a hug. Ranald was a little surprised, but Sir Hector soon let go and turned to Elspeth,

'And who's going to introduce me to this fine young lady?'

Ranald took a step to the side and waved in Elspeth's direction as she stretched out her hand.

'Hi, I'm Elspeth, nice to meet you.'

'Well Elspeth, Ranald kept you quiet and well hidden from us all. Welcome to Fykle Lodge. Let me introduce you to the rest of the house party,' and putting a guiding arm around her shoulder, Sir Hector lead Elspeth into the drawing room, where there was a general melee while he did the introductions. Max walked over to catch up with Ranald.

'We're pleased you are back in one piece, you certainly had Dad and the rest of us worried when you went missing the other night. What on earth were you up to on the hill?'

'It's a long story; one best saved for a quiet night and a bottle of whisky. But that's enough about me, what about you and Pippa? You kept your cards close to your chest on that one, you sly dog.'

'Yes, I surprised myself really, I think it was the day Pippa spent with you in Oban, which galvanised us together. We went for a walk up the Drum and when we got to the top the sun was shining, it was beautiful, romantic really and it just seemed like the most natural thing to do.'

'Well, well done. You make a lovely couple and I am sure you will be very happy together.'

'And how about you? Elspeth is a good-looking girl. How long have you been seeing each other?'

'We've been friends for some time although only just become an item. In fact, Thursday night on the hill was the catalyst which made me see sense and brought us together.'

'So very recent then!' said Max raising his eyebrows.

'Anyway Ranald, we've known each other a long time and Pippa is very fond of you, particularly the way you have always made her welcome at family events. So I was wondering. If it's not too much bother, would you like to be my best man?'

Ranald was lost for words, caught off-guard, not expecting to be asked, but, now was not the time to quibble. It was a magnanimous gesture and Ranald was flattered.

'I would be delighted to.'

'Good. In that case you can be the Master of Ceremonies tonight for our engagement party, it's your first official duty.'

Ranald laughed, 'You are getting more and more like your father all the time.'

\*

Lady Sally walked over with Elspeth, who had done the rounds and been introduced to all.

'Come on follow me, I will take you both to your room,' leading them up the main staircase and onto the wide landing where she threw open the door to the second room on the right and showed them in.

Once alone, Ranald grabbed Elspeth's hand and lead her over to the window and pointed towards Arragher.

'See those mountains. I've been all over them in the last few days, I've been chased by a helicopter, shot at, stalked and watched fires rage, all for the sake of a painting I was never even going to keep.'

'I know you silly fool,' replied Elspeth looking up at Ranald. He leant forward and gave her a kiss.

\*

With little else to do, Ranald and Elspeth went for a walk. The day was still sunny and warm, so they wandered down to Loch Fykle and the landing pontoon, where they found Stuart, fishing for slob trout in the brackish water.

'Hi, how are you doing?'

Slightly startled, Stuart turned around with a jump.

'Oh, it's you Ranald, I heard you made it off the hill in one piece. There was some strange old goings on up there on Thursday night. It sounded like a battle was raging, with all that gunfire and what not.'

'All that gunfire?' repeated Elspeth, slightly alarmed.

'Nothing to worry about my dear,' intervened Ranald, trying to brush the comments to one side.

'Anyway,' continued Stuart, 'Ewan and I took a walk up there yesterday, over the pass and down to Raick Forest to see the damage. We were wandering along the boundary when we came across your old Mannlicher, propped up against a tree.'

'Oh well done. I left it there on Thursday.'

'Aye, well we thought as much, so we bought it back and you will be pleased to know it is in the gun cabinet.'

Stuart paused, not sure if to continue or not, but he was enjoying Ranald's discomfort in front of Elspeth.

'There were no rounds with the rifle, I guess you shot all those bullets, I gave you?'

Elspeth looked at Ranald questioningly.

'A couple of shells perhaps. Anyway, it's time for us to wander back, to get ready for the ceilidh. I presume you are coming?'

'Yes of course. I'll be there to toast the Laird's son and his wifie to be.'

*

By the time Ranald and Elspeth returned to the Lodge, the ceilidh band had arrived and were setting up in the dining room. Lady Sally had decided a buffet supper would be best and Fiona had been cooking all day, preparing the feast, as pots and pans rattled in the kitchen. Ranald and Elspeth enjoyed tea and cake in the drawing room, before retiring upstairs to get showered and ready for the celebrations.

Ranald slipped into his kilt and fine Prince Charles jacket, while Elspeth squeezed into her new slinky black dress. They made a good-looking couple, descending the stairs and walking into the hallway, they found Sir Hector busy laying out drinks on a table. Ewan was in charge of tipples and by six o' clock the band started to play some melancholic ballads in time for the first guests to arrive.

*

Sir Hector and Lady Sally were in their element, ushering their neighbours and friends towards the drinks table where Ewan and Stuart served champagne cocktails, before encouraging them into the drawing room where Max and Pippa were receiving guests and Fiona circulated with canapes. By seven o'clock they had a full house and a merry gathering, with Ewan and Stuart, keeping the champagne glasses topped up with welcoming smiles.

Ranald stepped forward, tinkled the side of his champagne flute with a spoon as the hubbub of background chatter slowly fell away, 'Ladies and Gentlemen. Ladies and Gentlemen. Oh, and of course Sirs and Ladies.' said Ranald, as a small wave of laughter rippled through the crowd. Ah, how easy it was to entertain the well champagned guests he thought, looking out across the sea of grinning faces, before he continued,

'There is a buffet in the library with a fantastic array of culinary delights cooked by Fiona, who has been slaving away all day. Where is Fiona by the way?

'In the kitchen,' someone shouted to a little laughter.

'Oh well, still toiling then. But well done Fiona,' to which some of the younger guests cheered to acknowledge her efforts.

'Anyway, the buffet will be open shortly, so please, in due course do make your way through. And then from around eight o'clock the ceilidh band will be revving up for an evening of twists and twirls and hopefully not too many sprained ankles, when the dancing starts in earnest.'

The champagne continued to work its magic and there was another cheer from the guests at the prospect of some highland flings.

'And finally,' continued Ranald. 'The reason why we are all here tonight. Where are they? Come on, no hiding please.'

The guests parted as Max and Pippa were pushed to the front.

'Here they are,' said Ranald, with Pippa blushing and looking coy, while Max simply smiled, radiating his happiness.

'Look at the happy couple with contentment spread all over their faces. Ladies and Gentlemen it would seem remiss not to congratulate them on their wonderful news. Please raise your glasses and let's toast the lovely couple. To Max and Pippa.'

'Max and Pippa,' everyone repeated, sloshing back yet more champagne.

'Right, the buffet is now open, so please do make your way through.'

'Well done Ranald,' said Lady Sally, as the guests started to filter into the library. Ranald wasn't particularly hungry so he held back and with a throng of people collecting in the hallway, he stepped into the dining room with Elspeth on his arm and found the band playing, *By The Banks of Loch Lomond*. Such gentle soothing notes radiating all around. Looking into Elspeth's sparkling eyes he gave her a tender kiss.

*

With the large dining table and chairs cleared the room looked different. Unfamiliar to what he had become accustomed to, Ranald let his eyes roam in the subdued light, adjusting to the murky surrounds while he enjoyed the ambience. Around his eyes wandered, over the long sideboard with the stag's head above, past the pretty ornate stone fireplace, the clock in the corner, the band at the far end and up the right hand side taking in the streamers and balloons, hanging from wall lights. And then, his eyes stopped flitting around while he blinked, his jaw dropping as he found himself staring in disbelief at the wall above the long display cabinet between the two windows which looked out across the lawn. Eventually, he plucked up courage and stepped forward with his gaze transfixed, because there before him, illuminated by the picture light, hung – *En Canot*.

Ranald was simply spellbound, in awe of its majesty and beauty as it dominated the room with its brooding presence.

Of course, he thought to himself, of course, yes of course. The copy, this is the copy of the original which he had left at Tumult Lodge. But regardless, Ranald and the painting now had a history together and he was drawn to it, like a moth to a light, slowly walking yet closer, captivated and in a trance while it cast its spell over him yet again.

Sir Hector and Lady Sally had also moved into the dining room and were now stood behind Ranald and Elspeth, likewise admiring the picture, until Sir Hector broke the silence,

'Beautiful isn't it?'

Ranald was suddenly jolted back to earth when the words eventually registered with his brain and on turning around realised they were not alone. Sir Hector continued,

'And is this the reason why you spent a night on the hill?'

Ranald was confused, completely taken aback with Sir Hector's direct line of questioning.

'Why do you ask?'

'Just a thought. I mean you were clearly interested in the painting and it was odd that you went missing all of a sudden.'

Ranald hesitated, not sure what to say and if he should spill the beans and let Sir Hector know all, but then calmly replied, 'But the picture is still here.'

Sir Hector paused, mentally playing chess with his words, careful how he broached the subject, until he made another move and spoke again,

'Well yes, this picture is still here. But, I am not sure if you were aware or not. There was another identical painting in the house?'

Ranald, swivelled around so that he was facing Sir Hector while his mind whirred into overdrive. Had he been in cahoots with Babek and the Count all along? The thought had never really occurred to him before, but it now set alarms bells ringing loudly within him.

Recovering his composure Ranald replied, 'Yes, I did know as it happens. And when did you become aware of the second painting?'

'Well the original was looted by the Nazis in the Second World War,' said Sir Hector evading the question.

'I was also aware of that. So how did you find the copy?' repeated Ranald.

'Well quite by chance really. Ewan was cleaning the stag carcass in the game larder when he noticed some dust on the floor, which he thought odd, because he had only recently washed it down. Looking up at the hatch he thought it had been disturbed, so he peeped inside and there it was.'

'So Ewan found it in the game larder?' queried Ranald.

'Yes, that's right, it was Ewan who discovered it.'

'Right,' said Ranald as the news sunk in. 'So what did he do with it?'

'Well, I had already been a bit interested in the picture, but, it was only when I did an internet search and discovered its provenance, that I reckoned that one of them may be the original and that Babek and the Count were up to no good, trying to smuggle it somewhere. To be frank, I was still pretty hacked off with the Count for shooting my Royal, so I got Ewan to swap them, just for a hoax really. Then you went missing, Babek and the Count left and it never really played out how I expected it to.'

Ranald was stunned, standing in silence, trying to piece together the consequences of Sir Hector's actions, 'So, when did Ewan swap them?'

'Oh, let me think now. Was it Wednesday? No, that's not right. He found it on Wednesday, late in the afternoon and it was early Thursday morning, when I discovered the pictures origins. So I asked Ewan to swap then during breakfast when everyone was in the dining room.'

'Right,' said Ranald as the information started to sink in. He was silent. Sir Hector looked at him inquisitively, until eventually Ranald's face broke out into a big wide gleaming smile,

'You see Sir Hector, I also discovered there were two identical pictures earlier in the week and like you swapped them, just for a joke really. It was only when I was in Oban on Wednesday morning and happened to see Babek and the Count on the Super Yacht with the painting, that I realised what was going on. I was then pretty sure that the one they had would have been the copy and the original was still at the Lodge, so I raced back with Pippa and hid it in the game larder, before trying to smuggle it out of the glen on Thursday with the help of Fanny.'

'I see,' said Sir Hector, 'Ewan and I wondered who had taken it. What were you going to do with it anyway?'

'Well, just hand it into the authorities. Like you, I knew it had been looted by the Nazis and thought it ought to go back to its rightful owners.'

'Very admirable,' said Sir Hector, 'but what happened?'

'Well, when I tried to escape with the picture I was chased, firstly by Babek and the Count and then some well-armed loones, who seemed pretty intent on stopping me at all costs. I was in Raik Forest and I couldn't work out why I was unable to lose them, until I realised, I was being tracked on my phone signal. By then, I was worn out and completely exhausted, so I decided to quit. With my smart phone turned off, I made my way to Tumult Lodge where I left the painting with the phone switched back on, so as to draw the loones in, before leaving for Bridge of Orchy were Elspeth was.'

'Oh,' replied Sir Hector, 'and as we know Tumult Lodge burnt down.'

'That's true,' said Ranald. Again his mind worked in overdrive. Eventually he spoke.

'You see Sir Hector. If I was right and the picture I hid was the original, then the consequence of Ewan swapping then again would mean that the one I took to the hill was the fake. If it's gone up in smoke with Tumult Lodge, then whoever was chasing me to recover it, may assume that it has been lost forever.'

Sir Hector listened and nodded.

Ranald paused. 'But of course, the original was actually sitting on your landing and is now hung on the wall in front of us.'

Sir Hector looked at the picture in silence, gradually absorbing the information while Ranald continued, 'So, if the fake was destroyed in the fire, then you may just be left alone with the real – *En Canot.*'

Sir Hector continued to stare at the picture, almost hypnotised by its allure, until at last he spoke. 'And, what is it likely to be worth?'

'I've got no idea, £10 million, £20 million, who knows? But a lot, I am fairly sure of that.'

Sir Hector was stunned, lost for words. He tried opening his mouth to speak, but nothing came forth. Lady Sally held his arm firmly, providing support and after a couple of moments of quiet reflection, Sir Hector managed to pull himself together, 'Well, that was very generous of Babek!'

His face erupted into an enormous smile. Ranald grinned as Sir Hector's humour proved infectious and soon the frivolity gained momentum, with deep bellows of laughter radiating around the room. Ranald casually threw his arm over Sir Hectors shoulder, while Lady Sally and Elspeth smiled and looked on. Lifting up his champagne flute, he turned towards Sir Hector, who could now barely contain himself, and said, 'A toast. A toast to Jean Metzinger and – *En Canot.'*

'To – *En Canot'* – shouted Sir Hector, hardly able to speak and almost in hysterics with tears running down his face.

*

The band picked up the tempo and with the guests congregating in the dining room, the ceilidh began in earnest.

'More champagne,' shouted Sir Hector to Ewan, who scuttled off with Stuart to replenish the stocks while the party began to gather some momentum. The dancing started with the Gay Gordon's as the happy revellers charged up and down the room. Strip the Willow followed, with no time for anyone to catch their breath, then a Dashing White Sergeant, an Eightsome Reel and by the time they were dancing the Duke of Perth, Ranald was in his stride, fuelled by champagne and whisky chasers he danced like he had never danced before, picking Elspeth up and spinning her around so fast that her feet barely touched the floor.

But, Elspeth was no shrinking violet, nor a slouch on the dance floor and as Ranald tried to twirl her again yet faster, she shimmied to the left, skipped through some neat foot work and with a fleckle of the heels, slyly slipped her toes between Ranald's cumbersome feet and sent him clattering across the floor. And oh, how did the guests roar with laughter to see the erstwhile artist, careering towards the sideboard with his kilt around his waist, exposed for all to see!

*

For the second time in as many days, Sergeant Ken McGubbins found himself sitting behind the wheel of his little Ford Fiesta, with the blue light flashing, while driving down the single track road towards Fykle Lodge, closely followed by a dark, sleek, Mercedes Benz. He pushed his wee car as fast as he dare, around the twists and bends, over the bumps, hugging the narrow road, while enjoying his moment of importance immensely. Turning into the drive between the two tall columns, he sped towards the Lodge and parked on the gravel area next to the east entrance. No one heard the knock on the door or noticed the blue flashing lights as Sergeant McGubbins patiently stood outside with the occupants of the Mercedes beside him.

With no response from a further pounding of the brass knocker, he turned the door knob, walked into the hallway and towards the dining room, where he met Stuart coming out.

'Is Sir Hector in?'

'Aye, he is just through there,' replied Stuart slightly surprised to see Sergeant McGubbins with two official looking gentlemen in ties and long coats.

The tall sandy haired man stepped forward, held out his hand to Stuart and said, 'Good evening,' in a thick, heavy French accent, 'I'm Monsieur Bardrock of Interpol, Lyon. I think it would be better if you brought him out here to speak with us.'

'Okay, I will go and get him for you.'

A minute later Sir Hector appeared in the doorway, hot and flushed from his exertions on the dance floor, with a beaming smile and glistening brow. However, his effervescent mood began to evaporate, when he saw Sergeant McGubbin's uniform and the blue flashing light reflecting through the window.

'Good evening gentlemen.'

The dark-haired man stepped forward to introduce himself, speaking with an exotic foreign tongue.

'Ulov Omiovh, of the Russian Federal Regulatory Service for the Protection of Cultural Heritage. I believe you have our picture – *En Canot* – by Jean Metzinger?'

Monsieur Bardrock took out a small bundle of papers from his inside pocket.

'I have here a confiscation order, made upon an application by the Russian Federal State for the repatriation of the work.'

'Aye, these gentlemen are right Sir Hector,' chipped in Sergeant McGubbins, 'it's been authorised by the Chief Constable of Argyll and West Dunbartonshire Police Force. He rang me personally and asked me to escort them.'

Sir Hector was silent, bamboozled by the turn of events and completely lost for words. Ranald walked through and joined him, to see what was going on.

'What's up, Sir Hector?'

He looked around completely deflated, opening his mouth, but unable to speak. Sir Hector persevered, tried again and eventually managed to blurt out,

'It's the painting Ranald – *En Canot* – they've come to take it away.'

'Oh,' said Ranald looking at the light-haired man for an explanation.'

He held up the forms and pointed to a box: Sir Hector Munro-Fordyce, Fykle Lodge, Argyllshire, Scotland.

'He's the recipient on the export licence submitted by Babek Popovich,' said Monsieur Bardrock. I presume you both know Mr Popovich?

Sir Hector nodded.

'Good. Now where is the picture?'

There was silence while Sir Hector came to terms with what was happening and then after making eye contact with Monsieur Bardrock, he sighed and finally came to his senses.

'Please gentlemen, follow me,' leading the party into the dining room and pointing to the wall where the painting hung, illuminated under the wall light.

'Ah – *En Canot'* – sighed Ulov, walking over and admiring the work through his longing eyes.

The band played on and the dancing continued, without anyone really noticing the picture being removed from the wall and taken away to the waiting car.

'I'll need to pop back tomorrow to get a statement Sir Hector,' said Sergeant McGubbins. 'I don't suppose you will be going anywhere?'

'We've been here for the last four hundred years. I've no plans to leave just yet.'

'Okay Sir Hector, I'll be back around coffee time.'

'As you like.'

Within a couple of minutes, Sergeant McGubbin's little Fiesta led the cavalcade down the drive and out of sight.

*

Sir Hector and Ranald stood on the doorstep and looked around at each other melancholically, saddened that – *En Canot* – had been wrestled from their grasp. Stretching out his right arm, Ranald, gently put it around Sir Hector's shoulder and with a comforting smile on his face, turned to look at him, 'It wasn't yours anyway.'

'I know Ranald, I know. You're quite right. I've lost nothing really. But, I had become quite attached to the painting.'

'Yes, we all had. Strange really, an inanimate object, little more than pigment splashed on canvas should end up causing us so much sorrow in the end. But it's not important; come on let's get back to the party.'

Turning around they met Elspeth and Max coming out of the dining room.

'What's happened Dad? Where's the painting gone?'

'Oh, it's nothing Max, nothing to concern you. Now come on,

let's go and celebrate your engagement. Where's Pippa? It's about time we had a dance together.'

With smiles back on their faces they returned to the dining room to re-join the ceilidh, the best ceilidh yet, the ceilidh which no one would ever forget. And on it roared into the early hours of the following morning.

# Chapter 25 – The End

The Countess arrived at Buenos Aries Airport, the Argentine, early in the morning to stay with her Uncle, Herman Brixham, who owned a ranch on the Pampas. She was excited by her appointment with the Sotheby's Cubism specialist, Ola Guarreda, who took her rolled up canvas and peered over it with a magnifying glass, before he went into his study next door to examine it closer with a colleague. The Countess waited for an hour in the reception area, while the attentive girl behind the desk bought her tea and biscuits. Eventually Ola Guarreda called her back into his office.

'And Countess you say that your husband, Count Von Kelheim, gave it to you as part of a divorce settlement?'

'Yes, broadly. I mean we are not quite separated yet, so I suppose it's a payment in advance, but it's just a matter of time.'

Ola Guarreda peered over his glasses and looked at the Countess thoughtfully as she continued, 'So, what are your thoughts? I mean how much do you think it may be worth?'

Ola Guarreda continued to look at the Countess in silence, and then decided to put her out of her suspense.

'Well, I have good news and bad news for you.'

'Yes?' replied the Countess expectantly.

'The good news is, the loss of the signature won't make a great deal of difference to the painting's value.'

'Yes,' repeated the Countess, with her hopes inflating.

'But, I'm afraid that's because, the picture is a fake. A good fake, I should add, but worth no more than a few hundred dollars.'

'Oh,' replied the Countess.

With her hopes dashed, she stood up to leave.

'Just one thing,' said Ola Guarreda.

'Yes,' replied the Countess.

'May I respectfully suggest, you employ a good divorce lawyer?'

*

The Count and Camille were on their way to the Castle deep in the Bavarian Black Forest, while Babek, Jacinta and Ursula had holed up in a London Hotel. Babek was unsure what to do next, but eventually, decided to confront his predicament and picked up the phone to call Belusha. It rang in the hallway of his mansion in Rublyovka, Moscow seven times before finally, it was answered by the housekeeper.

'Hello.'

'Yes Hello. It's Babek Popovich. Is Belusha in?'

There was a long pause, until at last the housekeeper spoke,

'I'm sorry to have to break the news. It all happened very suddenly. Mr Belusha passed away last night, quietly in his sleep. We are not sure when the funeral will be, if you want to attend.'

Babek put the phone down. There was suddenly some light at the end of the tunnel.

*

Ranald and Elspeth arrived back in Glasgow at around four o clock in the afternoon, after a leisurely drive from Argyll, ambling along the pretty road which meanders beside the banks of Loch Lomond. Between them they had worked out Babek and the Counts scam to smuggle – *En Canot* – from Russia and they laughed at the way it had spectacularly failed. With the help of Interpol, The Russian Federal Regulatory Service of Cultural Heritage now had the picture and no doubt in the full course of time, it would be returned to the Nationalgalerie, Berlin from where it was originally stolen by the Nazis in the 1930's.

*

Elspeth helped carry Ranald's bags into his maisonette and had a cup of tea, before she left and drove home to unpack. Returning to

Huntly gardens at around six o'clock with a takeaway supper, she let herself in, walked up the stairs and entered the living room to find Ranald in front of his easel, peering out, over the Glasgow skyline. Walking over to greet him Elspeth started to massage his shoulders, before she leant forward and gently kissed him on the cheek.

'That's lovely darling,' replied Ranald, as he swept ochre number three and crimson red paint across the canvas...